Divorce Lawyer: A Satyr's Tale

Sidney B. Silverman

July 13, 2013

To Phyllis:
Mein Phyllis!
What else can I
say?

Love
Sidney

1

On Peter Morrissey's office walls hung framed photographs of his former clients. All women. They were signed and attested to the excellence of his services. The photos were part of a ritual. After the signing of a retainer, Peter would pull out a camera and snap a picture of his client. When the case ended, the client would scribble a letter of praise and sign the photo. It was then framed and hung.

Why did Peter represent wives? At the end of the case, courts often ordered the husband to pay the wife's legal expenses. Husbands, aware they would have to pay their own and their wives' expenses, advised their lawyers to keep the bill low. Peter had often heard from past male clients: "It's bad enough I have to pay you, but at the end of the case, the judge will make me pay that other shyster. So go easy. Don't run up the charges."

The wives had no such scruples. They urged their lawyers: "Leave no stone unturned. Get that bastard. Believe me, he can afford to pay."

Peter was having a bad day. He sat in his large corner office, enthroned in a black-leather, high-backed swivel chair, considering what his next move should be. He had a heavy build at six feet two and 220 pounds. His red hair streaked with grey gave no sign of receding. His features were big, his head in particular. His nose was more delicate than the rest of him, and his lips were unusually full.

Peter's law office was in a skyscraper on the northeast corner of Fifty-Ninth Street and Lexington Avenue. The building, newly constructed, was architecturally undistinguished. Its name, International Plaza, was chiseled in large letters above the entryway. It was a misnomer. There were few, if any foreign tenants, and the building had no plaza. A bullet-shaped dome crowned the structure.

Peter thought it looked remarkably like a phallus, especially at night when it was lit.

At the end of the day, Peter was alone and trying not to feel frightened. On that morning, he had received a notice from the Grievance Committee of the New York City Bar Association that charges had been filed, alleging that he had violated the Code of Professional Conduct. If found guilty he faced disbarment. The code was designed to impose standards of conduct, which would ensure that the profession "remains a noble one." Its rules represented, in the eyes of the legal establishment, the minimum level below which no lawyer could fall.

The code had ten rules, likened to the Ten Commandments handed down by the Lord to Moses and enforced with religious fervor by a group of high-born, old-school, white males determined to restore the dignity of lawyers to the standard existing at the time our nation was founded.

The tenth rule, cited in the notice, "prohibits a lawyer from demanding sexual intercourse as a condition of representing a client or coercing, intimidating, or exercising undue influence to obtain sex." The prohibition was relaxed for consensual relations, but even then lawyers were strongly urged to refrain from sex with clients. The rationale: In the event of a spat between the lovers, the lawyer's duty of loyalty might be compromised. In matrimonial actions sex is barred, even consensual sex, unless the client and lawyer had previously been lovers.

The Clinton-Lewinsky brouhaha had not escaped the rule makers. To close a loophole, sexual relations was defined as including "the touching of an intimate part of the lawyer or another person for the purpose of sexual arousal, sexual gratification, or sexual abuse."

The notice said Molly Dixon, a former client, "alleged" that Morrissey and she, in the course of her divorce action, had had sexual intercourse. Dixon's allegation was supported by an entry in a hotel's log: they had checked in at 8:00 p.m. and checked out two hours later. The entry gives rise to an evidentiary inference: if a man and a woman occupy a hotel bedroom, it is presumed they were not there to play chess.

The notice invited Peter to discuss the charge and asked for a list of his female clients going back five years.

Peter knew he was in trouble. One consensual affair would be punished lightly; at most, he'd be given a reprimand. If, however, the committee learned of others, and there were many, he'd be disbarred. Peter folded and unfolded the letter. He shook his head in disbelief. Yeah, they'd made love. They were right about that, but it only happened once. And it certainly wasn't rape. Not by a long shot. *Disbar me for a single, harmless infraction? Not bloody likely*, he thought. *New York Magazine* named him among the top twenty-five divorce lawyers five years in a row. He was chairman of the Matrimonial Law Committee of the very association bringing charges against him. The governor sought advice from him. He even had a consultation with Hillary. How about his thirty-five years helping battered women? Did that count for nothing?

The only thing that can bring me down is hubris. I have to be careful. Mighty Peter. Well, the gods won't win. I'll fight. I've worked too long and too hard to end my career in disgrace.

Peter checked his watch. William Duffy was late. Duffy was going to save his ass. That's what Duffy did—criminal defense. Morrissey had called him earlier that day and told him about the disbarment notice. He must have been between cases, because he'd agreed to meet that day after business hours in Peter's office, even though the action was only an administrative proceeding, not Duffy's usual top-drawer criminal case. Duffy said that they'd decide at the meeting whether it was up his alley.

When Duffy arrived thirty five minutes late, the first thing he said was, "Nice office you got here, Peter. Some day when I'm a hotshot lawyer earning big bucks, this is the kind of place I'll park my ass."

Peter smiled. What else could he do? Duffy was abrasive and always on the attack. These attributes helped make him an excellent trial lawyer, but why, Morrissey wondered, were they always on display?

Duffy was almost Peter's size of six feet two. Except he was thin compared to Peter's heavy frame, with only a wisp of the blond hair that had, in earlier years, covered his head. His jaw was square, his eyes bulged, and his nose was tinged with veins caused by too much drinking. Duffy had a high regard for duty; he never touched a drop during working hours.

Peter handed him the notice. "Well, I'll be damned," Duffy said, "Divorce lawyers screw their clients every day in every which way, but if it's done for fun, they're disbarred. Who's this fink Molly Dixon? You don't have to tell me whether you screwed her, just when and how many times."

"Precisely once. Several years ago. The circumstances were unusual. She said she wanted a divorce but was too embarrassed to say why. It was one of those days when the phone never stopped ringing. I told her I needed to know the reason otherwise I couldn't draft a complaint. She refused to tell me. I suggested dinner at my club, hoping that in that sanctuary, she might overcome her shyness and discuss her case. 'You'll see,' I said, 'a few drinks and dinner will put you at ease.'"

"You got it wrong," Duffy said. "Molly suggested a dinner date, not you. Inviting her out is the first step down the slippery slope of seduction. Try to think. Didn't Molly suggest a quiet meal? Just the two of you. Maybe a home-cooked meal. You smelled a hot dame and rejected dining in her house. You offered a public spot, your club."

"Nah, it's not true. It won't work anyway. She was living with her husband. What's wrong with inviting a client to dinner?"

"We'll live with it. Go on. I'm all ears. I just love to hear about two old folks fucking. It encourages me."

"Over drinks she complained she was unable to arouse her husband. She tried everything but nothing worked. 'I'm unhappy. I can't sleep. You don't know how helpless I feel lying next to a man who turns away. My marriage is loveless.'"

"Now we're getting somewhere. She's a bitch in heat. 'Take me, take me, I'm yours!' Let's skip the bullshit. Talk to me about seduction. Her seduction of you. What did she say and do to encourage you?"

"She discussed her ploys to arouse her husband. She even demonstrated them on my finger...well, I asked her to. The recital excited me. I wanted her to do all those things to me. She sensed the effect. By the middle of dinner, we were groping each other under the table. I told her before she begins an action accusing her husband of being asexual, she should make sure her techniques were effective. I said, 'You may not need a divorce lawyer but instead a sex therapist or a sex surrogate.' She asked what sex therapists do. I said, 'They discuss your techniques and how they can be improved.' She asked 'What's the difference between a therapist and a surrogate?' 'A surrogate,' I said, 'will hop into bed and work with you hands on to improve.' 'I don't want to talk,' she said, 'I learn better by doing. I'll take a surrogate.'"

"She asked me to recommend a surrogate. I recommended me, which she readily accepted. She clapped her hands, leaned over the table, and kissed me. I said that surrogates charge big fees. If I take the case, I'll add my charges to the bill. Think of the irony. Your husband will pay for my services as a surrogate *and* a lawyer. She said, 'I love it.'"

"You're going too fast," Duffy said. "If Molly had said, 'I want a therapist,' you were out of the picture. She directly and clearly propositioned you when she said 'I want a surrogate' and kissed you. Then and only then did you succumb."

"Yeah right. We checked into a nearby hotel. She was wild. The next day, she signed a retainer, and shortly thereafter, we started the divorce action. Look Bill, you're my lawyer and my friend. I'll tell you the truth. I'm a satyr, the male counterpart of a nymphomaniac. All women attract me. Fat, skinny, young, old, beautiful and ugly, and everything in-between. My lust has certain similarities with alcoholics. They don't care whether it's Chateau Lafite or a jug wine."

"I drink too much," Duffy said, "but only on my time. You know what I am? A functioning alcoholic. All my friends know that. But you're wrong about not caring about what I imbibe. I only drink the good stuff. Enough about me. Is that voluptuous, sensuous Molly's mug on display in your rogues' gallery?"

Peter removed a photo from the wall and handed it to him.

"Holy shit! Look what that temptress wrote: 'To Peter. Your services in all respects were excellent. I could not have gotten through the trauma of divorce and resumed my life without your heart-warming attention. Your devoted and admiring friend-client, Molly.' What a field day I'll have with her! First she plays to your weakness by telling you every sensuous thing she does to her ice-cold husband and then rats on you. 'Your services in *all* respects were excellent.' That includes time between the sheets. Not bad looking either. Look at that thick head of salt and pepper hair. I find hair sexy. Maybe because I'm nearly bald."

"Wait, there's more," Peter said. "The rule says if Molly and I had sexual relations before she became my client, we can continue our affair throughout the case. The night we made love she was not yet a client. She became one the next day when she signed a retainer. But there's more. It's complicated."

"Hold that thought. She comes to see you seeking legal advice. You have sex. The next day she signs a retainer. Was she your client before she signed a retainer? Punitive rules must be strictly construed. At the moment coitus began and through the end of your surrogate services, she was *not* your client. Not until she signed a retainer. You're saved, unless piss-head Dixon's disclosure emboldens others. Don't bother to tell me whether there were others. How old was Molly when the affair started?"

"She was in her early fifties, about ten years younger than I."

"Disbarred, my foot," Duffy said. "You should get a gold medal for spreading joy to your middle-aged client, abandoned by her husband."

"Before you hand out kudos, I billed her for that first night. It was akin to a preliminary meeting. I, like most lawyers, bill for the first meeting, but only if the client thereafter becomes a client. Would you say she was a de facto client? Look, I'm anxious. Will you take the case?"

"You billed her to schtup her? Did you charge her for the hotel room too? What were you thinking?"

"We did discuss the case. What's done is done, and yes, I charged dinner and the room as an expense."

Duffy looked as if he were a disappointed parent who was going to let the transgression go for the time being. "You ask if I'll take the case? It will be as much fun as I can have with my pants on. As far as the early session, she didn't sign a retainer at dinner or in bed. That happened the next day, right?"

Peter nodded then asked, "What will you charge for 'having all this fun'? "

"I would do it for nothing, but then you might hesitate to bother me to the detriment of the case. Upon paying me, you own my services and can call anytime. You're successful. You can afford the fee. I'll give you a professional discount and a second discount because you're my pal. How about twenty-five thousand? No extra charge for appeals or any other related matter except, of course, for out-of-pocket expenses."

Peter wrote out a check, handed it to Duffy, and thought, *He said he would take the case for nothing because we were friends, but ironically took my $25,000 for the good of the case. Do I like him? We'll see about that.*

"OK, Peter, my boy, before we discuss strategy, let's read the rule word by word. Do you have a copy?"

"I do. I also have the decisions interpreting the rule."

"I don't want those now. Let's concentrate on the language of this cockamamie rule. I'm going to read it slowly, the entire rule regardless of whether it applies to our case."

Duffy read aloud and slowly

A lawyer shall not:
(i) as a condition of entering into or continuing any professional representation by the lawyer or the lawyer's firm, require or demand sexual relations with any person;
(ii) employ coercion, intimidation, or undue influence in entering into a sexual relations incident with any professional representation by the lawyer or the lawyer's firm; or
(iii) in domestic relations matters, enter into sexual relations with a client during the course of the lawyer's representation of the client.

[The rule] shall not apply to sexual relations between lawyers and their spouses or to ongoing consensual sexual relationships that predate the initiation of the client-lawyer relationship.

"The rule says 'demand' sexual relations with any person," Duffy said. "Has it ever happened that a female lawyer demanded sex with her male client? Get real. It says 'person' but it means 'women' and is directed to protecting them. Instead, it insults them. It assumes women are helpless little things easily manipulated by men."

"I agree," Peter said. "The rule should read *women*. But that's not relevant. I've read the rule over so many times, I've memorized it. It addresses women who are clients and may be dependent on their lawyers. It says, 'She may look up to her lawyer. Depend on him. The lawyer should not take advantage of his position of trust.' The rule also creates a protected class—women in the process of getting divorced. Many have been battered both physically and mentally. Molly wasn't one of those women. That's the problem with line drawing. Fall within the line, you're protected. Molly falls within it if she was my client at the time we made love."

"Do you think," Duffy said, "a woman suing for divorce needs protection, so that even if she seduces her lawyer like Dixon did, you should be disbarred? In my experience wives are not monolithic. Some are tough, hate their husbands, and transpose their feelings to all men. The last thing they're willing to consider is a lover. No man has a chance, certainly not a big, fat, red-haired lawyer like yourself. Others blame themselves for a wrecked marriage. They lack confidence, self-esteem. They're too fearful to embark on a new relationship. Then, there's what falls in between."

"Bill, I don't think a frontal attack on a rule protecting women undergoing divorce is a winning argument. Courts will see them as prey for a crafty lawyer. I like your defenses better. She seduced me, and at the time, was not my client. We had a consensual encounter between a man and a woman. Nothing more. And it was never repeated."

"What about the bill for the seduction? Do you think the Grievance Committee has it? Let's say a Hail Mary it doesn't surface."

"I don't bill her. That's not the way my practice works. At the end of the case, I file an affidavit listing my services, time spent, hourly rate, and expenses. The affidavit goes to the husband and his lawyer. If there's no dispute, the judge awards me the fee sought. It there's a dispute, the judge resolves it. The bill was small, as the case was quickly resolved. Molly's husband didn't object to my fee. Here's my affidavit. There's five hours listed for a "consultation with client.""

"The problem is if we claim she was not a client when you had sex, the 'consultation charge' becomes relevant. Let's hold strategy discussions until we are further advanced," Duffy said. "Don't say anything to anybody. Disbarment proceedings are confidential unless you're disbarred. Open your mouth, and your practice is ruined. The notice asks if you're willing to meet. I'll call and meet. I like a chin-chin with the other side. I'll call you after the meeting."

As Duffy left, Peter looked out the window of the darkened city. He was twenty-five grand poorer. He was still in trouble. He was still on the prowl. If a new client walked in right now, God knows what he might be tempted to do with her.

2

The next morning, Duffy deposited Peter's check and called Richard Stern, the lawyer representing the Grievance Committee. Stern said he was a former assistant district attorney and knew Duffy by reputation. "What's a big-time criminal defense lawyer like you representing a low-life divorce lawyer in a piddling administrative proceeding? There's no jury to deceive. A strait-laced lawyer presides and acts as judge and jury. He's motivated by the facts, and they are overwhelming. Business must be slow, or Morrissey must have paid a humongous fee for you to take on his lost cause."

"Lost cause? My ass," Duffy said. "The complainant is an old bag of a whore. My client fucked her, if he indeed did fuck her, because she begged him to. Disbar a lawyer because he's gener-ous, considerate, and kind. Off the record, Morrissey should get a distinguished lawyer award. I took the case to show that your puri-tanical, outdated rules are frivolous and deny equal protection to divorce lawyers victimized by their clients. I'm going to get rule number ten declared unconstitutional."

The two lawyers, having acted out a first-call bluff–and-blus-ter ritual, agreed to meet at Stern's office the following Thursday.

At the meeting, Stern sat at the conference table in his office overlooking Battery Park, the tip of Manhattan, with Lady Liberty in the distance, and said to Duffy, "After receiving Ms. Dixon's complaint, I met with her. Her story was compelling. I reported it to the Grievance Committee. Henry Dinsmore, who heads the committee, said we needed more than one witness before bring-ing charges against a lawyer with a clean record. He asked me to search the docket sheets of divorce actions in which Morrissey rep-resented the wife. It's a needle in a haystack task. My assistant, Lisa Fox, who had heard Ms. Dixon's story, was motivated. She dug and came up with twenty-five names. She met with all of them and took copious notes. It's usually my task to make the case to the committee. This time I deferred to Lisa. She was livid. Reading from her notes, she persuaded the committee to bring the action. Here's a copy of her notes. They're bound, with a table of contents and an index. There's no editorializing. Most everything is quotes. Your client's violations were flagrant. Maybe, after you and he read the report, we can cut a deal. There's nothing to try. He's guilty as hell." Duffy gaped at the loose-leaf binder. Indeed, it had a table of contents with the names of twenty-five women, all presumably Morrissey's clients, discussing his conduct. The words "sexual intercourse," "lover," "rendezvous," assignation," and "Carlyle Hotel" leaped out from the pages, and Duffy knew this was going to be more complicated than he thought—and more trouble than it was worth.

He thought, *It's always good practice in criminal cases to get an early offer. Chances are it won't get worse and might be improved. Even if the case comes in stronger against the defendant than anticipated, you can always grab the offer. Prosecutors don't like going back on their word.*

"OK Richard, what's the deal?" he asked.

"Morrissey resigns from the bar and agrees never to apply for readmission. There will be no publicity. The case will be closed and sealed."

"That's not an offer. It's a guilty plea. I'll advise him to reject it, but the decision is the client's, not the lawyer's. I've been surprised before. I'll convey your offer. I'll also review Ms. Fox's notes with him." Duffy's response left the offer open without any time limitation. "One request. I'd like to meet Lisa."

Stern left the room and returned a minute later with her. She was short, stout with a pinched face, and mousey-brown hair. Duffy guessed she was thirty-five, give or take. She was dressed in a pants suit, a style that was de rigueur for professional women her age.

"Well, aren't you a knockout?" Duffy said. "How about I pick you up after work? I know a small, cozy bar where we can have drinks and dinner. Afterward, how about you come home with me?"

Her mouth turned down; her eyes flashed anger. She practically spat out her response. "Yeah, right. Sure…You're as slimy as your client."

"That's the point," he said. "Women are not helpless creatures easily manipulated by men. Did any of the women you interviewed tell Morrissey to go to hell, like you told me? Or did they encourage him by smiling and flirting? My instincts tell me you're sophisticated. You know consensual sex is not an offense against society."

"I'm not a woman facing the trauma of divorce," she said. "And you're not my lawyer."

"OK. Let's assume you were my client, would you have accepted my proposition?"

"I would smack your face. Look, Mr. Duffy, not all women are weak. Some said no to Morrissey. The code protects those who are not strong, the very ones your client succeeded with. That is, if you consider bedding down a wounded woman a success."

"Let's get on to a different subject. What did you tell Morrissey's former clients about why you wanted to meet with them?"

"The truth. A complaint has been filed against Morrissey. There are hundreds of complaints filed against lawyers. It's my job to investigate. I then showed my badge and said I'd appreciate their help but that cooperation is voluntary."

"There's always some fallout from a filing," Stern said. "We're careful to limit the leaks. Many former clients refused to be interviewed; we didn't, of course, contact any present clients. All the women interviewed, as you will soon find out, were pleased with Morrissey's *legal* services. His victims were mature and experienced. I'm not saying he acted in an acceptable professional manner, but nobody was hurt. No injury, no foul." ·

"Stop with your sporting analogies," she said. "Morrissey's a professional. He's held to a higher standard than Tiger Woods. Many women facing divorce are in a crippled state. They've been tossed into the street. Along comes a smooth-talking Irishman who makes a pass. The woman, drowning in self-pity, is too weak to turn away. Maybe this will be her last chance at love. He plays along until he finds another. There's plenty of trauma. The code prohibits sex between a lawyer and his client. It's our job to enforce the law, not revoke it."

Notes in hand, her eyes seemed to focus on something specific on the page. "This is strange. The women didn't fit a pattern. Some were old, older than Morrissey, some smart, others not so smart. There was one who was obese, and another who was anorexic. I bet he's a sex addict."

"Lisa," Stern said with a patronizing smile, "in your official capacity, you're the defender of the Code of Professional Responsibility, not all of womankind. Let's not go overboard. Disbarment is a severe punishment. But if Morrissey suffers from an addiction, that could be a mitigating factor."

Duffy was eager to change the subject. It was dangerous for a defendant if the prosecutor developed a personal animus. Lisa disliked Morrissey and was out to get him. "When is the hearing? How long will it take? Do you intend to call all twenty-five women?"

"Hearings are scheduled promptly," Stern said. "Within sixty days of the service of the notice. If you need more time, our office will not oppose a reasonable adjournment. As to the number of witnesses, we expect to call only Ms. Dixon. We reserve the right to call more and to call rebuttal witnesses. We'll let you know promptly after we decide."

Stern looked at his watch. When he looked up, Lisa had left the room. Duffy's departure was formal. He thanked Stern for the meeting and warmly shook his hand.

Duffy hailed a cab, took out his cell, and called Morrissey to relay the substance of the meeting. In view of the imminent trial, Duffy suggested they meet on Saturday at Morrissey's office. "I'll fax Lisa Fox's notes to you. Have the files out on all the women she interviewed. I'm hopeful we'll find several willing to testify for you? If not, you'll have to search for others. I prefer to confine the list to those already interviewed, but that might not be possible. Oh, by the way, the Fox has a hard-on for you. That's the bad news. Her boss seems sympathetic. He commented that if you're a sex addict, that might be a mitigating factor. Tiger Woods checked into a clinic in the south. Maybe you should spend a weekend there. It might help in two respects: It shows you recognize you have an addiction, and that you have taken steps to control it."

Duffy's report hit Morrissey hard. It was a blow to the chest. He slumped in his chair and put his hands over his heart. He agreed to the meeting but asked for Fox's notes to be delivered by hand in an envelope marked "Confidential."

"Too many curious people in my office," he said. Then, as a parting shot, he added, "The Fox may have a hard-on for me, but from what you tell me, she sure as hell doesn't have one for you."

"Glad you still have a sense of humor. See you Saturday."

Since receiving the notice, Morrissey was unable to concentrate on work or anything else. He remembered the advice given to him by a wise old lawyer, one of his early mentors. "Make sure your house is in order. That includes your family life and financial affairs. I lost a big potential client, because the day we were meeting, my broker kept calling. I had speculated in commodities, not realizing my transactions were ninety percent margined. That day the phone didn't stop ringing. I thought I was busted. I never heard from the client again."

Peter, like his mentor, was distracted. He feared making blunders in pending cases. *I'm in no condition,* he thought, *to represent anybody. I've got good lawyers working for me. I'll turn over day-to-day responsibility to them. I need time alone. No, not alone but with Katherine. I'll have dinner with her. Twins got each other's back. We have a sixth sense, a gut reaction to danger. How many times had she warned me to curb what she called my "libidinousness"? "Get help. See a shrink. It's going to ruin your life. We're a monogamous society, and you're an outsider." I should have paid attention but didn't.*

There was ESP between Peter and his sister. Katherine had been right about his ex-wife, Joan. She said, "She's bright and pretty but the wrong wife for you. We're shanty Irish and she's an upper-class WASP. She's as strong-willed as you are. The two of you will vie for the limelight. And then there's your pathological hypersexuality. You won't seek professional help. Marrying Joan is a recipe for disaster."

Did Peter pay attention? No, but to his credit, he never tried marriage again.

Katherine was young when her husband died, leaving her with little money and two small children, a boy and a girl. She did not remarry. She worked as a freelance writer and editor. She earned barely enough to pay the rent on her apartment and feed her family. Peter had no children of his own. He assumed responsibility for the care and welfare of his sister and her family. He paid for the children's education and for summer camp and trips. Her son, James, was an intellectual. He was an associate professor of English literature, married, and the father of three children. Peter treated his nephew's children as generously as if they were his own grandchildren. *And Lisa Fox thinks I'm a monster?*

Peter was fond of his nephew, but his niece, Jean, was his all-time favorite. He had taught her to read and discussed her boyfriends with her, a subject off limits even to her mother. Peter encouraged Jean to apply to law school. When she was accepted to Harvard, Peter missed her but made up for it by visiting her twice a year. She asked his advice before choosing her husband, a Harvard Law classmate.

"Do you think it's a mistake to marry another lawyer? We'll talk about law all the time. How dull."

"Nonsense," Peter said. "You'll have a rule. Work stays in the office. Thomas is smart, funny, and from my observations, you get along well. Don't worry if things don't work out. I'll represent you for free."

Peter needed to talk to someone. He called Katherine and made a dinner date for that evening. That would be enough of a break. He had to read Fox's notes before he went to bed.

As he turned the pages, he grimaced. On every page. Twice on some pages. Why was he such a fool for women? One client said he had "begged" for sex, claiming it would help the case if he got to know her better. Was he an abject beggar? Really? Didn't women want to know they're desired? Wasn't that what he was trying to do by coaxing them? After much soul-searching, the woman who said he had begged had submitted. Several said they were not emotionally strong at the time, and although they didn't want him (or any other man), they gave in. One former client said he pushed her into a closet and kissed and fondled her. It was only when she threatened to scream that he released her. She wanted to fire him, but the case was going well. What would she say to her new attorney? "My former attorney attacked me. I hope you won't." Also, she may have been complicit. When Morrisey commented on her figure, she smiled and said, "Aren't you cute?" She should have said, "I'm here to discuss my case, not my body."

Peter thought of the definition of sexual relations. The groping in the closet was, in the eyes of the law, sexual relations. *A guy can't have fun*, he thought. *What was fun for me may not be fun for a woman. Damn, when there's resistance, it isn't fun for me.* Rape was wrong. No question. He would never sink to that level. But forcing himself on a woman who didn't want him was akin to rape. Shameful. How many times had he vowed not to mess with his clients? Hundreds. At any friendly approach, his resolve turned to jelly. It took a criminal action—a pseudocriminal action—to bring home to him how outrageous his conduct was. And yes, how deserving of punishment it was.

Peter put thoughts about his other victims out of his mind. Molly Dixon was the Grievance Committee's only witness, and even though she had written Peter that sweet note, she had turned against him. Her case had ended several years ago. Why had she waited so long? Why was she doing this to him? Should he call her and ask? Would he be tampering with a witness? Better not to add a new charge.

The other interviewees were not being called. Presumably, she was the only one willing to testify. By praising his "services," she had tarnished her testimony. Duffy would drive that point home.

Peter set out for Katherine's apartment. He guessed they would eat at a neighborhood Italian restaurant, but his sister had other ideas. "Tonight Peter, we'll dine alone. I picked up dinner at Zabar's. I sense you need to talk."

He nodded and poured two glasses of white wine. Over dinner he described his encounter with Molly and the pending disbarment proceeding. He admitted there were too many Mollies to count. Katherine listened and said not a word until he had finished.

"Having sex with your clients was wrong. You have a tendency to objectify women. That too is wrong, aggravated by the fact you are a sensitive and smart man. Let's not forget, however, you have done a lot of good things for women. You've helped victims of domestic violence. For how many years now?"

"More than thirty-five years. I've given so much dough to the umbrella organization, Safe Horizon, they call me 'Saint Peter' and made me chairman of the board. You know what's strange? I lust after all my clients but have only compassion, no sexual desire whatsoever for these poor women."

"Of course you wouldn't take advantage of the defenseless. I remember the gala fundraising dinner for Safe Horizon. What was it...ten years ago? You took a table for twenty. Robert Morgenthau was the guest of honor and talked all about you. Oh Peter, I was so proud of you when he said, 'Peter Morrissey has gotten more orders of protection than any fifty lawyers put together. When a marshal was unavailable to serve the order immediately, he risked his life by serving it on a violent man, warning him it's prison if he ever comes near the victim.'"

She patted her brother's hand. "Your good deeds outweigh your bad. And I don't minimize the bad. Now I'm not saying that because you help poor women; you have a right to prey upon wealthy divorcees. What I'm saying is that in the ledger sheet of life, your balance sheet reflects more good deeds than bad. Pick your head up and hold it high. You're a good man. Be sure and get your good deeds before the judge."

"We have always been kind to each other," he said, "and sometimes being kind includes being frank. If you rob a bank and give the money to the poor, you're still a bank robber. If caught, you'll go to jail. There's no Robin Hood defense in the law."

"Peter, you won't be able to do a thing for these women if you're disbarred."

"You know what? The law won't give a damn. My work helping women has no bearing on whether sex with Molly Dixon violated the code."

As they talked, Peter's thoughts drifted back to his early years as an associate at Cahill, Gordon. The firm encouraged its lawyers to provide legal services for the poor. Peter volunteered to help battered women. Their scars and bruises caused him to take arms against men who beat up women. He assisted the police and the DA's office to get arrests and convictions. He had only compassion for the victims. He helped them get housing and start new lives. He was as attentive to their needs as to his paying clients.

Katherine did not raise the subject again, but after Peter left, she called Duffy, whom she dated twice after his wife died. It turned out that he was not aware of Peter's volunteer work with battered women. "Penalty is an issue in the case," Duffy said. "The judge has wide discretion. One extreme is disbarment; the other a slap on the wrist. Peter's community service would impress the judge. I was an assistant US attorney under Morgenthau. I know him well. He won't testify. He's an old-world moralist. I think, however, I could get him to send a letter about Peter's work helping battered women. A letter from him or someone from Safe Horizon would be dynamite. I'm glad you called. Katherine, let's stay in touch."

3

Duffy came to the Saturday meeting dressed in a golf shirt, khakis, sneakers, and a baseball cap. Despite his playtime wear, he was all business. On Fridays many attorneys dress casually. Peter did not fully embrace "casual Friday," as the tradition was called; he always wore a jacket. That Saturday, he put on his best Friday uniform: a blue blazer; natty, red-and–white, open-collar shirt; white flannel pants; and penny loafers. Although his outfit suggested a day at the country club, he was eager to go to work.

"Let's go over the twenty-five interviewees," Duffy said. "We'll put the Fox's notes in two separate files. Pile one is women you plowed; pile two, ones you didn't. I hope we have some who resisted your charms. My plan is to interview the ones who resisted and pick the best, and if there's only one, so be it."

He continued, "The code defines sexual relations broadly. A lawyer is barred from having sex with his client. *And* from fondling her breasts, ass, or crotch. Taken literally, a pat on the behind might be enough to get you disbarred. In pile two are the ones you didn't seduce or grope. How many of those do you think there are? I counted six."

"That's what I got, but one, Helen Jones, lied. She told Fox we didn't have sex, and when Fox read the broad definition of sex, she remained firm. She said, 'There was "no hanky-panky."' I recall she was particularly passionate. Maybe Fox is setting a trap."

"I wouldn't put it past her. Let's take no chances and ignore Helen. She mentions a 'wish list.' What's that all about? "

"At an early meeting, I ask clients to tell me the financial terms they hope to get. I divide them into applicable categories: real estate; securities; pensions; bank accounts; alimony; child support—custody, joint, or exclusive; and personal property, such as cars, furniture, and jewelry. We call it a wish list. We match the final results against the list. Helen, as did many others, agreed we did better than the list. In matters that counted, we equaled or did better. Mary Flowers is not on the list. I guess she wasn't interviewed. Or if she was, Fox left her off. I never touched her. Not, mind you, through lack of effort. I tried. She refused my offers for dinner and dancing. She liked the result I got for her but not me. It's a point you should stress. I worked hard for all my former clients, regardless of whether we had sex."

"Any reason Mary didn't succumb?" Duffy asked.

"Yeah. She's an editor at Random House. She was in love with her boss. Shortly after the divorce, they married. Her ex-husband was also having an affair. He, too, promptly remarried. I remember her laughing when she turned me down. She said, 'Definitely no. Cheating on my husband is morally reprehensible. Cheating on husband and lover is a one-way ticket to hell. I'm bad but not all that bad.'"

"Let's look at the photos of the client-witnesses we're considering. She must be reasonably attractive. If she's ugly, a judge might say, 'Of course he ignored her.'

"Look Bill, why worry about others? Molly's the only witness against us. Maybe we deal only with Molly and not call any witnesses. Why open Pandora's box?"

"I'm not about to call a witness who will hurt you. If we don't have a good witness, we won't call any. Something Stern said put an idea in my head. 'No injury, no foul.' It doesn't quite fit, but it comes close. I'd like to show that you served all your clients well. Whether they went to bed with you or not was a matter of indifference as far as your services were concerned. I'll get that from Molly on cross-examination. But, I'd like more if we can find it. A good witness is one who is smart, attractive, and independent. She's proof that a 'no' to sex had no impact on your services.

"The first order of business is to select our witnesses. I'll meet with them in my office. Let's wait on Mary Flowers. Fox may claim surprise, because she didn't interview Mary. It's best to stick with the interviewees. I don't want to open the door to more witnesses. It's a big plus for us that the committee is calling only one."

"Why do you want me present at the session? It will be embarrassing for the client and for me."

"You'll be there to introduce me and then make a graceful exit. When each interview is over, I'll call you. You can say goodbye and thank her. Then we can discuss whether or not she would be effective.

"When the case comes up for trial, and the prosecutor concludes his case, I think—but I may change my mind—you will be our first witness. Then again, depending on the flow of the case and my judgment on how helpful our fact witnesses are, they may bat first and you clean up. You will show contrition and reform. To show good faith, you'll enroll in Sex Addicts Anonymous. Yes, it exists. Weekly meetings are held at the Church of the Heavenly Rest at Fifth and Ninetieth Street. Philip Gross heads the program. It's modeled after A.A. You will actively participate. Never miss a meeting. Gross will testify for us if you play ball."

"I despise holy rollers," Morrissey said. "If I have to do it, I'll sing praise to the Lord. Give me strength to overcome my weakness. I'll wave my hands toward the heavens. I'll do anything to get out of this putrid, stinking hole. "

"There's more coming. I've lined up a neuropsychologist. He will testify as to the role of the brain in addiction. It plays a dominant role. You see, Peter, it's not your fault. Blame your brain, blame nature, blame anything at all but not you for your preternatural sexual appetite. He will comment on your voluntary commitment to Sex Addicts Anonymous. He will find your acts reflect a sincere desire to control your addiction and obtain sexual sobriety.

"Our final witness or witnesses will be the client or clients we select unless they come first. I know it's nerve-racking when the lawyer is inconsistent, but I've got to remain flexible until we see which way the tide is turning. The witnesses will stress your superb work, despite the fact they told you to fuck off. They will say—I hope—that your flirtation was 'flattering.' 'It came at a good time.' Just when their egos needed a boost. They didn't take you seriously, because when they said no, you didn't persist. Their interest was focused on their divorce, on you as a divorce lawyer, not a lover. It's hard to disbar a competent lawyer. That's just a bare outline.

"I'd like you to sign a wish list for me just as your clients do for you. We'll coordinate your wishes with numbers with the most desirable result; for example, dismissal of the case at ten, disbarment at one, and a five-year suspension at five.

Morrissey smiled then said, "Stop teasing me. It hurts." What he said did not register with Duffy. He pulled out his cell phone and snapped a photo of Peter. "When the case is over, I'll ask you to sign the photo and say something wonderful about me. I'll hang it in my bathroom. Every time I'm on the crapper, I'll think of you.

"Oh," Duffy said, "there's an important matter we haven't discussed yet. Character witnesses can be important on the issue of penalty. Guys have been convicted and escaped the slammer because the sentencing judge was impressed with their good deeds. I remember a judge saying 'To incarcerate you would deprive society of your services. That's not what justice is all about.'

"Katherine called. She told me about Safe Horizon. That's the kind of stuff that moves a sentencing judge. I wish more of my clients' relatives would call. They know more than I do about my clients and sometimes more than my clients."

Peter said, "I didn't think about character witnesses. Being a lawyer immersed in his own case, my vision is myopic. I think only of relevance. In the eyes of the code, helping poor women doesn't give me a license to screw my clients."

"Of course not," Duffy said. "But it does go to penalty. Robin Hood wouldn't get the same sentence as Willy Sutton."

"I'll get it before the referee as part of my opening. I'll ask whether he'll accept letters from character witnesses. Although not part of the trial on merits, I'll plant your good work at the start of the case."

As the two men parted, Duffy said, "See you on Saturday at around nine thirty. That is, if I can get the gals to come. I'll schedule the first meeting at ten. Bring along the wish list of each client we'll be interviewing and the final judgment in the case. I'll want to remind each former client what a great job you did."

"While you're at it, Bill, there is only one wish on my personal list. Get the case over with quickly. It's taking a toll. I can't concentrate on work or anything else. Settlement is the fastest way to end a case. I'll agree to anything provided I can keep on practicing."

"That's the problem. Stern wants you to resign. There's no wiggle room. If I counter, he'll detect weakness and won't budge. Over with quickly? The only way is a quick trial. You'll have to hold out for a few months. "

4

Duffy called the five clients and told them, "The case involves an important civil liberties issue. Should a lawyer be punished for having a consensual affair with a client? The bar association threatens to disbar any lawyer, who, while representing a woman in a divorce case, has sexual relations with his client. The one exception is if they had sex before she became his client. Morrissey had a consensual affair with a client. She subsequently turned against him. You know a little bit about the case, because you were interviewed by the prosecutor's assistant. You talked to her. Will you talk to me?"

All five agreed to meet on the following Saturday. He scheduled the meetings an hour and a half apart anticipating each would take not more than an hour. The extra time would be spent with Peter brainstorming the witness's prospective testimony.

Duffy portrayed the information as good news. Peter did not agree. He hated asking clients to help him in what he believed to be a lost cause. He had violated the code almost from the time he opened shop as a divorce lawyer. As a divorcée and bachelor, he indulged his insatiable appetite for sex. At first, he dated women introduced to him by friends. Then he found a new source: his own clients. Sex with them was easier as they required much less wining and dining. There was another advantage. The relationship had a natural termination point: the end of the case. Peter didn't want to fall in love or have a messy split. He also had no patience for a time-consuming seduction. His clients didn't need much encouragement. They looked up to him as their knight-errant and more—a man who would romance them and avenge their mean, unfaithful husbands. They wanted nothing more. Peter turned down offers to meet "the perfect woman" so many times that friends finally gave up. Over time, his love life revolved around his clients. Whenever he felt shitty about his sex life, he thought about his work as a 'champion of the cause of battered women.' *I'm not a sexist or a misogynist. I'm a good guy.*

Peter had been happy until Molly Dixon and the bar association struck. Now he was depressed. As he read through Lisa Fox's notes, he was profoundly embarrassed. Maybe he should accept Stern's offer and resign from the bar. He was at a crossroads. It was time to speak to an independent person, one he trusted. That person was his niece, Jean. He called her and said he had to talk. "I hope it's not your health," she said.

"No, the bar association wants to disbar me. I hate to burden you, but you're a lawyer and a woman."

"Tom's out of town. How about dinner at my place at seven? It's strange. You always counseled me. I'll try to do the same for you."

At dinner Peter described his sexual problem. He began with his marriage to Joan. "She was wonderful. The divorce was my fault. I sought out other women. Only a few and on rare occasions. Enough to upset Joan. I don't have the foggiest notion why I cheated, but cheat I did. Joan gave me a chance to reform, but I failed. After the divorce, I started to take up with clients. Lots of them. Now one, Molly Dixon, complained to the bar association, and it investigated. What it found is not pleasant. I have a copy of the investigator's notes. Do you want to see them?"

"No, I don't. Did you coerce any of your clients? Don't bother to answer. I've known you all my life. Of course you didn't."

He was too ashamed to say the truth, so he lied flat out. "Every relationship was consensual." He didn't need to tell his niece everything. "In fact Duffy believes Dixon seduced me." Morrissey then discussed the Dixon affair. He mentioned the tactic of using the leader of Sex Addicts Anonymous and a famous neurologist as expert witnesses. He said Duffy was planning to call five former clients and himself as fact witnesses.

Jean listened quietly and took some time before she issued an opinion. "Lawyers get disbarred for embezzling funds, dereliction of duty, committing crimes. You did none of these things. What are you accused of? Having an affair with a willing client? That's nothing. Duffy is probably engaged in overkill. Let's not second guess him. Peter, you've been a father to me. I was always proud of you. Whatever you decide, I'll still be proud of you. But I'll be prouder if you fight. Of course you're going to use your pro bono work for women in your defense."

"Of course," he said.

He thanked Jean, kissed her goodnight, and returned to his home in the Pierre Hotel on Sixty-First Street and Fifth Avenue. His apartment, which consisted of a bedroom, living room, bathroom, and kitchen, was on the twentieth floor. If he stood to one side of his living room and twisted his neck, he could catch a glimpse of Central Park. A decorator furnished his apartment in dark tones and overstuffed chairs and couches. Its message: this is a bachelor pad.

Peter saw his phone light blinking. He was the only person in the world without his own voicemail system at home. He loved certain old-fashioned ways that his money could still buy. The hotel operator told him, "A Mr. Duffy called reminding you of the meeting tomorrow with the five visitors. Any change, call him right away." *I guess*, he thought, *Duffy must have sensed my ambivalence. God, I hate this case. Lawyers should defend clients, not be targets themselves. Well, I'm learning one thing: how my clients feel as trial approaches. From now on, I'll have more empathy for them.*

It happened most years on or near Peter's wedding anniversary, what he called "My Anniversary Dream." As he lay in bed that night, he closed his eyes and reminisced about Joan Gifford, his ex, whom he hadn't seen in over twenty years. He felt it coming on and let himself drift off to sleep.

They had met when they were in their mid-twenties. Peter was constantly searching for women. A friend told him about an anti-Vietnam War gathering in a basement room in a church on Park Avenue. "There'll be lots of attractive young women. You'll do well."

The room was strewn with banners. Facing the audience was a Martin Luther King quote: "If America's soul becomes totally poisoned, part of the autopsy must read Vietnam." Other banners read: "Dow shall not kill." "Making money burning babies." "Girls say yes to men who say no."

Joan took charge of the meeting. She was blonde and fair-complexioned with big brown eyes and had a snub nose, high cheek bones, and thin lips. She was tall, big-boned, and plump. Overall, she was attractive in a way that was typical of young, Midwestern, Christian women. She hailed from Highland Park, a rich and segregated suburb of Chicago.

Joan worked as an assistant producer of a TV news program. Her broadcast experience was evident. She called the meeting to order and gave a short introductory speech. She talked about the high concentration of blacks fighting in Vietnam, the wholesale exemptions of white males. She attacked the use of chemicals as causing the mass murder of children and civilians and destroying the countryside. The war, she said, was fought for imperialistic reasons and not to prevent the Soviet Union through a domino strategy from conquering the world. She called for an immediate end to the war.

Joan introduced a black Vietnam veteran followed by a Catholic priest and an NYU professor. Peter listened with half an ear. He was distracted; he couldn't stop staring at Joan. He wanted to be alone with her. He had started at the rear of the room but kept moving forward. By the time the meeting ended, he was at the very front, close to Joan.

When she was done speaking, Peter introduced himself to her. "To tell you the truth, I've been so wrapped up in myself and my job at Cahill, Gordon that I've ignored the protest movement but not the war. I'm in the reserves, but my unit has not been called. I'm praying it never will. I won't go if it's called. I won't risk my life in that war. I'd like to get involved in the movement but don't know how. How about a tutorial at P.J. Clarke's? It's just a few blocks away."

"I'm not a missionary, but I do encourage people to become active. I'll go to Clarke's but only stay a short time. I'm working the early shift."

On the way to Clarke's, Peter asked how Joan got involved. "I was too young for the Civil Rights Movement," she said. "This protest is, in a way, a continuation of the earlier movement. I doubt our leaders would be so eager to send more and more troops to the war if our troops were all white. The fact that the enemy is brown makes the use of napalm and Agent Orange acceptable. Would we use those chemicals against, say, the Germans?"

Over beers, the subject changed to Joan's early life. She described Highland Park, as an all-white, upper-class community. Her parents were narrow-minded bigots. "They associate only with other rich WASPs. They and their friends measure tolerance by the size of the Christmas bonuses they give their black maids."

Joan was happy to leave her home and found a better one at Mount Holyoke. Her roommate in her senior year was now her best friend, Sally, a black girl from Newark. "At graduation, my father didn't greet or look at Sally, and my mother made some ridiculous comment about Sally's dress being pretty. They refused to have dinner with Sally and her parents."

Joan liked her job but hated the work environment. "Women are second class. We're paid less than men and find it much harder to get promoted. One of my bosses called me 'girl,' pinched my behind, and tried to fondle my breasts. It made no sense to complain to a higher-up. They think groping is a game. I didn't know what to do, so I said, 'Keep your hands to yourself, or I'll tell your wife.' I hope you're not a groper."

If only she knew, Peter thought, *she'd have thrown her beer in my face.* "Look, I'm a red-blooded heterosexual man, mad for women. I wait, however, for them to grope me. Most times, the wait seems to take nine hundred years, as long as Methuselah lived."

Joan laughed. "You must be exaggerating. You're so big. So much to grope." The ice was broken. It was midnight before Joan said, "It's late. I've got to go. I'm afraid I've failed. You've learned nothing."

Peter was emboldened. "That's fodder for our next date. How about dinner tomorrow?"

"Call me. I have to check."

They exchanged phone numbers. Peter hailed a cab and took Joan to her Westside apartment. No groping took place in the cab or at the front door of Joan's apartment.

The next night they had dinner. Thereafter they saw each other whenever they had free time. Although they made no formal commitment, they dated no one else. They necked and petted, but Joan ruled out intercourse. "I'm a modern, progressive female, a women's libber and a free spirit. I'm also a product of my Midwestern upbringing. I'm not a virgin, but I hate one night stands. I know how I feel about you, but I'm confused about your feelings. Sometimes I see you staring at other women. I get mixed signals. Are you lusting or just looking?"

"Joan, I love you. I want to marry you. We must make love now, or I'll die of unrequited love. Let's elope right now. That's my commitment to you. Are you convinced?"

She took a moment to answer, and during that moment, his heart sank and rose, sank and rose, until she finally answered. "I'm convinced. Why didn't you say that earlier? Come to Highland Park with me over Thanksgiving. You'll meet my parents. They're awful. I'll introduce you as my fiancé. My mother will set a date."

They made love that night in Peter's studio apartment on E. Ninety-Third Street and Second Avenue. She was passionate. Peter called her a gift from the gods and declared himself the happiest man in the world.

Peter made the pilgrimage to the Gifford home, and Joan had prepared him for the large colonial family house, the simple but expensive furniture, and the Oriental rugs in all the important rooms. Joan had showed Peter photographs of her parents but had not mentioned that both had nicknames. The father baptized John Gifford III was named after his father and grandfather. As a boy he was called "The Third," which when he was very young, he pronounced as "Tish." It became his nickname. He asked Peter to call him Tish. "All my friends do."

When Peter was introduced to Florence Gifford, she held his hand tight, and with a coy smile on her face said, "When we get to know each other better, I hope you'll call me Mitten."

Peter survived the long weekend helped by passionate sessions in Joan's bedroom. Mitten said she would set the wedding for June, on the "first Saturday our club is available."

"There are lots of good law firms in Chicago," Tish said. "It would be wonderful if you and Joan moved to Highland Park." Joan sounded the first discordant note of the weekend. "Dad, if Peter decides to work in Chicago, I'll divorce him."

Mitten kissed them both as they were leaving. Peter had been perfunctorily kissed many times, but never could he remember a kiss as ice cold as Mitten's. He wondered if she knew what a rat he was.

Peter didn't have to move to Chicago for the marriage to end. He just had to be himself. Being married to Joan cured his womanizing, as he hoped and prayed it would but only temporarily. He thought, *a satyr is a life sentence. After all a leopard can't change his spots, and the wind can't stop blowing.*

There was no need for a divorce. They were only married for two years. No children. So, they got the marriage annulled. Joan alleged he concealed the fact he was a hypersexual. That was part of it. There was more.

Katherine had warned him that Joan needed to be under a spotlight. "She loves herself more than she is capable of loving anyone else. I sense she disapproves of me. If I'm right, by extension she disapproves of you. Maybe, despite her scorn for Highland Park, she's having trouble accepting our working-class, Brooklyn background."

Katherine was probably right. Joan accused him of lacking class, not being dignified, especially when he was too friendly to waiters, maids, or other working-class people, though she professed to be a friend to the poor. "It's your lower–class, Brooklyn background. I wish you could repress it."

Now, thirty five years later, Peter was nearing the end of *Portrait of a Lady. He* opened the book, and thought about Isabel Archer. If morals were defined as how we behaved toward others, and ethics as how we should live our lives, then Isabel possessed exemplary morals and ethics. She made a bad mistake in the form of a horrific marriage to Gilbert Osmond. She had a chance to end that liaison and marry either Lord Warburton or Caspar Goodwood. Both loved her dearly. What did she decide? To stick with the rat she married because of her affection for his daughter. As he finished the book, Peter spoke to Isabel. "Think of yourself. Forget Osmond's daughter. You owe her nothing. But then you wouldn't be Isabel."

As he drifted off to sleep, he thought, *it's easy to write about really good people but hard to live as one.* Joan was no Isabel Acher, but she was real, not a figment of a novelist's imagination. He lost her in part because of his sexual obsession. He refused to seek help. He had lost his wife, and now his sickness threatened to end his career.

5

Over breakfast on Saturday morning, Peter thought about the five witnesses Duffy had dubbed "The Holy Virgins." He chuckled when he thought about the first, Gloria Bienstock, a lesbian. She wanted out of her marriage in order to marry her partner, Betty Driscoll. "As soon as the divorce becomes final, Betty and I are headed to Massachusetts and wedding bells." Peter wondered about gay marriages ending in divorce. New York did not then recognize gay marriages. Would its courts have jurisdiction to entertain a divorce action? What rules would apply? *C'mon Morrisey, get back to business.* Would Gloria make a good witness?

She had sued for divorce in 2008, claiming that her husband, Eric, was unfaithful. At that time New Yorkers still needed grounds for divorce; the only available ones being adultery and cruel and inhumane treatment. Peter considered his role prominent in changing New York's divorce law to make divorce possible without proof of fault. His bar association committee drafted the new law, and Peter explained its provisions to the state assembly and senate, which approved the change. Peter was present when Governor Patterson signed the bill and was given the very pen the governor used. Peter was often mentioned in news stories about the law.

His thoughts returned to Gloria. She had no evidence of Eric's infidelity other than her own ipse dixit, unproven assertion. "He's having an affair with his assistant, Emily Axelrod," she said. "I know it."

Peter hired a private detective to tail Gloria's husband. The detective followed Eric and Emily to a farmhouse in Pennsylvania, where they spent the weekend. *Strange,* thought Peter. Knowing that a divorce action was pending, Eric was careless. He probably didn't give a damn. It must be hard living with a woman in love with another woman.

Eric had counterclaimed for divorce. He alleged that his wife was having an affair with a woman and named Betty Driscoll as the correspondent. He contended sex between women was adultery, a recognized ground for divorce. Was gay sex adultery? There were no decisions either way, so Eric's case would make new law. Peter thought it made sense. What's the difference if a woman or a man makes love to a married woman? Both acts are outside the marriage contract and should be treated the same.

Gloria, at first, refused to allow Peter to serve a formal denial to the counterclaim. "Betty and I are proud of our relationship. We will never deny it."

"No, no," Peter said. "An admission that you've been having an affair with Betty will kill your chances on the financial terms. Our judge is old fashioned. He equates gays with freaks. I'll file a general denial on the ground that the counterclaim is vague and ambiguous."

Gloria called Betty, who asked to speak with Peter. She wanted to know about the implications of a general denial.

"A counterclaim has to be answered," he said, "A general denial is not made under oath. It's considered a formality. If Gloria admits her relationship with you, I guarantee she will suffer financially. The judge assigned to our case is intolerant, not socially or politically correct."

Betty asked to speak with Gloria. The two accepted Peter's strategy. He could see that money trumped pride.

The judge refused to hear any evidence that Gloria was gay. "It's incredible," the judge said. "You have been living with this woman for twenty-five years. And after all those years, you claim she's gay? I thought I had heard everything. Don't raise that issue again if you know what's good for you."

Gloria was awarded a divorce and a better financial split than she had hoped for. Eric's counterclaim was dismissed.

Peter had made no effort to seduce Gloria. It was doomed to fail, though he did think about a ménage à trios. He'd watch Gloria and Betty going at it, and then he would join in. Both women would seize him, and he'd make it a doubleheader. He wondered whether the addition of another woman, not his client, would exempt the act from the code. He did not share his thoughts with Duffy.

Back to reality and the other candidates. He would tell Duffy that Gloria was gay. The fact that he did not make a pass or that she resisted him was not evidence that he had behaved or that she was strong. The weight of her testimony was zero, most likely negative. The judge, when the truth about her sexuality came out, would think they were trying to trick him.

Peter turned to the second witness, Alice Burns, a tenured professor at Barnard College. Her husband, Nicholas, was a professor at Columbia. They both specialized in English literature. Nicholas had fallen in love with a young teaching associate. Alice refused to condemn him. "Nicholas is exceptional," she said. "A figure as large as a Nietzschean philosopher of the future. He does not have to follow the rules."

On their first trip to court, Peter offered her his hand when they got out of the cab. Her "no thank you" conveyed the meaning: how dare you attempt to touch me. When Peter made a direct pass, Alice said that Fitzwilliam Darcy, or Mr. Darcy, as he was known in the Jane Austen classic, was her ideal man. "You, Mr. Morrissey, are no Mr. Darcy. Have you read *Pride and Prejudice*? I think not. Don't you ever dare again to flirt with me."

Peter knew that Alice held him in contempt, and that she was not one to dissemble. If she agreed to testify, which was problematic, her hostility would come through. She would find a way to hurt him. He'd advise Duffy to keep her testimony short. He flirted. She rejected him. He continued to represent her. That's it. *Pray that she'll hold up in cross-examination.*

The third was Margaret Gould, an heiress who wanted to unload her third husband, a gigolo, Anthony Armstrong, on the cheap. Cheap to her was a million dollars. Anthony was younger than Margaret and had a thing for her Park Avenue apartment. And her homes in Newport and Palm Springs. She accused him of caring more about her real estate than about her. He did not deny it. Soon after their marriage, Anthony made the mistake of refusing to have sex with his wife.

Margaret sought her divorce in 2005. At that time divorce was granted on a finding of fault or a separation agreement containing all financial terms on file for a year during which the married couple lived apart. In 2010 Anthony's sexual neglect would be considered a "constructive abandonment" and a ground for divorce. Peter had to deal with the law as it was in 2005.

Anthony was willing, indeed eager, to sign a separation agreement but put a price tag on his signature of $10 million. "I'll roast in hell before I pay that wastrel anything above a million," Margaret said.

Peter didn't understand the principle. "If you're worth $500 million, what's the difference between a million and ten million? Some people confuse princi*pal* with princi*ple*." Margaret was one such person. She stuck to principal.

Peter sized up Anthony as gay or at least bisexual. He thought about bringing an action to annul the marriage on the ground of fraud, namely that Anthony had concealed his sexual proclivity. "Suppose Anthony had told you he was gay?" he asked Margaret. "Would you have married him?"

"Anthony's not gay. I have several gay friends, and they know who's gay and who's not. They say 'Anthony's not gay.' I believe them."

"So, you were suspicious. Suspicious enough to ask others. He sure is asexual around you. You're a sensuous, attractive woman. If Anthony abstains, something's wrong. My idea is to seek an annulment alleging fraud. Anthony concealed his homosexuality. Our objective: if we win, he gets nothing. If he signs on the dotted line, he gets a million. I'll speak with his lawyer and tell him we have evidence that Anthony is a deviant."

As Margaret looked for something in her purse, Peter smiled wickedly and approached her with his arms open, ready to embrace her. Although all women excited Peter, wealthy women had an added effect. They were perfectly dressed, groomed, perfumed. They seemed aloof but Peter believed it to be a disguise. They want everything, including passionate sex.

Margaret did not fit the mold.

"Get back to your desk. Don't you ever come near me again, or you're fired."

Peter returned to his chair, and Margaret continued where they had left off. "Anthony was highly sexed before we married and for months thereafter. Then he changed. After several failures, he became indifferent. I suggested Viagra. 'It will be a short time only, and you'll be back to the old Anthony.' He refused, claiming fear of the side effects. He suggested abstinence until he felt the urge. Almost two years have passed. I'm sick of abstinence. OK, speak with his lawyer, Myron Cohen. Do you know Mr. Cohen?"

"The divorce bar is small. I know everyone in the field. Look, I know you think very little of me and will think even less if I pull this off. Would you prefer we forget it?"

"Don't be an ass. You're a highly regarded divorce lawyer. That's why I hired you. I can see where you might be attractive to some women. You're not my type. Not even close."

Peter withered at her response. After she left, he called Myron Cohen. They agreed to meet for breakfast at the Regency. Peter wasted no time. He opened with the spiel he saved for schlocky lawyers. "I'm a big believer in fees for lawyers. Your client is a ne'er do well, a spendthrift; he has no money, and if he did, he wouldn't want to give any to you. Courts routinely make the husband pay the wife's legal expenses, but how many times do you recall an award against the wife and in favor of the husband? Trust me, Myron. If the case winds up the way it should, you'll get a humongous fee. If Anthony doesn't play ball, neither he nor you will get a dime. Don't interrupt me, and don't say 'no' unless you have something against huge fees."

Cohen concentrated on his cup of coffee. Peter went on.

"Anthony is queer. Worse, he lacks discretion. One of Margaret's gay friends said Anthony propositioned him. He told Anthony to go to hell, but the friend's not so sure about a mutual acquaintance. For the right price, we'll get a witness. If I were to get the marriage annulled, Anthony will get a big fat zero. And so will you. Margaret would prefer not to bring the suit. She's a socialite and avoids scandals. For that reason if he signs a separation agreement, she'll give him one million dollars, and he can keep all the toys she has given him, including the Ferrari.

"Don't negotiate. A counteroffer will be considered a rejection, and the annulment complaint, now in draft form, will be finalized and served. You have a rough assignment. It's going to take time and all your powers of persuasion. Succeed, you'll be well paid. I'm no bluffer."

Upon parting Cohen said he'd be back, but he wasn't sanguine. "Give me some room to negotiate." Morrissey said he would if he could, but that he had none. Cohen read Morrissey's equivocal comment to mean there was room. Maybe an additional $100,000.

Two weeks later Cohen called. "Great news. He'll do the deal but for an extra $100,000. He says tell Margaret he'll use the $100,000 to make charitable contributions." *Margaret*, Morrissey thought, *will have no doubt that the beneficiary of the extra money would be Anthony.* But it was a clever ploy. It would give her a way out.

"OK. You did your best. I'll try and sell it to Margaret. Draft the agreement with Anthony's signature and send it to me. Add a $50,000 fee for you."

Margaret agreed but complained about the legal fee. "Why should I pay Anthony's lawyer's fee?"

"Think of the fee as an inducement to get Anthony to sign. Cohen's job wasn't easy."

"Oh, I get it. It's a bribe. Lovely bunch of guys. How much is your fee?"

When Peter said he shouldn't get less than Cohen. Margaret nodded then said, "I figured as much."

Peter looked straight at her. "Under certain circumstances, I'd be willing to provide a discount."

Margaret laughed. "Peter, you couldn't even begin to buy me. Wipe that smirk off your face."

He reverted to his parting ritual. He handed her the photo and asked her to sign it. "Please don't use any scatological words."

"I won't, but don't hover." She wrote: "Thanks for your help."

Well, here is a solid witness. He flirted; she resisted. But Margaret was atypical. A wealthy, independent woman. What Duffy needed was a housewife, weakened by rejection and leaning on her lawyer. Margaret wasn't even close, but she was the best so far.

Joyce Ryan and her husband, Jim, had lived in a brownstone in Greenwich Village. They were an odd couple. He was short, ugly, and shrewd. He made a lot of money from an export business whose most profitable product was weapons. If the price were right, Jim would sell nuclear bombs to the Taliban. The law was a knock away from his door. Joyce was about six inches taller than Jim, attractive, and dumb. She kept a diary and indiscriminately entered personal items. A typical entry might read: "Made pot roast. Had sex with Jim."

Richard Huffington, an architect who specialized in remodeling brownstones, met the Ryans at a party, and Joyce hired him on the spot. When Jim objected, Joyce said: "I look on the house as mine. You own everything else. Richard has a great reputation. He did Muriel's house, and you loved it. It will cost money, but you're rich. Just sell a few more guns to the terrorists and put the proceeds in your Cayman Island bank account."

Jim was angry at himself for telling Joyce anything about his business. If he ever tossed her out—which he wanted to—she could blackmail him. He caved partly out of fear and partly because the house needed an upgrade.

Richard spent about a week in their five-story home and another two weeks preparing the plans. He then met with Joyce. The plans were spread on the kitchen table. As Richard reviewed them, he accidentally touched Joyce's arm. Other touches followed, which were plainly intentional. Joyce praised the plans but was more excited by Richard's attention. Her two children were at school. She and Richard were alone. The move to the bedroom was swiftly accomplished, and what had started as a remodeling of a house turned into a remodeling of Joyce.

When the construction began, Jim, Joyce, and their two children moved out of the brownstone and sublet a nearby apartment. Joyce, however, was in the house practically every day. She and Richard played a new game, making love out of sight of the workmen. All six bedrooms were used.

Months later, when all the work had been completed, Joyce threw a party. The guests admired the changes and were introduced to Huffington. In making the introduction, Joyce said, "This genius of an architect—he's really an artist—is responsible for it all." Throughout the party Joyce stayed by Richard's side.

Jim noticed her gazing at Richard with a look she had once turned on for him and became suspicious. That night he picked up Joyce's diary. Sure enough, she recorded having sex with Richard ten times.

Several nights later, Jim asked her if she was still seeing Richard. "Why should I see him? His work is finished."

"Come on Joyce. It's confession time. You and he were having an affair. You fucked him ten times. At least. It's in your diary."

Joyce attacked Jim. Although he was short, he was strong and subdued her. "You're a hypocrite!" she screamed. "You've had dozens of affairs but are just too dishonest to write them down. You've neglected me, scorned me, made fun of me. You're jealous because a brilliant guy like Huffington finds me attractive."

In fact, Jim was not jealous. He had wanted for some time to divorce her but feared a divorce might expose his business practices. If his dealings came to light, he could be convicted of violating the US weapons and tax laws. His wife's affair had provided a way out.

When Joyce calmed down, he put his plan into effect. "Joyce, it will take a long time for me to forgive and forget. Perhaps a year. You may have thought I was unfaithful but I was not. Here's what I propose. We'll get divorced. I'll sue on the ground of adultery. You'll admit your affair with Huffington. I'll set generous settlement terms for you, but we'll ignore them. We'll tell no one about it and continue to live together as man and wife. But, if you're unfaithful again, I'll enforce the divorce."

Joyce was flummoxed and afraid. But she admitted her affair and did not contest the divorce. As long as it meant nothing. They'd been married for fifteen years. The fake divorce was just to make sure she stayed in line. That was how dumb she was. The financial terms were much less than she would have otherwise received, even without the added threat of blackmail. Jim was now free to discard Joyce whenever he wanted without fear of disclosure.

That night Joyce's diary had only one entry. In large, underscored type, she wrote: "Made Love to Jim upside down, sideways, and inside out."

Jim's business attorney, Steve Stump, represented Jim. Stump chose an associate in his office to represent Joyce. The divorce was granted. Six months later, for no reason, and certainly no further adultery, Jim kicked Joyce out. He paid her back alimony and child support. Jim's ploy had worked on a gullible woman.

When Joyce turned to Peter, she said, "I'm divorced and didn't know it. I never would have agreed to those stinking terms if I had known the divorce was for real."

"You're in luck, my dear, because your husband made a fatal error. You didn't have your own lawyer. You were represented by your husband's lawyer's employee. The divorce itself can't be nullified because of your admission of adultery, but we have a chance to better the terms."

On her wish list, she specified the financial terms she wanted but added, "I really want Jim back." She failed to grasp reality: Jim didn't want her.

After taking her photo, Peter reached out his arms and tried to embrace her. "Get away!" she screamed. "Jim said he'd take me back, but I have to be true to him even though we're divorced. I want Jim. I have to be good."

She was paranoid on the subject of being faithful to a man who wanted nothing to do with her. *Too bad*, Peter thought. *We could've had lots of fun.*

Peter was hostile when he met with Stump. "What made you think you could play my game? You're an idiot for choosing your associate, a guy you control, to represent Joyce. She's naïve, and she needed an experienced, tough fighter who will hit below the belt. A lawyer like me. I see your client paid Joyce's legal fees. What did you do? Pocket both fees? You should be disbarred."

Stump stammered out a reply. "I didn't charge."

"Then you're a bigger fool than I thought. My advice. Accept the blame and get Jim a serious lawyer. He's in big trouble." Morrissey knew that Stump, in order to keep his client and protect himself against a malpractice suit, would not step aside. He added, "I can settle the financial terms with you as well as another lawyer, but first I have a favor to ask. Joyce wants to go back to Jim."

"I assure you that will never happen. Jim has moved on. He has another woman. Business is good. Your client may be able to get better terms."

"Speaking of business, if we cannot agree on terms, I'll have to inspect all his illegal sales to our terrorist enemies, and whether he paid taxes on the proceeds. Joyce says he kept his money in the Cayman Islands. Is that true?"

"He sells only to the Palestinians. They're freedom fighters. Israel's enemy, not ours. Many loyal Americans support the Palestinians, and so do large charitable foundations. They pay for the weapons. As far as his Cayman Island account is concerned, it is a perfectly legal practice. He pays all the taxes he owes. The practice is known as 'tax planning.' You'll get nowhere going down that path."

"That's a nice argument. The judge who granted the divorce will handle Joyce's fraud case. The judge is a Jew. I'm sure he'll understand that Jim is just a warm-hearted businessman out to help a downtrodden people establish their own country. The judge, who pays his taxes like the rest of us, will also sympathize with Jim's *tax planning*, assuming that's what it is. Here's what my client wants: Act quickly. She may change her mind when she learns Jimboy has another *friend*." Peter gave Stump the terms on Joyce's wish list. He added a fee for himself of $50,000.

In short order the financial terms were modified. As Joyce signed her photo, Peter placed his hands on her shoulders. She pushed his hands away. "Sorry Peter, it's not going to happen."

Joyce appeared to be a perfect witness. Peter had tried and been rejected. Her case was not one for divorce but for modification of a divorce judgment. The code, however, was not limited to divorce. It covered "domestic relations matter," which Joyce's action certainly was. If they had had sex, and Joyce had complained, the Grievance Committee would have claimed a violation.

Joyce showed that a sexually active woman "in a domestic relations matter" was able to resist her lawyer's attempts at seduction. Yet Peter's instincts told him Joyce would make a bad witness. She was driven to be "good" by her insane thought that if she were, Jim would take her back. In practice sessions she was unable to stick with the story Peter had scripted for her. When asked why she was seeking better terms, she blurted out, "I cheated on him. I didn't deserve anymore."

Joyce had been an actress before she married Jim, but she couldn't have been any good. Peter almost gave up when he hit on a plan. "Joyce, I'm hiring you as an actress to play yourself in this very proceeding. I'll pay you Actor's Equity's minimum wage, provided you learn the script, and when forced to ad lib, you follow our game plan. Here's the script. The principal points: you knew nothing about what you were entitled to; you relied wholly upon your lawyer; when he said that's about what you'd get if the case went to trial, you accepted his advice. After all he told you he was an experienced divorce lawyer. He wasn't. He failed to disclose that this was his first divorce case, and that he was employed by Jim's lawyer. Had you known these critical facts, you would have sought independent counsel."

Peter then handed Joyce a written outline of her answers to possible questions. Joyce memorized the script. In rehearsals she suppressed the answer she wanted to give. She said over and over again, "I relied on my lawyer." Peter was confident she would stick to the script if the case went to trial.

For Peter's case Joyce was not the perfect witness. Would she remember the answers she had to give? Peter doubted it. Duffy could always "hire" her. Peter decided he would leave it to Duffy.

The last candidate was Ruth Block. She was the bitterest of Morrissey's many bitter clients. Her husband, Herman, was a smooth-talking swindler. He had induced Ruth's parents, her relatives, their friends, and many others to manage their money. His performance was nothing short of disastrous. He invested mainly in new public offerings. The stocks were highly speculative. Shortly after purchase, almost all the companies failed. To conceal his dismal performance, Herman reported substantial profits by claiming that the few successful investments represented the entire portfolio. Those who withdrew profits were paid out of the money contributed by others. When Herman's Ponzi scheme collapsed, he was indicted for securities fraud, convicted, and sentenced to fifteen years in prison.

Ruth did not stand by her man. She sought a divorce and refused to visit him at the federal prison in Butler, North Carolina. Fines, penalties, and judgments obtained in civil actions claimed all of their joint assets. Ruth would have been penniless but for her husband's one protective act. "I take big chances. Let's leave your money in bonds, so you'll always have something to fall back on, if something happens to me."

Ruth transposed to other men her hatred of her husband. Peter had no chance. Ruth, at first, refused to allow Peter to take her photo. When she gave in, it was on the condition that Peter stand across the room. "It's not just you, although right now it is you. I don't want any man getting close to me."

The divorce was easily obtained. One ground, under the old law, was a prison sentence of three years. Since Herman was sentenced to fifteen years, he did not bother to contest. Herman had no assets, so Ruth sought nothing from him. She signed her photo and added, "You were OK."

Peter wondered what Duffy would make of Ruth when they met in a couple of hours.

He checked his watch. Duffy expected him at nine thirty and no later. He got to Duffy's office with a minute to spare but failed to see how any of the witnesses would help him out of the goddamn mess he was in. It was going to be a monumental waste of time.

6

Duffy beseeched his clients to come to meetings on time. A late arrival would be penalized by adding the late time to the bill. That worked for his clients. He could not impose the rule on volunteers, this morning's visitors.

Gloria was scheduled first. She arrived at ten thirty—thirty minutes late. While they were waiting, Peter described the circumstances surrounding each prospective witness, much as he had mused about them earlier when he was alone in his apartment. Duffy waited for Morrissey to finish before commenting. "The purpose of this meeting," Duffy said, "is to determine whom we want to call. If it makes no sense to call a witness, we won't. Knowing what we both know, I'll keep it simple. You only had an affair with Molly, because she wanted you to. You coerced no client and served each well. That's all I'll try to get from each prospective witness."

Gloria arrived with a wry smile on her face. "I'm sorry to be late. My wife, Betty, wanted to come. I told her not to, since I would call her from time to time. Also, I said you would speak with her. It took time for me to persuade her. We both like Peter very much and want to help. Hello Peter. Good to see you." Peter thanked Gloria for coming as she and Duffy retreated to his office.

Duffy listened to Gloria's story of how wonderful Betty was, and what a pig her ex-husband was. "Peter," she said, "handled my case with sensitivity. Wisely advised me to keep my relationship with Betty under wraps. The judge never knew I was in love. He prohibited Eric's lawyer from raising the issue. The judge was a Neanderthal, but I got great terms. The bar association's rule prohibiting consensual sex would be funny if the consequences were not severe. I believe that two adults can do anything, provided they consent."

Gloria called Betty, repeated her conversation with Duffy, and put her wife on the phone. "One reason," Betty said, "lawyers are the butt of every joke is that they're centuries behind the times. Did you ever hear of anything more ridiculous? Two mature adults cannot express their natural feelings because one is a lawyer representing the other in a divorce action? Gloria is ready to testify. Peter was at all times a gentleman. I'd like to tell the judge or whoever presides that the rule, not Peter, is wrong. Two adults should not repress their sexual desires just because others impose rules contrary to nature."

Duffy looked at his watch. 11: 20. Almost time for his next witness. He called Peter in. He thanked Gloria for her help and lightly kissed her on her cheek. "That was so romantic, Peter. If only you had kissed me while I was your client, I might have married you instead of Betty."

Duffy and Morrissey walked with Gloria to the door. "I heard the elevator stop," Duffy said. "It's time for the 'Alice Burns show.'"

Professor Burns entered dressed in a plain blouse and skirt. On her feet were low-heeled shoes. "Well, if it isn't Paolo reincarnated. Of course, you don't know who Paolo is. You think Dante is a restaurant on the West Side. For your information, Paolo, a great lover just like you, had sex with his sister-in-law, the wife of his brother. Then his brother murdered him. The bar association only wants to disbar you. Life in prison would be more fitting. I don't believe in capital punishment. Your tools are developed. I'm sure of that. It's your mind that's retarded. What's the last book you've read? Never mind. I'm sure it was porn."

Addressing Duffy, she said, "Is Mark Antony to be present?" Duffy shook his head no and escorted Alice to his office. *I like this witness,* he thought. *Sure she hates Morrissey but the case is not about popularity. She said no and he respected her decision. He represented her to the best of his ability. That's all we need from her. I'll do my best to persuade her to testify.*

Duffy had read Dante's *Inferno.* "I make use of the stanza describing the fate of fortune tellers. Their heads are turned backwards, so they are unable to see what is ahead. My practice is criminal defense. My clients always ask about their chances to win. Very few ever win. If they were innocent, they wouldn't have been indicted. Ninety-eight percent of indictments result in convictions. I answer their question by saying 'I avoid prophesying.' I quote the relevant verse and claim that, as an observant Catholic, I fear for my fate. " Alice smiled. Duffy's reference to Dante won her over. She almost liked Duffy.

Encouraged by the smile, Duffy turned the conversation to Morrissey.

"How would you rate Morrissey as a divorce lawyer?"

"My divorce was uncomplicated. My ex is a genius. The usual rules do not apply. I accepted that when I married him and again when he asked for a divorce. Morrissey did a good job. I said that on my photo which he asked me to sign. His behavior was, however, outrageous."

Alice's last answer segued to his next question. "Tell me about Peter's flirting."

Alice grimaced. She clasped her arms across her chest. Paused. Took a deep breath. Then, in a voice dripping with anger, said: "He's a baby. Maybe he's sick. I never encouraged him. Why would I? And yet despite all the unwelcome signs, he was always moving close to me. Several times he put his clammy hands on me. Ready for Peter's masterstroke? One day he returned from the bathroom with his fly unzipped. When I pointed it out, he said, 'I had trouble zipping. Would you help?' I said if he didn't zip his pants immediately, I was walking out. You might think he would get the message. But no. He carried on with his filthy ploys until I threatened to fire him. If I testify I'll have to say his conduct was clownish. The only neutral thing: he didn't resort to force."

"Professor Burns, in this legal proceeding, I'll ask the questions, and you answer only the question asked—directly and without embellishment. If you can't repress your hostility toward Peter and are determined to destroy him, don't bother to testify. What's it going to be?" Duffy was angry. He glared at her with fire in his eyes. Part of his anger was at his client, for being such a boor.

Alice backed off. "I agreed to come here. I've wasted your time. Peter didn't hurt me. I'll testify according to the rules."

As she was leaving, she turned away from Peter, who offered his thanks. In parting she said to Duffy, "As I said on the phone, I'll help, but I'll tell the truth. Will that help? What do I know? I'm a professor of English literature, not a lawyer."

Joyce was the next to arrive, oozing sympathy. "Those bastards have no right to pick on you. They're just jealous of your high fees. I can't get over that you got $50,000 for my case. Especially when you worked maybe ten hours. Well, I didn't have to pay it, so why did I care? Jim was pissed. He called it blackmail."

Duffy turned the conversation from legal fees to the results. "Peter did well, but how did *you* do? It's always risky to take a chance and go to trial. The terms of a final judgment may be better than a settlement or worse. I understand Peter got a great settlement. You must have been very pleased?"

"You bet I was. I got everything I wanted, except Jim. That's my job, not Peter's. I'm working on it. I'm following Thomas Jefferson's advice: 'have no entangling affairs.' It was Jefferson...or was it Washington? I get the two mixed up."

"I, too, don't know who said it," he said. "I'm sure it was said but foreign affairs, not sexual, was meant."

"Oh, what's the difference? An affair is an affair whether it happens here or abroad."

"Touché," he said, although he thought the pun unintended. He took Joyce by the arm and led her to his office.

She was a compulsive talker. She told all about the architect, how Jim found out about it by reading her diary. "I'm an open book, just look at my diary." How her husband was ready to forgive her provided she didn't slip again. She claimed to be good. "Never so much as even thinking of another man."

She was hurt when Jim, without any warning, threw her out. She protested. Showed Jim her diary, which contained nothing since he took her back except about the two of them.

"I told Peter about sales of weapons to Hezbollah and the Cayman Island account, because Jim had lied to me. Right after I was tossed out, I met Jim at our son's graduation. He said I looked gorgeous and asked whether I was still on the straight and narrow.

When I said I was, he said, 'Stay clean, and I'll take you back.' I'm clean as a whistle. But Jim hasn't given up that whore he's living with.

"He fooled me about the divorce. He said it didn't matter. When he said we'd live together like man and wife, I believed him. I didn't know I was divorced. I believed we were still married. Do I believe him now when he says he'll take me back? Jim says, 'Fool me once, shame on you. Fool me twice, shame on me.' Well, shame on me if Jim is lying. I'm trusting him. Jim *will* take me back if I don't transgress, and if he gets tired of the whore he's living with."

"Tell me," Duffy said, "were you an actress?"

"How did you know? I sing and dance. I was off-Broadway, close to my big break when I met Jim. He came backstage. Asked me to a late supper. I fell in love. We got married, and I became pregnant. I missed my opportunity to be a star, but look what I got in return."

"If a script is handed to you, would you memorize it and be the star of our show? You're a professional, so we'll pay you. If asked, you'll tell the truth: you're getting paid for your time. If you're not asked, don't volunteer. Now the $64,000 question. Did you have sexual relations with Peter as defined in the Clinton-Lewinsky affair? Did Peter touch your private parts or did you touch his?"

"Of course not. I stayed pure so that Jim would take me back. From the time Jim asked me to leave, I've remained faithful to him. Nothing has transpired between me and another man."

"Did Peter flirt?"

"Sure. But when I told him my plan to remain pure, Peter stopped. Also, he's definitely not my type. Although I'm tall, I like short men, like Jim. Peter's so big, he frightens me. Probably his penis is also big and would scratch my liver. Stop laughing. And don't put that in the script!"

Joyce would be great on direct. Just the kind of witness the case needs. Dumb witnesses get caught in cross. He'd have to prepare her well. He was thinking of possible areas of cross when Margaret arrived.

She was perfectly dressed and perfumed. Duffy was bowled over. *Why is it*, he thought, *upper-class women have a mystique, an indefinable appeal?*

Peter and Margaret exchanged pleasantries. She was polite but reserved. *Well, what else would you expect from a woman worth $500 million?*

When they were alone, Margaret praised Morrissey's tactics. "My husband was a bandit. Out to rob me. Peter played a dirty trick, but it worked. Anthony deserved worse. I got rid of him on bearable terms. After making a big mistake, who could ask for more?"

"Peter is facing disbarment," Duffy said, "because he and a client had a consensual sexual relationship. The code of professional responsibility prohibits a lawyer in a matrimonial action from having sex with his client, even though both consent, and even if the client is the prime actor, as she was in Peter's case. The stuffed shirts who rule our profession believe women in divorce cases are easy prey, off limits to their lawyers. You probably like stuffed shirts?"

"How did you know? Yes, I also like pompous lawyers, especially those who pontificate about high moral standards and probably masturbate while watching pornographic movies, I mean, off hours, of course."

"Did Peter flirt? I know he got nowhere with you."

"Of course he flirted, but he took no for an answer. About half a dozen noes. Peter is harmless. The bar association is wrong. The divorce bar needs Peter. He's one slick operator."

She agreed to testify. Duffy thought, *If I keep it brief, she will make a good impression.* He was not afraid of what she might say in cross. Peter was not being disbarred for 'dirty tricks.' As he was thinking about Margaret, Ruth Meadow, the last witness, arrived.

Duffy knew plenty of people who were seriously depressed and still walking around. None as low as Ruth. Although they were strangers, she cried before he could ask a question. In between sobbing she cursed her ex. "That bastard! He stole my parents' life savings. He did the same to our friends and relatives. He looted our children's and grandchildren's funds. He embezzled from charities. I'd like to kill him. And myself."

Duffy said, "I know all about your husband's case. If I were the sentencing judge, I'd have thrown him in the slammer for life."

He paused for a moment, waiting for her to calm down. Then he turned the conversation to Peter. "Just compare the two. Peter had consensual sex with a client, and I'm convinced she seduced him. What punishment is he facing? Disbarment for life. I keep asking myself, 'What did he do wrong?' Look, you've got a lot on your plate. Maybe you'd like to finesse Peter's problem? Why should we burden you?"

"I said I would help, and I will. Peter's trial will be a diversion. If he wins, who knows, I may even smile. What do you need from me?'

"Did you have sexual intercourse with Peter? Did he touch any intimate part of you or cause you to touch him?"

"No to all your questions. Peter was a gentleman. He was all business. I got nothing from my husband, but there was nothing to get. Peter's fee was minimal. I'd like to do him a favor."

"We'd like that. You'll be a big help."

Why hadn't Peter seduced her? She was too much of a victim, like the battered women he was so celebrated for defending.

It was late afternoon when the interview sessions ended. "There's so much tension," Duffy said to Peter. "I have to walk a fine line to avoid a charge of tampering. I want to put words in each witness's mouth, but I fear the consequences for the case, and hell, for myself. Can you imagine the delight of a prosecutor, one of my many enemies, who learns I tampered with the evidence? I'd be indicted for obstruction of justice. If convicted, I'm disbarred, I lose my citizenship and spend three years in summer camp. I sweat after each session."

"Let's adjourn to the Palm," Peter said. "Promise me, Bill, no more talk about our five witnesses. Before the Grievance Committee reared its ugly head, I actually liked myself. Now I hate myself, everyone else too and especially our five witnesses."

"Don't be so hard on yourself. You're not perfect. You have faults like the rest of us. Your offense is minor and technical. It will be over with soon and forgotten. I could use a drink or five and a big steak. We need to relax. "

Photographs of celebrities decorated the walls of the restaurant. Peter said he was thinking of suing the Palm for stealing his decorating idea. "Bill," Peter said, "what do you know about common law copyright? I want to talk about anything but my case."

Being a bachelor, Peter ate out a lot. The Palm was one place he could dine alone and feel comfortable. He had the status of a regular and was warmly greeted by the maître d' and the wait staff. Peter regarded the Palm as his second club. A place where he felt at home.

"That's fine with me. What do you say we talk about women?"

"Bill, can't you be kind? I'm going through hell."

Both men ordered very dry martinis. Duffy had a second and ordered a bottle of a Malbec from Argentina, saying, "It's inexpensive but good. I feel compassion for you." They also ordered steaks and split orders of cottage fries, onion rings, and sautéed spinach.

They talked about politics, sports, and gossiped about lawyers. Both were Democrats who hated Romney, Republicans in general, and the Tea Party in particular. Duffy liked pro football. He rooted for the Jets. Morrissey followed professional basketball. He was once a Knick fan but now watched only to cheer when they lost. He had plenty of opportunity. They discussed lawyers whose reputations exceeded their skill. By the time dinner was over, Morrissey proclaimed Duffy 'the best criminal lawyer in the business.' Duffy returned the compliment by naming Morrissey 'the king of the matrimonial bar.'

Duffy looked wistful as he drained the bottle of wine. When the waiter asked if he wanted a second, he thought about it, looked at Peter's disapproving face, and ordered a glass.

"Peter, there's one question I need to ask. I'm sorry, old man, but you must answer. Did you know having sexual relations with a client violated the code?"

"Yes, of course I knew. If I said no, I'd look even more the fool than I already do and a liar to boot. Furthermore, there's record evidence that I knew. The minutes of my committee reflect we reviewed the rule. As chairman I said, 'The rule is necessary to maintain the integrity of the bar and should be vigorously enforced.' And it's recorded in the minutes, so I'm stuck. You won't question me on intent but Lisa Fox will. She knows there was more than one Molly. Maybe hundreds of Mollies. Suppose Fox, on crossing me, goes down the list of the twenty who claim I had sex with them. She asks me, 'Is it true you had sexual relations with so and so?' If I say no, the woman who said I did will be subpoenaed. When she testifies add perjury to my other offenses. Bill, I'm screwed whatever I say."

"You don't have to say anything. Many times I've advised clients not to testify. Peter, just suppose I don't put you on the stand? I know I said I would. But suppose I change my mind? Fox's' notes are hearsay. They are not admissible in evidence. She can use them to cross-examine you, but that's it. If you don't testify, her notes are *functus non officio*. No court, no administrative proceeding, can even look at them.

"Fox informed us and the judge that Dixon was her only witness. Now if you testify, she can call witnesses to rebut your testimony. But if you don't testify, she's stuck with Molly. Maybe it's best you don't testify. Let's see how the case develops. By the way how's Sex Addicts Anonymous?"

"I've been to one session. I told my story. The group applauded me. One said, 'Being frank was the first step toward a cure.' They booed when I said I was up for disbarment. Several said they would tell the judge an addiction can be controlled. One man spoke for five minutes. The thrust: punishment leads to recidivism. The addict must be given a chance to show his addiction is under control. Tomorrow night is the second session. I'm to speak again as to whether I slipped or even was tempted. Bill, after talking to the creeps at the meeting, I'm convinced: I'm not one of them. They're obsessed with porn and whores. They spend hundreds of hours fantasizing about sex and masturbating. Porn bores the shit out of me. Whores are a big turnoff. The act of seduction raises my blood pressure. I'm hypersexual but not a sex addict."

"You're probably right. I'll speak with Philip Gross. He's headed Sex Addicts Anonymous for about ten years. He'll have a lot to say about this! A sex addict may well be something different.

After I speak with Philip, we can decide whether you need to attend other meetings. Wouldn't it be great for Gross to testify that you're not an addict, just a normal man with a normal sex drive? Shit, I meant to tell you about my meeting with Max Wolfe. I met with him yesterday."

Duffy paused to take a sip of wine. "He's the neuropsychologist I've told you about. He has testified several times for me on the defense of insanity. Don't worry. He's not going to say you're insane. He will explain addiction. Assuming you come across as I indicated, he will rank the gradation of your illness as weak, average, or strong. He'll rate you as weak. Call for an appointment early next week."

Peter had experience with expert witnesses. In matrimonial cases, if the parties own real estate, it is sold, and the proceeds are divided. If, however, the property is awarded to one party and value is disputed, it has to be appraised. Value then becomes a point of contention. It is usually decided by appraisers who sign their report adding the initials M.A.I. short for Master of the Appraiser Institute. Lawyers jokingly refer to the designation as "made as instructed."

Morrissey was confident that experts give testimony to help the side paying the bill. He asked the only remaining question: "How much will Wolfe charge for the whole package?"

"My educated guess is not more than five thousand. Of course, no part of his fee can be contingent. To protect his independence, it's important that he be paid up front."

After Duffy had drained the glass of wine, Peter signaled for the check. Two slightly tipsy men left the restaurant and headed for home.

Peter was usually jolly when he got home, but that night he couldn't turn on a smile for the doormen or the elevator operator. He had purchased his apartment in a bankruptcy sale in 1990 during a dip in the market. The purchase price, $750,000, was below market value, but the maintenance was high—$5,500 per month. In exchange Peter got many extras: maid service, room service, a concierge, and the use of a gym. Living at the Pierre buoyed Peter's spirits. He knew his home was in one of the premier buildings in the world. He also enjoyed the look of envy in the faces of some when they learned he lived there. Since Peter had no family, only material things, he placed much value on them. Peter turned on the television, picked up the newspaper, and tried to forget his problems. He could not. He was anxious, tired from lack of sleep and fed up. Maybe he should cut a deal, give up law, and retire? He knew he was guilty, more so than anyone else knew. He deserved to be disbarred. Why fight? Then he heard a voice in his head. "Peter, you hurt no one. Duffy has a good strategy. Don't run away." It was the voice of his niece, Jean.

7

A week later Peter sauntered into the waiting room of the neurology department of New York Hospital, announcing to the receptionist that he was there to see Dr. Wolfe. While he waited he couldn't concentrate on *The Economist* or *The New Yorker*. He put the magazines down and turned inward, cursing his obsession for bringing him down, thinking of it as having a separate existence. He was beginning to see it at Sex Addicts Anonymous, even though he didn't think he was the same kind of addict as the others. Was there a difference between an obsession and addiction? Maybe Dr. Wolfe could tell him.

His sex drive had destroyed his marriage and any hope for a long-term relationship. Now it was threatening to destroy his career. "Was it wrong for a lawyer to have an affair with a woman he was representing in a divorce action?" As he pondered the question for the fiftieth time, a puffy-faced, rotund, bald-headed man with piercing eyes and a drooping mouth entered the waiting room.

"I'm Dr. Max Wolfe. Come with me. My hearing is not great. I'll ask you to speak in a loud voice. Our meeting is taped so I won't miss anything. I will also take notes out of habit.

"Duffy has briefed me on the case. For me to be helpful, you'll have to be forthcoming. Hold nothing back. What you think is unimportant may turn out to be critical. Before I testify, I'll give the tape of our session to Duffy. It's protected in his hands. The law considers it privileged—not to be disclosed. It's probably privileged in my hands, but Duffy wants to wear a belt and suspenders. When the case is over, Duffy will give you the tape. You are free to do with it what you wish. I tell you this, because I don't want you to fear disclosure. What you say will remain confidential. Are you ready?"

Wolfe began with a description of the brain and its function. He said it was necessary for Peter and the court to understand its role. "The reason will become clear when I reach my testimony in chief. The discussion sets the background for the questions I will ask you and the opinion I will provide the court."

Peter paid no attention to Wolfe's rambling about the brain. *I'll hear it again in court.* His thoughts turned to his ex-wife, Joan. He could have had a life with her. Children and grandchildren, weddings, celebrations, and family get-togethers. The years and years of lonely nights and weekends would be full of laughter and joy. Did Dr. Wolfe want to know why he seeks sex? *I'm unloved. No, that's not right.* He had affairs during his marriage. Will this pompous doctor see him as he was? A pig. A selfish pig.

Wolfe finished his discussion of the brain and turned to addiction. Peter's interest was piqued.

"Some addiction, which we call 'strong form,' may not be susceptible to treatment. That is why in order for me to help, I must determine the degree of your addiction. My questions are designed to obtain the basis for a sound conclusion. An erroneous one will not serve your interests. It will be shot down by the other side and rejected by the court. You will have wasted your money, and I will have impaired my reputation. If you are forthcoming, I will tell you if I can help. If I cannot, I will not charge for my time. Do you have any questions before we begin?"

Peter said, "Lawyers are accustomed to asking questions, not answering them. I will try to answer fully, but there are many things about my obsession that are unclear to me. I'm compelled to seek sex with women, any and every woman. I lack discernment, taste, discretion. I have sexual relations without love or intimacy. I know of no one else like me. What's wrong with me? Do I deserve to be punished?"

"Mr. Morrissey, you're jumping to the end. I will, however, answer you now. A mature man who has sexual relations with fifty or more women of all ages and shapes, including his clients, exhibits troublesome conduct. Your conduct cannot be justified. Do you still want to continue?"

When Peter nodded his head, the questioning began.

"At what age did you begin masturbating, and when, if ever, have you stopped? Please don't read anything into my question. Masturbation is a normal activity."

"Look, it's complicated. What about wet dreams?"

"We'll get nowhere if you play wiseacre. My question was directed to masturbation. Save your dreams for a Freudian analyst. May I have an answer and not a deflection?"

"I began when I was about fourteen. I continued on and off depending upon the availability of women. Sex on my own is a poor substitute for sex with a woman. I stopped at the time I got married at age twenty seven. As you know I've had sex with many different women, too many to count. I have no need to masturbate and don't."

"During periods when you were without a woman—I assume there have been such—did you have sex with prostitutes?"

"No. Prostitutes are a big turnoff. Some poor woman who hates your guts makes love to you solely because you pay her. I've been accused of objectifying women, because I'm only interested in sex. Alcoholics abuse wine, and druggies abuse drugs. I guess I abuse women but not the downtrodden. Prostitutes get my sympathy, not my patronage."

"Do you read pornographic books, magazines, or go to X-rated movies?"

"Occasionally, I pick up *Playboy* or *Hustler*. I don't subscribe to either or to any pornographic magazine. It's a rare day when passing a stand, I buy a magazine. I'm not a habitual reader of porn. In fact, I find it boring. I've read Henry Miller's *Tropic of Cancer*, It's partly autobiographical. He and his friends made love to every willing woman and prostitutes as well. The book is considered a classic and a model for a new literary genre. Miller is hailed as a genius. Fortunately for authors they are not governed by a code of professional responsibility."

"Do your thoughts often turn to sex?

Peter scowled, pointed his index finger at the doctor, narrowed his eyes, all signs that the doctor had hit a sore spot. "I spend a lot of time working. Some days more than ten hours. I attend concerts, the opera, and read. Do I sometimes think about sex? To help me get to sleep, I replay a childhood fantasy."

"Don't be defensive. If I don't delve into your inner thoughts, I won't be able to help you. Note my question relates to 'thinking' not to actual sexual encounters."

Wolfe turned off the tape recorder, and in a confidential tone, told Peter that on instructions from Duffy, the doctor was not to address actual sexual encounters. "If I were to ask about sex with women other than your clients and not about your clients, Duffy contends, I'd be accused of shielding you. If I include your clients, your answers destroy your defense, that is, if I were asked about them on cross. In order to protect you, I will not ask about actual encounters. I will base my findings on mental symptoms and signs, not physical acts."

Peter was incredulous. "I thought I was sick, because I made love to a multitude of women. Your approach is like evaluating an alcoholic without asking what he drinks and how much."

"In my expert opinion, alcohol and sex addiction are very different. Your addiction, if indeed it is an addiction, is not to a substance but to women. All normal men crave sex. Some are hypersexual; others are asexual; and then there are all the gradations in between. The abnormal ones are those who spend their days dreaming about sex and reading and looking at pornography. Their obsession prevents them from leading productive lives. My opinion will be based on how, if at all, your sexual activities dominate your life. Mild addiction, which occupies free time, poses no problem. A strong form of addiction, which takes over your life, requires intensive psychotherapy and medical treatment. Before we go back on the record, I intend to explore your sexual fantasies, and the time you devote to sex. Is it controlling your life? It is important for my report that you be forthcoming. Let's go back on the record."

The doctor turned the tape recorder back on. "Do you have sexual fantasies? How often do they occur, and how long do they last?"

"There are several. One predominates. It started when I was about fifteen. I come back to it even now when I have trouble sleeping. For me it's soporific and nothing else. What's the relevance?"

"I won't know until I hear it."

Should I clean it up? It's embarrassing. I've never told it to anyone, and now this perfect stranger wants access to my inner thoughts—my almost fifty-year sex fantasy. Yes or no? I have no choice. "The fantasy is not only about sex; it's also about me. At the time it originated, I was a gawky teenager with a face full of pimples and a head of unruly red hair. I had reached full height but was skinny as hell. In my fantasy I'm transformed. My hair becomes dark and thick, parted on the left side, the rest combed into a high pompadour held in place with a greasy styling gel. My idol was Marlon Bando whose raw, brooding look I affected. I imagined I was like Brando, a male beauty with androgynous good looks. A man few women could resist.

"My schoolmates talked about becoming professional athletes or making lots of money in business, medicine, or law. I thought only about sex. Maybe if I got laid just once, I'd be like everyone else. I made a list of young and older women living in my neighborhood. With each entry I imagined what making love would be like. And in every case, the answer was the same—wonderful! I was willing, nay eager, to have every single one. The problem was: who would want me? I was no Marlon Brando. But I picked Selma Gold, the nineteen-year-old sister of my next door neighbor and best friend Bernie."

"See here, Peter, if you are reporting on an actual sexual encounter, I don't want to hear about it. My focus is on your imagination."

Morrisey said nothing happened between Selma and him, except in his mind. He claimed that he lacked the nerve to approach her. "If I had, she would have laughed and made fun of me. Parts of the story are, however, based on facts. All of what I am about to relate about Selma and me being intimate is pure fantasy. I overheard my parents talking about Selma. My mother said, 'She's giving Helen fits. Selma turned down college, dates cops and firemen. She stays out until two in the morning. Helen thinks she's man crazy. She worries about pregnancy.'

"I don't know whether my mother's gossip had any truth to it.

"One day, Bernie came over and said his parents had left for a vacation in Florida. And that his sister, Selma, broke up with her boyfriend. And was in a bad mood. So he was staying far away from her. The rest of the story I made up.

"Every Saturday morning Bernie biked to the gym for pickup basketball. The next Saturday I watched from my window until I saw him ride off. Then I crossed the street and rang the bell. The door opened a crack, enough for Selma to see it was me. The conversation would go like this:

"'Bernie's not here,' she said.

"'It's not Bernie I want to see, it's you' I replied.

"'Well, I don't want to see you. You're a snot-nose baby. Go bother some fourteen-year-old girl.'

"'I gotta twenty-year-old mind and body. I hear music. I'm a very good dancer.'

"'Twenty-year-old mind and body, my ass. You're an idiot! But Bernie did say you're a good dancer. OK, come in, but stay in the living room. I'll change the record.'

"She went to her bedroom, put on a samba. I followed her. When she saw me, she looked angry and said, 'Didn't I tell you *not* to leave the living room?'

"We stayed in her room and danced. Me, still in my heavy jacket. We danced wildly and well. When the music ended, I gently kissed her on both sides of her mouth near but not on her mouth. I had seen Cary Grant do that in a movie. She was breathing hard, shook her head, and said, 'Take off your jacket. You must be hot. I'm hot too.'

"She turned and sashayed into the bathroom.

"She returned wearing a black, rayon nightgown barely reaching her knees. She placed a small plastic-wrapped packet on the table next to her bed. 'If you're too warm,' she said, 'you can undress.' Without waiting for a response, Selma unbuttoned my shirt, reached into my pants, and raised the shirttails. In the process she grazed my penis. She unbuckled my belt and took a step back and waited. I stripped to my underwear.

"'Do you tango?' Selma asked. I nodded yes. I had lost the power of speech. 'Well, if you do a mean tango, you'll get a reward. The king of the beat is Juan D'Ariezo. When you hear his recording of 'El Flete,' you'll know why.'

"We tangoed as well as could be expected from two amateurs who had never practiced this sensuous, highly stylized dance together. We pivoted, crossed forward and back, twirled, danced face to face, back to back, sideways. We embraced with our arms, hands, and fingers. Each time our bodies touched, we separated.

"When the record ended, Selma slipped off her gown and pulled down my underwear. 'What a big stiff prick you have. Did little ole me do that to you?'

"She led me to the bed, unwrapped the packet, removed the contraceptive, and mumbled, 'This thing is a scumbag. I'll put it on you. Then we can fuck in safety provided your broomstick don't break it.'

"When we finished, Selma checked the contraceptive. 'Good, it held. I live another day. Damn, how I worry about getting pregnant. Now get dressed, and get out of my house. Let's see how fast you can do it.'

"'When will I see you again?'

"'Never. I could be arrested for corrupting the morals of a minor, even though it was you who corrupted me. I never want to see you again. Scat!'"

Wolfe asked whether, over the years, the tale had changed.

"The basic framework stays the same," Peter said, " but depending on whether I'm still awake, Selma and I continue to have sex right up to the day before her wedding. Several times I lengthen the story to include sex with her after she's married."

"Do you daydream about sex during the workweek?"

"No, unless I want to take a nap."

"Do you associate sex with violence, either in your encounters or imagination?"

"Sorry to disappoint you, but I'm not into sadomasochism, real or imagined."

"With what frequency do you engage in sex?" Wolfe asked.

"Whenever I can. Some weeks, I make love as many as four times. Other weeks, as infrequently as once. It's a rare week when I don't indulge."

"In the weeks when you have sex four times, is your desire for sex satisfied?"

"That's der pointe. I never have enough. I want more. I enjoy intercourse more than anything else. It has little to do with the partner. If she's willing I have fun. Sex is my passion. I'm always willing."

"In weeks when you have little or no sex, are you anxious, edgy, agitated?"

"Yes, I'm all those things and more. During dry periods, I tend to eat and drink more. I'm also less effective at work. To me sex is a fix. Without it I'm depressed. Come to think of it, with it I'm also depressed. I worry. Why can't I settle on one woman? I tried marriage, but it didn't work."

"Tell me about your marriage."

Before Peter could answer, a young doctor entered. "Sorry to interrupt, but it's an emergency. Dr. Farris asked me to get you immediately."

"These things happen. Everything's an emergency except very few things are. If I judge the call will take more than fifteen minutes, I'll get word to you, and we'll reschedule. I know we're on a short fuse. I'll do my best. While you're waiting, you might find my article in *The Journal of the Neurological Sciences* interesting." Wolfe reached across his desk to a pile of journals and opened the top one to the first article. He handed the journal to Peter. "It's the lead article. You can tell, since it's the first article referenced on the cover." The young doctor, gently but impatiently, steered Dr. Wolfe out of the room.

Doctors are no different, Peter thought, *than the rest of us. Their egos have to be fed. The patient could have died while Wolfe was searching for his article.*

After a quick glance at the article, he saw that he couldn't understand a word of the technical jargon and returned the journal to the desk. He looked through the other magazines and found a battered copy of *Playboy*. He picked it up. The mailing label on the cover was addressed to a Henry Wojecoski. Must have left it here. Peter thumbed through the magazine, stopping to look at the centerfold. Then, he put *Playboy* down just before Wolfe returned.

"That was short," Wolfe said. "Less than fifteen minutes. The neurosurgeon was in the process of removing a tumor from the left hemisphere of the brain and wanted to avoid impairing speech. The damn fool didn't know, although it was on the patient's charts, that she was a true lefty. In such cases speech is located in the right hemisphere. I'm often asked to consult by surgeons, not for my expertise, but for my reputation, as protection against a malpractice suit. Where's the journal I gave you? Have you finished the article? How'd you like it?"

Peter looked at the doctor in disbelief and thought, *I'm paying him. I don't have to kiss the ass of this tin god.* "Like it? The article is technical and the prose turgid. I put it down after the first line. It's not for lay readers. I wonder which hemisphere in your brain thought I would like your impenetrable article. What do your colleagues say?"

Wolfe was hurt. He had played the wrong game with the wrong person. He had hoped to rise in Morrissey's esteem. Time to get back to business. "Enough distractions. Let's get back on the record. Before our break I asked you about your marriage. Tell me about it."

Peter concealed his hostility. He needed Wolfe as an expert. He'd better play it straight. "Like most things in my personal life, it was crazy. I proposed to Joan almost as soon as I met her. You see, when I was with her, I thought of her only. I didn't notice other women. I was twenty-seven. It was the first time one woman held my interest. And no wonder. Joan was smart, pretty, and not the least bit self-centered. She was involved in the anti-Vietnam protest and her work in TV. I was an unhappy army reserve. I was flattered she made time for me.

"I didn't want our first date to end. She had to start work early, so it ended much too soon. We made a second date for the next night. Thereafter we saw each other all the time. Let me anticipate your next question. No sex. In fact, we waited until I proposed. I remember thinking my obsession with sex was over. 'I'm normal; no longer a satyr.' Our courtship was the happiest time of my life. I was committed to Joan for the first six months. Then I slipped. Joan was alarmed as she observed me change. I remember her saying, 'You flirt outrageously with every woman. One or two would be bad enough, but you reach out to all of them. You embarrass me when I'm present. When I'm not I hear through the grapevine how charming you are, that you're the life of the party, chatting up all the women. Peter, why can't you be dignified like other men? Stop flirting. It hurts me, and it is so childlike.'

"I swore to her I was faithful and just had fun talking to women. A few months later, I could no longer offer that defense. One woman slipped me her business card. I called. We met in the afternoon. After the affair I suffered from remorse. I took an oath never to call that woman again. I kept my pledge, that is, as far as that woman. I slipped again and again. Seduction excited me just like it did before I met Joan. I tried to stop but could not. Being married made me hate myself for actions I could not control."

"How did Joan find out?" the doctor asked.

"She sensed something was wrong. I was depressed with good reason. Joan was wonderful in every way; I was a complete idiot. I didn't deserve her. I confessed: 'You're the best woman in the world. I'm the lowest of the low. I was depraved when I met you. I wanted women without surcease. Any woman. Personality, looks, age made no difference. Then I met you. My life changed. I thought about telling you about my past. But why? Being with you made me a new man until it didn't. No fault of yours.'

"Shortly after my confession, our marriage was annulled. I've had regrets all my life."

"Have you sought help for your sexual condition? Maybe with treatment you can be cured."

"Not formally. I did discuss my mental state with a friend who is a psychoanalyst. He said men had different libidos. 'You suffer from a hypersexual disorder. There's nothing to worry about. Have fun; forget guilt. As long as your relationships are consensual— and make sure you keep it that way— enjoy sex. Think positively. One encounter is fun. Many are lots of fun. You function at work and socially. So don't worry. If I were you, I wouldn't consider marriage. Monogamy is an unnatural state, even for normal men. For you it's impossible. Marriage is a prison without a lock and key.' I wish I had had that discussion before I had met Joan.

"'You'll need help,' my friendly analyst added, 'when you force yourself on objecting women, expose yourself, peep at women, or read a lot of porn.'"

"I said I only engaged in consensual sex, kept my fly zipped, was not a Peeping Tom and rarely read porn. The analyst called my sexual proclivity 'a personality defect.' 'You don't need analysis, you need to find the right woman.' Then he laughed and suggested a nymphomaniac. A satyr and a nymph make excellent bedfellows."

"You say you're a functioning addict," Wolfe said. "Suppose you have a conflict between work at the office and a date, how do you resolve the conflict?"

"Work takes priority. In the event of a conflict, I'll call my date and postpone our tryst for a later hour, or if not possible, reschedule for another evening. My answer is not hypothetical. It has actually happened. Sex has never interfered with my work. Sex is recreation. It comes when I have time."

"That concludes our session," the doctor said. "I'll review the tape and my notes, and let you know if we need another session." Wolfe turned off the tape and stared at Peter for several seconds. "Many professionals believe there's no such malady as sex addiction. Those who do would not describe you as a sex addict. I'll prepare a formal report and opinion. I'm not flexible. My opinion is my opinion. I'll tell you my conclusion. You're not abnormal. Your sex drive is high but in the range of normality. Those who indulge less than you would like to have even more sex than you. Your classification: borderline hypersexual. Let me put this in perspective.

We classify someone with no sex drive as asexual. Is such a man mentally ill? Of course not. He's at the lowest end of the range. At the upper range is hypersexual. Does a hypersexual suffer from a personality disorder? Not in the judgment of the American Psychiatric Association. After Duffy reads my report, we'll meet. Based on how he has structured the defense, I'll find out whether I can be of help or not."

8

Duffy's office was in a brownstone on the northeast corner of Thirty-Sixth Street and Lexington Avenue. The building served a dual purpose. The ground floor through the second was exclusively offices. Duffy lived on the top two floors. His personal office was on a parlor floor that consisted of three rooms. The front room served as a reception area and an office for Duffy's secretary. The next and largest room was Duffy's office. In back of his office was a storage room. The second floor contained five offices for lawyers working for Duffy. The ground floor was divided between two large rooms. Secretaries and filing cabinets occupied one room; the other was a large conference room and library.

When Duffy bought the building, his wife and their four children occupied all five floors. When his wife died of cancer, and the children moved into their own homes, Duffy converted the lower floors into offices and moved his firm in.

Duffy and Morrissey were huddled in Duffy's office awaiting Wolfe's arrival. His report was not what Duffy had anticipated. He planned to urge mitigation of Morrissey's actions by claiming he suffered from hypersexuality, a personality disorder, and a form of mental illness. The illness, Duffy would argue, was curable with a course of psychotherapy and medication. Morrissey had voluntarily undertaken both. There was, Duffy would contend, no need to disbar Peter for one piddling offense when the action he was taking would prevent repetition.

Wolfe's report provided no support. It stated that hypersexuality was not included as a mental illness in the *Diagnostic and Statistical Manual of the Association of the American Psychiatric Association*. A subcommittee had considered hypersexuality as a form of mental illness but rejected it. The problem was one of definition. How much sex was too much? Anecdotal evidence was that many men engage in sex on a daily basis. Others, who are less active sexually, fantasize about a more active sex life. How could what some men achieve and others dream about be a mental illness? And what was normal activity?

Wolfe's report reviewed professional studies on sexual behavior. None contained empirical evidence of the number of times "normal" men engage in sex. The association faced a dilemma. Should it pathologize an activity that may represent, at most, a high libido? Should it make a moral judgment on what it considered normal? The association, at an earlier time, claimed homosexuality was a mental illness. It recanted, to its great embarrassment.

The report discussed personality disorders, a form of mental illness. Its symptoms include mood swings, stormy relations, social isolation, angry outbursts. These led to significant problems in social and work situations. Morrissey, Wolfe concluded, had none of the symptoms and none of the problems.

The report discussed Morrissey's lust for women. It saw no reason to control it except as it applied to clients. That could be accomplished by therapeutic sessions training the brain to bar encounters with clients.

Duffy played the lawyer's game of devil's advocate with Morrissey. He argued that with mental illness out the window, he was left to defend a normal guy who intentionally violated the code. Gone were any extenuating circumstances. He could imagine the committee's summation. "How many women clients will have to be victimized before we realize that the lamebrain theory of brain control won't prevent him from preying upon clients?"

Was another expert available? Duffy thought not. He had given the committee's attorneys Wolfe's name and curriculum vitae. They would smell a rat if a substitution were attempted.

On the other hand, Morrissey found it easy to defend the report. Why? He liked it. He would seek psychotherapy and develop an aversion to sex with clients. Fox's notes had hit home. Around many of his clients, he was a fool and a pest. He was determined to control his behavior if only he were given a chance.

"Wolfe will soon be here," Peter said. "Let's question him and see how he holds up. Right now if I don't testify and wreck our case, all the committee has is a single instance. Through cross you'll establish she propositioned me. Then comes Wolfe. We're in good shape. What about Gross? We're seeing him tomorrow, right?"

"Yes, but I don't know what he can add."

"A lot," Peter said. "He can tell tales of full-blown sex addiction. Those afflicted have symptoms and problems that scream insanity. He can provide the practical, hands-on side to Wolfe's scholarly views. He said I'm normal. My experience is not at all like the others. He asked me not to attend any more meetings as I was confusing the group."

Dr. Max Wolfe arrived all smiles. He greeted both men warmly before turning to Duffy. "How did you like my report? Your client doesn't suffer from a mental illness. You can argue that he's normal. Isn't that better than crazy?"

"Not in defending a case. A mentally ill person's actions can be excused. Morrissey's conduct amounts to a willful and intentional violation. As long as he remains a practicing lawyer, in the eyes of the Grievance Committee, he's a threat to his female clients."

"You miss the point," Wolfe said. "Morrissey is not an addict. Let me illustrate the difference with an analogy to a real addict— one hooked on alcohol or drugs. The addict's brain adjusts to the intake of the substance, requiring ever-increasing doses to obtain satisfaction. He needs more and more to reach his happy state. It's called tolerance. The addict's life is dominated by his addiction. When an addict quits, he suffers withdrawal symptoms. Among alcoholics it's referred to as 'delirium tremens' or D. T. The condition leads to a return to abuse. An addict is never cured. He remains in a state of remission, susceptible to a relapse.

"Let's now focus on Peter. He does not require an increasing number of sexual encounters to achieve satisfaction. His hobby, and that is what sex is for him, does not dominate his life. He engages in sex in his free time and puts work ahead of his pastime. Since Peter is not an addict, he can learn through psychotherapy to control his sexual drive. His brain will be trained to make an adjustment: clients are verboten."

"Morrissey," Duffy said, "is not particular about whom he makes love to. He sets the bar so low that every woman can get over it. What about indiscriminate sex? What about objectifying women? Aren't they symptoms of a mental illness?"

"No, what you raise are questions of morality. Moral weaknesses cannot be pathologized. Do I believe that sex without love is wrong? I'm not a priest. I make no moral pronouncements. That's a task for the individual, his family, friends, and religious counselor. There is a big distinction between addiction and bad behavior. In Morrissey's case the brain plays an important role. It regulates personality, appetites, and desires. I'm prepared to say Morrissey needs therapy. A therapist will help him adjust the wayward ions located in his cerebral cortex. In short order his sexual desires can be brought under control so that he will have no sexual desire for clients."

"Dr. Wolfe's opinion has present-day application," Peter said. "Several days ago I interviewed a new client. She was sensuous and made no effort to conceal her full figure and finely shaped legs. She batted her eyes at me. Before the present debacle, I would have closed the door and gone to work. Instead, I looked away. I felt nothing, that is, except disdain. Do you think, Max, my brain is already working toward the goal?"

"No question. Your brain alerted you to a present danger. It turned off your libido. What would otherwise have been a temptation you could not have avoided became one you could not accede to. Duffy's a wonderful lawyer. I've seen him in action many times. This time he's blinded by a defense that cannot be scientifically supported. My testimony will be far more helpful to our case. Sex addiction is not referenced in my profession's standard manual. I regard it as an omission. A sex addict is one who spends hundreds of hours per month reading porn, seeing X-rated movies, engaging in self-masturbation, having sex with prostitutes. He evidences obsessive-compulsive behavior invariably accompanied by severe negative consequences. Among other health-related issues, it causes stress to family and friends and adversely affects his social life and work. The requisite treatment is a period of abstinence, therapy, and peer-group counseling. Sex addiction is a serious personality disorder and should be classified as a mental illness."

"Once again I agree with Max," Peter said. "At meetings of Sex Addiction Anonymous, I've met the very kind of men Max has described. I've listened to their stories. There're pathetic. I have nothing in common with them. In fact, I've been asked not to return. Sexual addiction is a mental illness, but it doesn't take the form of lust."

"You were not present when Peter and I met," Wolfe said to Duffy. "You have the tape of the session. So you know Peter abhors the practices so dear to sex addicts. He finds porn boring, has empathy, but no desire, for prostitutes. Does not masturbate. His weakness is women in general. To Peter sex is a form of recreation, a means to fill spare time through an activity he finds exciting, not unlike an otherwise engaged person plays golf. Is Peter's leisure-time activity dangerous to him or society? As long as sex is consensual and doesn't rule his life, it's a purely personal matter. To take a contrary position, one would have to contend that intercourse should be rationed. If too much sex is unhealthy, would you claim that the male who abstains or the celibate priest is an exemplar? "

"Well, you two are persuasive guys," Duffy said. "I'm coming over to your side. Gross has no advanced degrees or even professional training. It's necessary for you to discuss sex addiction. Are you prepared to put a label on Peter's condition other than sex addict? Are you prepared to opine as to a cure? "

"Of course I am. I'll discuss sex addiction in all its permutations. I will say Morrissey is not an addict. His habit can be corrected by therapy and willpower. Influenced by therapy Peter's brain will send messages controlling his behavior so that his craving is limited to women who are not his clients. His treatment is much easier and more effective than any proposed for sex addicts. With age Peter will poop out. Once he learns to control his lust and recognize that his clients are off limits, Peter may continue to have all the sex he can handle at no one's expense. My take on life: We pass through only once. There's nothing wrong with seeking pleasure and avoiding pain provided only you abstain from women whom you have a fiduciary duty to protect."

"I like a defense built on truth—or at least what we believe in," Peter said. "If we go down, so be it. What do I believe? We'll win. I haven't told you this before, Bill, but I was giving thought to giving up. Now I feel full of strength. We're not going to lose."

"This discussion," Duffy said, "has made me rethink the defense. Ignorance is no defense, or is it? Who would think two people over fifty agree to have sex and one, a lawyer, gets punished only because the other is his client? Look, a defense lawyer has to be flexible. 'If the glove don't fit,' said Johnny Cochran in defending O. J., 'try a different pair' or something like that. I'll make a one hundred eighty degree turn and claim Morrissey's normal. His involvement with Molly was an aberration brought on by her promiscuous behavior. Why should I even concede Morrissey needs treatment? I'll jump off that bridge when I come to it. Let's see how the trial goes."

The meeting had begun with three grim faces. It ended with all three smiling.

9

Avowed sex addict Philip Gross arrived at Duffy's office a few minutes after four. He was short, bald, had a round face and body, large blue eyes, a ready smile, and a ruddy complexion. He wore a blue suit, blue shirt, and a bright red tie. His overall appearance was that of a cherub.

After Peter introduced Philip to Duffy, Peter asked two questions. "Would you be willing to disclose what you went through to control your addiction?

"And, if Duffy thought it would be helpful in my case, would you tell the story in court?"

"You have generously agreed to contribute $5,000 to Sex Addicts Anonymous. Yes to both questions."

Philip's answers were not surprising. Addicts were always advised to speak about their dependency, their battle to overcome it, their success, and their efforts to rejoin the human race. Candor, without shame, was an essential part of rehabilitation. Philip was eager to tell his story.

"I was living life at the very bottom. I spent over one hundred hours per month reading pornographic books and magazines, watching triple X-rated movies, viewing Internet porn, and engaging in telephone sex chats. Pornography occupied my free time and then some. I avoided romantic encounters with women other than prostitutes and with those only infrequently. In lieu of healthy sex, I derived arousal and satiation from pornography, punctuated with masturbation. When I was not actively engaged in pornographic activities, I fantasized about them. In my underworld I observed hundreds of others afflicted with my same condition. 'All guys do the same' was the way I rationalized it. But I knew better. My habit was ruining my life. In moments of truth, I called myself a pervert."

Gross paused. Took a handkerchief from his pocket. Wiped his nose and asked for a glass of water. Duffy asked if he wanted a drink stronger than water. When Gross said no, Duffy opened what looked like a door to an ordinary closet. In fact, it concealed a wet bar. Duffy filled a glass with water and handed it to Gross and left the door ajar.

During the pause Peter's mind raced to the trial. *If Philip's story is heard, it will underscore Wolfe's testimony that the American Psychiatric Association erred in not including sex addiction as a mental illness. In contrast my conduct will seem harmless, maybe normal. Well, slightly abnormal.* He looked at Duffy and wondered what he was thinking. "Please continue," he said.

"One morning I vowed to avoid porn. My usual route took me along Eighth Avenue past the dirty bookstores, movies, and peep shows lining that street. On my trip to and from work, I took Ninth Avenue, a street lined with restaurants, bars, and specialty food shops. After dinner, I read *The Brothers Karamazov* and kept reading until I was ready for bed. Alyosha was an angel. Kind and loving. His elder brother, Dmitri, was a libertine. The middle brother, Ivan, was an intellectual. I couldn't be an Ivan, but I could try to be an Alyosha. I went to sleep with one thought in mind: 'How would Alyosha react to a given situation?' I would try to emulate him. I'd reform. Give up porn and lead a moral life.

"When I awoke, I thought about that nice math teacher I worked with, June Goldstein. I thought to myself, 'By God! Reading Dostoevsky made me think about a woman as a person, not an object.' I vowed to ask June for lunch."

"I don't get it," Duffy said. *Wolfe's report said that addicts need professional help?* "You're addicted to porn. Just by reading a book, one I read in high school, you have an epiphany and decide to change your life?"

"No. I didn't succeed. I needed lots of therapy and group support. The first step, however, must be taken by the addict on his own. Shall I continue?"

Both men nodded, and Philip went on.

"I was frightened and ambivalent about inviting June for lunch even though teachers lunching together is common in our school. I was working toward becoming a principal but was a history teacher. When we met my hands were trembling so much, I had to squeeze them and hide them behind my back. I knew June would say yes. The request was no big deal, but I was delighted by her answer: 'What took you so long to ask?' Lunch was so pleasant that I hated to see it end. We agreed to meet the next day and soon every weekday thereafter. The weekends remained a problem. Plenty of free time and no June Goldstein. I slipped, returned to some of my old haunts but with a difference. I didn't like them and criticized myself. 'You're no Alyosha, you're a quitter, a recidivist, a person unworthy of having a friend like June.' The alternative, a weekend date, was daunting. Lunch was circumscribed by our schedule. After lunch we had classes. A date on the weekend had no natural ending. What if June wanted to make love—a feeling I sensed—could I perform with a real woman? What if I failed? Would my relationship with June end? I needed help.

"I learned about Sex Addicts Anonymous, a group modeled after Alcoholics Anonymous. Attendance was free. Meetings were held on Sunday night in the downstairs meeting room of a large church. I decided to give it a try."

"I don't mean to rush you," Duffy interrupted, "but I have a problem too. As I approach the end of the day, I need a drink. Just one. Will you join me, Philip? How about you, Peter?"

Both men declined. "Nobody's perfect," Duffy added. "The three of us are afflicted by different demons."

He bounded to the wet bar and filled a glass identical with the one he filled with water for Gross. This time he poured Scotch and no water. Took a big swig and asked Gross to continue.

"At Sex Addicts Anonymous, the new man tells his story after being introduced. I was it. I hesitated, used euphemisms, and left large gaps. The others rushed in, completed my sentences, supplied missing facts, and told my story better than I could. It was clear. They had suffered the same agony. I gained confidence from the fact that I was not alone. I took a deep breath and said, 'I'm in love. Her name is June.' I described how I had determined to give up porn. And my fear. Should I tell her I'm hooked on it? The answers were inconsistent. Some said: 'Your past is not her business. Don't wash dirty laundry in public.' Others said: 'A lasting relationship should be built on truth and trust. Hiding the past leads to deception. You're not cured and never will be. The best that can be said is that your addiction is in remission. June can help, but only if she is aware of your struggle.'

"The honest approached prevailed. Alyosha would be truthful. I told June how special she was. How our relationship had made me want to change. In the past, I had spent free time in the dark, deep recesses of the world of pornography. Since meeting her it was a thing of the past. 'Now I care only about you. I'm sure that with tea and sympathy, I will stay that way. Do you like me enough to lend a hand?'"

"I know something about women," Peter interjected. "You were too direct. You should have taken a middle-of-the-road position and gradually led up to your weakness. Before hearing bad news, women like to be waltzed around. How did June take your blunt approach?"

"You're right. She was appalled. 'I'm a feminist. I hate pornography. It degrades women. You stare at THEIR body parts as though they were nothing more than an object. She's somebody's mother, wife, or sister. What am I to think of you? What would you think of a woman who spent her days staring at penises? When we became friends, I thought you might be gay. I could accept that. We could be friends. I could never be friendly with a sex pervert. And that is what you are.'

"I reported back to the group. Many advised to give her up. Only one offered positive advice. Barry had faced a similar situation with Phyllis, the woman he eventually married. She had spurned him when he had told her about the role of pornography in his life. Barry overcame her hostility when he sent her a letter along with a dozen roses. He admitted he was despicable, hated himself, and was unworthy of her friendship, and pleaded for a second chance. And asked for her help."

Duffy rose. He held his glass for the others to see. "I'm so riv-eted I forgot my drink. The ice has melted. It's water. Don't mind me; I'm just going to freshen this up."

In fact, as Peter observed, Duffy's glass was empty. *It's a good thing, court unlike office meetings, ends at five.* The witching hour for Duffy. Peter asked Gross to continue, and with a shrug in Duffy's direction, he indicated he should be ignored.

"Barry gave me his telephone number. 'Phyllis is my wife. See if you can get June to our house. We'll help.' Long story short, that dinner was twenty five years ago."

Peter said, "Now if you cut to the happy ending, we'll have good testimony. Duffy and I have endless patience, but judges are different. You've given a good picture of the trials of a sex addict. We're ready to hear the conclusion."

"I'm the principal of our school, and June is the head of the math department. Our two children are in college. My only encounter with porn is my association with Sex Addicts Anony-mous. I counsel, mentor, and work with other addicts."

"You're not going to skip twenty years just like that," Duffy said. "You'll have to say something like this: 'Six months later, we got married. We have two marvelous children,' et cetera. We'll work on it."

Peter was astonished. He thought Duffy was involved only in his drink. He thought about what Wolfe had said about tolerance. Apparently, two drinks were nowhere near Duffy's limit.

"A few more questions. Don't go yet," Duffy said. "The Griev-ance Committee's lawyer has referred to Peter as a 'sex addict.' How do you define the term 'sex addict'?"

"Someone obsessed with imaginary encounters. Afraid of actual encounters, flesh and blood. Once he has a successful real-world sexual relationship, he's on the road to recovery."

"Bravo! What was the group's reaction to Morrissey's tale?"

"When Peter told us of his problem—he craves all women—we thought this man has a healthy, sexual appetite. We wished we were like Peter. I asked him not to return. 'You're not a sex addict, and you're confusing the group.'"

Gross talked a bit more and then finally left. Duffy started to reconsider the case. "Experts lack hands-on experience. Their opinions rest on theory. Gross's problem is that he lacks credentials. Putting Wolfe and Gross together enhances both of their testimonies. An expert opinion and empirical evidence unite to make a stronger force than either one standing alone. You're hypersexual, not a sex addict. You have the will to resist clients. With psychotherapy, just like Wolfe said, sex with clients will become anathema. Probation, not disbarment, is the appropriate remedy."

"You told me," Peter said, "that the Fox said I'm a sex addict. That provides the perfect shoehorn to get Gross's testimony in. The judge will see what sex addicts are like. In comparison I'll come off—what did Wolfe say—like 'a man with a strong libido,' just like thousands of lawyers. What's the bar association going to do? Disbar us all? The only remaining issue…It's against the canons of ethics for a lawyer in a matrimonial action to make love to his clients. The violation stands unrebutted."

"I think most rational people will agree," Duffy said, "as long as it's consensual, it's nobody's business. And if the client seduces you, the lawyer should not be punished. 'The law is a ass,' said Shakespeare but not that big of a ass. We'll find out shortly. The next time we meet will be in court."

"We had a good day. I'll see you in court, if not before."

Peter levitated out of Duffy's office. The dark, heavy funk dogging his life had lifted. He hailed a cab and gave the driver the address of a shelter for battered women run by Safe Horizon. Peter had recently helped Peggy Doolittle; he wanted to check up on her.

Peggy started turning tricks at fifteen. Her pimp, Huey Douglas, gave her shelter, food, drugs, pocket money, and when in the mood, abusive and sadistic sex. In return Huey claimed all of Peggy's earnings. She secretly held back part. When Huey found out, he took a whip to Peggy and lashed her in front of the other young girls in his stable. "Never, never, hold back on me. Let this be a lesson to all of you. I'll whip the next one even more."

Peggy called a hotline and was directed to a nearby shelter. The counselor called Peter. He obtained an order of protection, and accompanied by a policeman, served it personally on Huey. Peter warned Huey that if he came within a hundred yards of Peggy, he'd spend years in the slammer. The policeman arrested Huey for aggravated assault. The charges were enlarged when drugs and a concealed weapon were found. At Peter's urging, bail was set at $100,000. Huey was held at Rikers Island pending trial. At his arraignment he pleaded guilty to all charges. He was sentenced to ten years in jail. The sentencing judge added a provision that if Huey ever came up for parole, notice to Peter would be given, and an opportunity for him to be heard.

Peggy received medical care, peer counseling, job training, and a comfortable room at the shelter.

Peter met Peggy in the common room. When they had first met, she was dirty, bruised, weeping, and unwilling to speak. "How wonderful you look," Peter said. "Your stay at the shelter will soon be up. I've arranged for interim housing for the next six months. After that you're on your own. Are you ready?"

"I've kicked drugs goodbye, and I'm never going back to the street. I've been taking courses on cutting and grooming hair. My instructor said I'm very good. I'm also learning manicure and pedicure. I've started working as a trainee at a unisex shop on Lenox near One Hundred Twenty-Sixth Street. My pay is not much, but it's all mine.

"Oh Mr. Morrissey, there's something else I got to tell you. I've met a nice guy. He's gentle although he's big and strong. He works as a prison guard on Rikers. I made him promise not to beat Huey."

Peter got the salon's address and phone number and said he would soon come in for a haircut and coloring. "For you there's no charge," she said. "Don't even try to give me a tip. You have given me a second chance. I will never forget you."

He was happy when he entered the shelter. He was even happier thirty minutes later when he left.

That night Peter thought about Peggy and Dr. Wolfe. He should have told Wolfe about his work with battered women. No. His concern was with Duffy's theory of lunatic behavior.

10

Duffy was alone in his living room sipping his third tumbler of Scotch. It would be his last of the day, as he adhered to a three-drink limit. Should he request an adjournment? Max Wolfe had thrown a curve ball, and Gross needed work. Richard Stern, the Grievance Committee's general counsel, had said at their only meeting that he would agree to a reasonable adjournment. Although it would be helpful to have more time, there was a downside: the request might alert the Grievance Committee that trial, not settlement, was imminent. The committee, like so many other overworked agencies, counted on settlements. Morrissey had violated the code. What was there to try? Only the penalty. Stern had likely anticipated Duffy would ask for a deal, a sanction less than disbarment.

At their meeting Stern had outlined his case and turned over Lisa Fox's notes. Stern had the right to examine Wolfe and Gross before trial, but first he had to ask. He hadn't, and trial was only three days away. How could Stern be ready for trial? *It's strategically more important,* he thought, *to catch Stern unprepared than to have more time to fine-tune his own case.*

Duffy abandoned thoughts of an adjournment. He'd spend the next two days whipping his case into shape and show up on the date set for trial ready to proceed.

The next day, Stern called Duffy. "We're swamped. So many complaints have been filed against lawyers. It's an epidemic. Clients lose a case, blame the lawyer, and file a complaint. Most times it's sour grapes. Not like in Molly Dixon's case where there's substance. Reviewing spurious charges is time consuming. For every fifty complaints we receive, charges are brought in only one. Lisa and I are exhausted. We told you Molly Dixon would be our only witness and turned over Lisa's notes. We've received nothing from you. When can you get us a witness list?"

Trials carried a great deal of risk. Experienced lawyers preferred to accommodate, not alienate the prosecutor. They might need the prosecutor's good will to work out a settlement if the trial were to turn against them. There were exceptions. Duffy decided this was one. "I've given you Dr. Max Wolfe's name and his curriculum vitae. I've also identified Philip Gross. You've not asked for a list of fact witnesses. Am I a mind reader? In two days trial begins. Give you a list, and the next thing you'll do is request an adjournment. I can hear you whining, 'We just got a witness list yesterday and want to take depositions of the expert witnesses. Two months ago we gave Duffy our witness list and the record of our investigation. He gave us nothing.' Too bad, Stern. Nothing personal, but you should have made your request a long time ago. You've put lots of heat on an innocent man. He wants vindication. Not next month but in a few days. We're ready for trial. Your request is too late. Either you go to trial or drop the case. What are you going to do?"

"Neither. I'll ask the referee for an adjournment. We'll get it. You're discourteous for denying my request."

"So there's no misunderstanding, I'm coming prepared for trial and will oppose an adjournment. To protect the record, I'm sending you a letter by hand stating my position."

On the corner of Madison Avenue and Twenty-Fifth Street sits a white marble building with fluted, Corinthian columns. Designed in 1900 by the architect James Brown Lord in the high classical style of the renowned sixteenth century Italian architect Andreas Palladio, it was home to the court known as the Appellate Division of the First Department. Its primary function was to hear appeals from the trial courts in New York and the Bronx. Additionally, in its grand rotunda, new lawyers got their first taste of the majesty of the law. There, they took an oath before the judges of the Appellate Division to uphold the law and were admitted to the bar.

The Appellate Division, through enforcement of the Code of Professional Responsibility, had the authority to expel the very lawyers it had admitted if it concluded they had violated the code.

Duffy met with Joe Berman, his top brief writer and researcher. "Joe, I'm taking Morrissey's case to trial. It's different from our usual case. If we lose Morrissey is disbarred, not jailed or hung. Here's the way it works. Clients who have a bitch against their lawyers squawk to the appropriately named Grievance Committee. Its staff, appointed by the App. Div., investigates, and if it believes the claim has merit, brings an action to disbar the attorney."

"I know what Morrissey did. Only a prudish bunch of vigilantes would burn that poor, heretic Morrissey at the stakes. Are there no checks?"

"The committee has to get a pass from a panel of six lawyers also appointed by the App. Div. The panel members are leading lawyers, not likely to rubber-stamp. There's a lot on Morrissey, including interviews with twenty five of his former clients.

"The clients got to tell their stories. Did Morrissey get a chance to tell his?" Berman asked.

"No. The committee didn't alert him to the claim. His first clue was a letter telling him he's up for disbarment."

"Sounds like Morrissey has been railroaded. Who's the judge?"

"The judge, or rather the referee, is a tight-ass WASP-y lawyer appointed by the App. Div. Sounds incestuous to me. Since when does the prosecutor's boss get to pick the judge? It's aggravated, because the referee is all powerful. If facts are disputed, what he finds is conclusive. So if we're going to win, we better win at trial. That's going to be tough -- I think the deck is stacked. It sure as hell doesn't shout due process to me. "

"Where will the trial take place?" Berman asked.

"In a mini-courtroom on the third floor of the App. Div's courthouse. The parties sit close together so that, unless you're careful, what one says may be heard by the other. The referee sits behind a large mahogany desk and a high-backed chair on an elevated platform. The referee should be referred to as Mr. Referee or by his last name. The Committee's lawyers, being ass-kissers, will call him 'Your Honor' or maybe 'Judge McGuire.' His name is Charles F. McGuire. He's a senior partner at Sullivan, Cromwell. I'll call him 'Mr. McGuire' or 'Mr. Referee.' Judges and temporary judges, for the most part, don't take to flatterers."

"Well, I'll start the basic research. When you need help, just holler."

At 9:30 a.m., a half hour before the time set for the hearing, Duffy and Morrissey arrived. Duffy preferred to be early as it gave him time to settle in, unpack his briefcase, and arrange his papers. Early in his career, Duffy had arrived late for court when his cab was in an accident. He jumped out of the cab and raced to the courthouse. He arrived breathless, sweaty, and late. As soon as he entered, the clerk called the court in session. Out came the judge, who growled, "Are you ready, Mr. Duffy?"

The outcome of that long-ago hearing was anticlimactic. Duffy had put so much effort into his failed attempt to arrive on time, he had little left for oral argument. He lost the case. From that day forward, Duffy took the subway to court and allowed plenty of time for delay.

Duffy estimated that if Stern's request for an adjournment was denied, opening argument and direct and cross of Molly Dixon would take up the first day. He asked his seven witnesses to stay ready. He provided estimates as to the day they would be called and said he would alert them by phone as to the precise time.

Stern, Fox, and Molly Dixon arrived five minutes early. Stern glared at Duffy. Molly Dixon, who was conservatively dressed in a dark dress, held a handkerchief which she used to dab her eyes. She looked straight ahead. *Why the hell is she carrying a handkerchief,* Duffy thought. *Is she going to weep and wail? I'd better be prepared for a scene.*

Duffy strolled the few feet to the committee's table. He greeted Stern and remarked on how gorgeous Fox looked. She turned in disgust and mumbled, "Get lost." He smiled at Molly. "Why the handkerchief? Are you preparing to cry for poor old Morrissey?" Just then the referee entered the room. Duffy remained standing, while Morrissey, Stern, and Fox rose to their feet. Stern and Fox greeted the referee with a "Good morning, Your Honor." Duffy was silent and returned to his seat. The referee introduced himself as Charles McGuire and asked the lawyers to call him by his first name. None would take that liberty.

McGuire asked if there were any preliminary matters. Stern rose. "Yes there is, Your Honor. Almost sixty days ago, we met with Mr. Duffy, identified our witness and turned over a copy of Ms. Fox's notes of her investigation. Having made full disclosure, we anticipated Mr. Duffy would reciprocate. We waited, and when we heard nothing from Mr. Duffy, I called and asked for a witness list and a short adjournment for preparation. To my astonishment Mr. Duffy upbraided me. He sent me a letter with a copy to Your Honor. In the letter he claims that by filing charges we signaled we were ready for trial and that my request for a short delay would prejudice Mr. Morrissey's right to a prompt trial as guaranteed by the Constitution.

"Judge McGuire," Stern continued, "The charges are straight-forward. I need to examine the experts in advance of the trial. I haven't the foggiest notion what an expert can possibly testify to in this factual case. Examining the experts before trial will eliminate surprise and result in a shorter cross–examination, thus saving the time of the court and the parties."

"Mr. Duffy," McGuire said, "your position is clearly stated in your letter. Unless you have anything to add, I am ready to rule."

If the judge had decided to rule against me, thought Duffy, he'd have given me a chance to answer. There are a few points I would like to make, but suppose I say something that causes the judge to change his mind? Best to shut up. "I await your ruling," he said.

"The hearing will go forward as scheduled with one modification. After each expert witness is examined by Mr. Duffy, I will call a two-hour recess to allow Mr. Stern to prepare his cross. I believe my ruling satisfies the needs of both sides. Mr. Stern, do you want to make an opening argument, or do you want to skip it and call your witness? I am familiar with the charges against Mr. Morrissey."

"Ms. Fox will conduct our case and wishes to make an opening statement."

Fox's statement took almost an hour. It was emotional in parts and flat and repetitive in parts. Some hit home, including these:

"Women facing divorce are in a weakened state. Not all but many. They have been cast away, abandoned, feel needy, and seek support. They worry about life after divorce. Will they be able to maintain their current standard of living? What about their social life? Will they be abandoned by their married friends, fearful that they may woo their husbands?

"Their lawyer is looked upon as a champion, a fiduciary charged with the task of rescuing them from a shipwreck. A lawyer must not take advantage of the vulnerability of his client to satisfy his sexual appetite.

"I hasten to add that not all women are easy prey. Many are strong. I anticipate you will hear from five of them. The same is true about most lawyers. Most are compassionate. They serve their clients and not their prurient interests.

"Our code recognizes the difficult position of a woman facing divorce and the role of her lawyer. She is weak; he is all powerful. In recognition of the disparity, the code absolutely and unconditionally prohibits attorney-client sex. It is found in the code of all fifty states.

"The evidence in this proceeding will show that Molly Dixon was mentally crippled when she sought help from Peter Morrissey, Esquire. She reposed trust and confidence in him. Morrissey repaid her trust with a virulent sexual assault. It began while they were having dinner at the Friars, Morrissey's club. He plied her with drinks. Told her it was necessary, if her case were to proceed, for her to have sexual relations with him. He refused to take the case if she said no. She resisted and began to weep. Morrissey became stronger in his unconscionable rage to satisfy his lust. He told her it was usual for his clients to have sex with him. He said 'All good divorce lawyers sleep with their clients.' Unless they made love, he would not represent her, and most likely no other lawyer would either. She cried. Begged him to make an exception in her case.

He refused. Having nowhere to turn, she averted her eyes and endured.

"The law is designed to protect the weak and to punish the lawyer who violates his trust. That is what this case is about and nothing else."

Fox put her papers to one side, grimaced at Duffy, and with a voice filled with contempt said, "Mr. Duffy has stated he intends to call expert witnesses. If the defense is designed to further the principles announced in the Code of Professional Responsibility, the experts should opine that Morrissey is a sex addict and looked upon his clients to satisfy his addiction. I hope the experts will offer relevant evidence, but I have little faith in Mr. Duffy's respect for ethical and moral standards."

Duffy was stunned. Fox's tale was very different from Morrissey's. "Did you bullshit me?" Duffy whispered into Morrissey's ear. When Peter shook his head no, Duffy thought about the many times witnesses cast the same event in radically different lights. There was usually some common ground. Here, there was none. *Well, if Morrissey is lying, he'll lose his license. Molly has no motive to deceive.* But there was the photo and her inscription. Something was amiss.

Now it was Duffy's turn. He began by defusing Fox's attack on his moral standards. Judges don't like personal attacks on a lawyer. He saw an opening to strike back. "Judges quite rightly pay no attention to childlike attacks upon one's opponent. I will not respond to Ms. Fox's insults concerning my ethical and moral standards except to say her statements are slanderous. If, in our only meeting that lasted no more than fifteen minutes, I said something inappropriate—I know of nothing of the sort—I beg Ms. Fox's forgiveness." Duffy then offered his hand to Fox and said, sotto voce, "That was a stunning opening." She refused his hand and looked away.

He shook his head in disbelief and resumed his argument. "My argument will be short as I believe you are more interested in hearing the witnesses testify than in hearing each lawyer's characterization of the evidence. I will discuss one document, a photograph of Ms. Dixon, signed and inscribed by her."

Duffy had weighed whether to drop the bomb before Dixon testified or wait to surprise her on cross. If he delayed the photo might shatter her credibility. If he referred to it now, Dixon and Fox would have time to concoct an explanation. He decided against delay. Fox's opening had poisoned the waters. Once she and Molly finished their dog and pony show, it might be too difficult to erase the image of a weak woman abused by her lawyer. Better to introduce the document now and derail her testimony before it began.

"I confess," Duffy said, "that I have a prejudice in favor of documentary evidence. Documents never forget; they never change sides. Their evidentiary value is the same regardless of the interest of the parties. In short on point documents are the most reliable evidence. With your permission I hand you a copy of a photograph of Molly Dixon and a statement, signed, sealed, and delivered."

Duffy also gave a copy to Fox. "You will note the inscription 'To Peter. Your services in all respects were excellent. I could not have gotten through the trauma of divorce and resumed my life without your heart-warming attention. Your devoted and admiring friend-client, Molly.'"

Duffy criticized lawyers who used a bludgeon to beat to death a good piece of evidence. It often caused judges and juries to sympathize with the witness. The signed statement, Duffy believed, destroyed the claim that Morrissey took advantage of a wounded sparrow. Duffy paused for a moment to let the thrust of the statement sink in. Then he turned to Morrissey's public service.

"There is another side to Peter Morrissey, other than divorce lawyer. For over thirty-five years, he has been active, and perhaps the most active lawyer in the country, in defending victims of sexual abuse. He donates to Safe Harbor, an organization that shelters and cares for women who are brutally assaulted, but more important, he gives of himself. He has a busy practice but finds time to spend about a hundred hours per year working for a cause he holds dear. He obtains orders of protection, serves them when a marshal is not immediately available, assists in putting assailants behind bars, and counsels victims. He is not only on the board of Safe Harbor, but for the past ten years, he has served as its chairman. I believe, Mr. Referee, you will never reach the issue of penalty, but if I am wrong, I ask you to allow me to submit letters attesting to Mr. Morrissey's extensive and excellent community service. The letters will come from dignitaries but also from the hearts of many of the women whom he has helped."

"Mr. Duffy," McGuire said. "I will keep an open mind on the penalty of disbarment. Our trial will center on the violation alleged by the Grievance Committee. If I deem it appropriate to consider Mr. Morrissey's good works, I will allow you time to place the letters before me."

Duffy had set a favorable stage. More, he felt, would be counterproductive. He turned to Lisa. "I eagerly await Ms. Dixon's testimony."

McGuire stared at the photograph, the statement, and then at Molly and Fox. Finally, he said, "Ms. Fox, call your witness."

11

"The Grievance Committee calls Molly Dixon."

Dixon stepped slowly to the witness chair, stooped over and with her head bowed. She fixed her eyes on Fox and clutched her handkerchief.

Lisa began slowly. She asked about Dixon's early life, her educational background (she attended a junior college in upstate New York). Dixon said she was not interested in a career other than marriage. When, in her first year at college she met John Dixon, she fell "head over heels" in love. He worked as a salesman in his father's Ford dealership. After dating for six months, John proposed, Molly accepted, quit college, and they were married.

Molly said their marriage was happy for the first twenty years. The only disappointment was that they could not have a child. Then Fox got to the circumstances leading Molly to seek a divorce and her relationship with Morrissey:

Q. You have earlier characterized your marriage as a twenty-year love affair. Did there come a time when this period ended?
A. Yes. It didn't happen all at once. Over time maybe ten years, John grew distant. We didn't have children, yet we referred to each other—when we were alone that is—as mother and father. I continued to call John, "father," but he stopped calling me, "mother." I was hurt. I felt inadequate. Perhaps John was blaming me for not bearing him a child. We were told it is not always the wife's fault. We could have been tested, but John said: "What was the sense of pointing a finger at one of us? We're happy. Let's leave it alone."
Q. Were you happy?
A. For the first ten years.
Q. What made you unhappy?

A. John ignored me. Not all at once but gradually. He stopped talking. Didn't want to go out, not even to the movies. After dinner he watched television and then went to sleep. Most nights he hardly said a word except to issue a command: "I'd like more meat!" I tried to watch television with him but didn't like his choices. Mostly ball games. I tried reading, but I'm not much of a reader. I thought about calling a friend and asking her to have dinner with me and see a movie, but I couldn't bring myself to do that. My life was entwined with John's.

Q. Now Molly, I don't wish to pry into your sex life, since that part of your life is private and should remain so. But in general terms, how, if at all, did your sex life change?

A. It was exciting when we first met. We didn't really do anything until we were married, but whenever I got close to John like when we were dancing or kissing goodnight, I felt his excitement, and it ignited me. After we were married, we had a wonderful relationship. It changed about the time he stopped calling me mother.

I knew, after twenty years of marriage, what John liked. I tried all those things and more, but the only response I got was a negative one. He remained as unexcited as when we started. I asked what was the matter? What more could I do? John said nothing and claimed: "I'm not in the mood." I asked if he would tell me when he was ready to make love. He said he would but never did or maybe was never in the mood. I tried again and again. I called my sister. I told her for the past five years John and I had not had intercourse. It was really ten, but I was ashamed to admit that. "It's time for a divorce," she said. "He must be cheating."

Q. What action did you take after hearing your sister's advice?

A. I spoke with John who said he was willing to stay together, but if I wanted a divorce that was okay too. John didn't give a damn whether we were divorced or not. After several months passed with no change, I got Mr. Morrissey's name from my sister.

Q. Would you describe what happened when you met Mr. Morrissey?

A. His office is very large. So is Mr. Morrissey. On the walls are framed photos of clients, all women. Some are famous. The photos say wonderful things about Mr. Morrissey. He pointed some out to me and said: "I hope when your case is over, you will be willing to comment on my services. Most of my clients do but not all." As we walked about his office, his hand brushed against my bottom. I couldn't tell whether it was accidental.

Our meeting was repeatedly interrupted by telephone calls. Mr. Morrissey rejected some and apologized when he accepted others. I offered to step out of the room while he was on the phone, but he asked me to stay.

"Finally," he said. "This is an unusual day. It's not fair to you. How about we meet after six at my club? It's the Friars a few blocks away. No calls, I promise. I also promise dinner."

I was thrilled. This big-time lawyer had invited me to dinner and at the Friars! I knew it was a hangout for showbiz folks. I immediately said yes. I asked if I should change my clothes. I didn't want to embarrass Mr. Morrissey. He said I looked fine, but I rushed home and changed. I was in the lobby of the club fifteen minutes early. He was late. I thought he had forgotten, or I had made a mistake. Then he walked in.

Mr. Morrissey greeted several important-looking people before he spotted me. He came right over. Offered me his arm. We climbed a broad-winding staircase to the main dining room.

Q. What did you and Mr. Morrissey discuss at dinner?

A. He wanted to know why I wanted a divorce. When I told him I was too shy to discuss details other than to say "my marriage is dead," he pressed. "If I take your case, I'll have to draw a complaint. You must tell me everything that has led to your decision. Everything you say is privileged, which means it stays with me."

I wanted Mr. Morrissey to be my lawyer. I feared if I didn't tell him everything he would think I didn't trust him and might not take my case. I had to drink a martini, however, before I got the courage to say my husband and I had no sex for ten years.

That wasn't enough. He pressed me on what I did to encourage my husband. I refused to speak. Mr. Morrissey said he had to know. "What you think is unimportant may turn out to be vital. You must tell me everything about your relationship with your husband if I am to help you. Don't be shy. All of my clients confide in me."

"I took a final gulp of my martini before I gained the courage to open up. But whatever I told him was never enough; he always wanted more details. He insisted I tell him what I did to excite my husband."

Q. I know you are under stress, but tell us what you told Mr. Morrissey.

A. I dressed in a certain way when an intimate moment seemed likely. I also did certain things to John, which I knew he liked. Not anymore. He turned away. Mr. Morrissey wanted descriptions of these things.

The waiter took our dinner orders, and Mr. Morrissey ordered a bottle of wine. I didn't want anything more to drink and said I felt woozy. When the wine came, Mr. Morrissey filled my glass. I didn't want more to drink, but I drank that glass and another.

Q. What effect did your answers have on Mr. Morrissey?

A. No matter what I said, he always wanted to know more. As I talked he placed his hand on my knee, under the tablecloth so no one could see, and moved it up my leg as far as it could go. I pushed his hand away. He put it back. I said to myself, "Dinner will soon be over, and the attack will end."

At one point he put his finger near my face and asked me to demonstrate on his finger what I did to John's penis. I jumped up and started to cry. Mr. Morrissey apologized. "Maybe another time," he said.

Q. How did the evening end?

A. Mr. Morrissey demanded that we have sex. "It's important to the success of our case that we have an intimate relationship. You saw the photos on my wall. Most of those women have had sex with me. Given the basis for your divorce, it is essential that we spend the night together. I must determine whether the sexual breakdown is your fault or your husband's. Unless you're willing to come with me, I won't be able to take your case. Other divorce lawyers will need the same kind of personal experience."

I was drunk. I needed a lawyer. I didn't want to go. I said yes but didn't really mean it.

Q. What happened in the hotel room?

A. We had sexual relations. After it was over, he said I was wonderful, and my husband is a fool. He told me to get dressed and to come to his office in the morning. He got dressed too. Outside the hotel he hailed a cab, dropped me at my house, and continued on with the cab.

Q. Did you show up at his office the next day?

A. Yes. What choice did I have? If I wanted a divorce, it was either Mr. Morrissey or another. I didn't want to repeat the whole humiliating process.

Q. Mr. Duffy handed the court a framed photograph of you containing the message: "To Peter. Your services in all respects were excellent. I could not have gotten through the trauma of divorce and resumed my life without your heart-warming attention. Your devoted and admiring friend-client Molly." What were the circumstances under which you wrote those words?

A. When the case was over, I came to Mr. Morrissey's office to sign some final papers. He showed me my photo and said it would occupy a prominent place in his office. He asked me to write something and sign my time. I didn't know what to say. So Peter told me. I wrote what he said. Those are his words, not mine.

Q. Do you know what the word "trauma" means?

A. Yes, it means upset, disturbance, something like that.

Q. Have you ever used the word "trauma" on any prior occasion?

A. No.

Q. On your photo it is written that Mr. Morrissey's "heart-warming attention" helped you "resume your life." After the divorce how would you describe your mental condition?

A. I was seriously depressed. I drank a lot, took too many pills, and had a breakdown. Analysis saved my life.

Q. What if anything did you tell your analyst about Mr. Morrissey?

A. I told her everything. How he got me drunk. The analyst said, "Lawyers have a bad reputation and are the butt of disparaging jokes. No wonder. Your Mr. Morrissey is a pig. He almost killed you. You should file a complaint with the bar association."

Q. What action did you take?

A. I filed a complaint and met several times with you.

"That concludes my examination," Lisa said.

"It's almost five," McGuire said. "We've been going since ten with only a short break for lunch. Let's call it a day and resume tomorrow with Mr. Duffy's cross. How long do you anticipate cross to take?"

Duffy wanted to prepare McGuire for a weak examination. "There's not much I need to cover in cross," he answered. "I should be finished by the lunch break."

Duffy and Morrissey hopped a cab to Peter's office. They barely talked, but when they reached the sanctity of Morrissey's office, Duffy unleashed. "How can I represent you if you hide the facts? 'She seduced *me*? Look what she wrote on her photo?' Shit, we're in, no, *you're* in deep shit. McGuire was moved by Molly's tale. Is there anything else you didn't tell me about Molly?"

"I'm looking at my notes. She had an affair with a neighbor, Charlie Monk, but only once, she said. She also had a passionate scene with her sister's husband, that is, until her sister appeared. She hasn't seen her sister since. Is this useful?"

"Useful, hell yes. But I don't trust you. Before I get excited, how come she told you all this?"

"Under the law at the time of Molly's divorce," Pete r said. "Adultery and cruel and inhumane conduct were the only grounds for a contested divorce. If a party could prove wrongdoing, he or she stood a better chance on the financial terms. Divorce lawyers, on both sides, routinely ask about adultery. Even if the case, as this one was, is uncontested. You don't want to be surprised at trial."

"You're not fucking funny," Duffy said. "Let me see your notes on Molly's encounters. Well, I'll be damned, we may be back in business, at least part way. Don't get your hopes up. The attorney-client privilege may prevent disclosure of things Molly told you."

"No, it won't," Peter said. "The privilege does indeed prohibit an attorney from disclosing confidential conversations with his client. It's also true that it operates against the attorney but not the client. Molly is free to disclose what she told me but not the other way around. There is an exception. If the client attacks her attorney, he can defend by disclosing confidential info relevant to his defense. In other words the attorney can use client confidential communications as a shield to protect himself."

"Makes sense. I'll call Joe Berman. He's my law man. I'll ask him to get the authorities and leave the printouts on my desk. Meanwhile, I have to start my preparation. Stay with me."

Peter and Duffy returned to Duffy's office. They ordered dinner in. Together they worked out Duffy's cross. They worked until ten before they were satisfied. "It's not great as you had led me to believe, or rather misled me, but it is the best under the circumstances. If her testimony is credited, it's impossible to claim she seduced you. But let's see how far I can go with Mr. Monk and her brother-in-law. See you tomorrow at ten."

12

Molly's testimony created a ton of sympathy. Even Duffy, hard-nosed as he was, felt it, and Peter, shattered by Molly's revelations and sensing his future in ruins, was remorseful. He had thought having sex with clients was the fun part of his practice. A bonus he was entitled to. After hearing Molly he realized his conduct could be hurtful. Drugs, alcohol, a breakdown. He should have never allowed lust to intervene. What was a game for him had hurt others. Badly. How had it taken him so long to see this?

The next morning, in a voice filled with pathos, McGuire asked Molly to resume the witness chair. He reminded her she was still under oath but added "not that you need to be reminded." He then turned to Duffy, and without saying a word, pointed to the podium where Duffy would conduct his cross.

Duffy began gently. He said he too had gone through a divorce. "Do you agree that some men suffer as much as women?" Irritated by his mild beginning, she turned aggressive and made a smart-aleck response. "How should I know? I'm not a man." Molly then laughed at her own joke. Duffy continued unperturbed. He had not realized how much his wife meant to him until after he was without her. He asked Molly if she missed her husband. Duffy was pleased when she said no. He remarked that one year after his divorce, he and his ex remarried. He asked if Molly considered going back to John. Again she said no. Duffy told of occasions after his divorce when he came into contact with his wife. The contacts revived memories of happy times. He asked Molly if she saw John after the divorce.

"Not in person, but I did call him and asked a question," she said. "I was appalled by the answer."

Duffy was too experienced to fall into a trap so obviously set. Instead of inquiring about the telephone call, he returned to his line of questioning to show Molly's indifference toward her former husband. Showing such a state of mind didn't win cases, but it did reflect on character. In a close case, where the judge must decide whom to credit, character plays a part.

Duffy asked if she made any inquiries as to John's health or wellbeing. Again she said no. In answer to the question of whether John had remarried or had a woman friend, she said she didn't know and blurted out, "nor do I care!"

"Well," Duffy mused. "You lived with a man for thirty years, and don't give a damn what has happened to him? Don't bother to answer, you already have."

> Q. I've learned from your testimony that John ignored your sexual advances. Did he hurt you in any other way?
> A. No. Isn't that enough

Duffy had appeared to be sympathetic toward Molly. She had been abused by her divorce lawyer. If his lawyer turned on her, sympathy would flow to her and hostility to him. Duffy had made a conscious decision not to attack her until he sensed the climate had changed. He sensed a change. Her negative answers and angry tone of voice were not endearing her to McGuire. The time was ripe for a frontal assault.

> Q. Since you were neglected by your husband, did you feel that you had a right to encourage other men?
> A. No.
> Q. Well, maybe "encourage" was the wrong word. Did you, without encouraging other men, have affairs during the course of your marriage?
> A. No. How dare you.

Duffy started to read from handwritten notes, but before he could get a word out, Fox rose and in a loud voice, much too loud for the small room and several decibels above her usual range shouted: "Objection, Your Honor. Mr. Duffy is holding notes. He owes the court an explanation as to whether he intends to use alleged confidential information that may have been allegedly obtained by Morrissey in the course of representing Ms. Dixon. I was warned. Mr. Duffy is a street fighter ready to violate sacred principles designed to protect clients from being blackmailed by their attorneys."

"Mr. McGuire," Duffy said. "I freely admit that I intend to make use of Attorney Morrissey's notes taken at the time he was representing Ms. Dixon. It is well established that the attorney-client privilege is waived in situations such as the instant one. Mr. Morrissey's license to practice is under attack based on charges filed by Ms. Dixon. As the New York Court of Appeals has held, Mr. Morrissey may use otherwise privileged information to defend himself against an attack by his client."

He then handed McGuire and Fox a copy of a Court of Appeals' decision and read the head note. "'Attorney is released from the confines of the privilege if disclosure is necessary to defend against claims of a former client.'"

In an obvious state of uncertainty, McGuire called for a twenty-minute recess. He warned both Fox and Stern that since "Ms. Dixon is under cross, you are prohibited from discussing her testimony. The better practice is not to speak with her at all until Mr. Duffy has completed his examination." McGuire then left the hearing room.

Fox grabbed Molly's arm and announced they were going to the bathroom. "I'll go with you," Duffy quipped.

When McGuire returned he announced what he described as his preliminary ruling: Duffy may make use of the otherwise privileged communications. McGuire granted Fox permission to file a brief opposing his decision and said, "If I'm persuaded you are right, I'll strike that portion of Ms. Dixon's testimony based on information told to her attorney."

Duffy was ready with his next question.

Q. After Judge McGuire called a recess, you and Attorney Fox went to the bathroom. While you were there, what did you say to Attorney Fox, and what did she say to you?
A. Nothing, except she told me to keep telling the truth.

"That's strange," Duffy said, "since you were *not* telling the truth before the recess. I ask the reporter to read the last question and answer before the recess."

The court reporter read Duffy's question asking whether Molly had had affairs during her marriage, and her answer was "no" followed by her comment "how dare you." Duffy waited for the stenographer to nod that she was ready to transcribe before asking his next question.

> Q. Apparently Ms. Dixon, you forgot about your neighbor, Charles Monk. Didn't you and Charlie have sexual relations many times? (Duffy fakes reading from the notes.) So many times that you thought about moving in?
> A. No, that's a lie. We had sex only once.

Duffy was satisfied with her answer. Morrissey's notes indicated that the affair was short lived as Charles was married to Molly's friend, Doris. It didn't say how many times. Molly's concession that it had happened once was enough to make her answer before the recess false. Fox's advice, harmless on its face, violated McGuire's order not to discuss her cross. McGuire got the point. Duffy did not press and went on with his question.

> Q. Is Mr. Monk a tall man about the size of Mr. Morrissey?
> A. Yes.
> Q. Did you tell Mr. Morrissey (more faked note reading) that you are attracted to huge men, because they tend to be outsized all over?
> McGuire was short. He stared and waited. Molly folded her arms and refused to answer. McGuire interposed and said, "I direct you to answer the question."
> A. Yes. I didn't say exactly what Mr. Morrissey wrote down but something of the sort.
> Q. Were you under the influence of alcohol when you bedded down with Charlie? (Duffy wanted to ask: "How many martinis did you have before having sex with great, big Charlie?" But he decided against being flip).

A. I don't remember, but it was in the afternoon, so it was unlikely we had had anything to drink.

Q. Prior to having sex with Charlie, did you describe to him your sexy tricks to arouse a man?

"Objection," Fox said. "This is the same ugly trick used against rape victims. What happened between Ms. Dixon and Mr. Monk has nothing to do with whether Mr. Morrissey violated the code."

"I share your concern," McGuire said. "I'm not sure about the relevance of Ms. Dixon's extramarital sex life. It's too early, however, to determine relevance. Your objection is overruled subject to connection. If it's not connected, I'll strike the questions and answers."

"Thank you, Judge McGuire," Duffy said. "It will be connected through other witnesses later on in the trial."

Duffy's reply pleased McGuire. He had learned to always flatter a judge when responding to a ruling. It was easy when the ruling was favorable; it was also easy when it was not. A typical response to an adverse ruling was to say: "Your Honor is correct in ninety-nine percent of the cases, but I would like to explain why this situation calls for a different ruling." Duffy's arguments were rarely persuasive enough for the judge to change his ruling, but they did not alienate the judge.

A. No, I didn't discuss my personal life with Charles. If Morrissey said I did, he's lying.

Q. I'm going to read from the definition of "sexual relations" contained in the rule we are concerned with. "Sexual relations means sexual intercourse or the touching of an intimate part of another person for the purpose of sexual arousal, sexual gratification, or sexual abuse." As defined in the Code of Professional Responsibility, did you have sexual relations with your sister's husband.

Molly burst into tears. Fox objected, claiming that Attorney Morrissey was on trial, not Ms. Dixon. "I understand your point, but Ms. Dixon must answer, otherwise I'll strike her entire testimony," McGuire ruled. "Ms. Dixon's conduct doesn't excuse Mr. Morrissey's. Nevertheless, she must answer. The testimony has a bearing on credibility."

Molly said she was confused and asked to have the question read. Thereafter she answered, "We didn't have intercourse, but we did kiss and touch each other."

Q. Did your analyst assign any blame to Mr. Monk for your breakdown?
A. No. She said only Morrissey was to blame.
Q. I know what the answer will be to my next question, but I must ask it to complete the record. Did your analyst assign any blame to what I would describe as "an incestuous relation" with your sister's husband?

Fox objected, claiming that the relationship was not incestuous as Molly and her sister's husband were not blood relatives. "Also she didn't have intercourse. They just, well, kissed."

McGuire turned to Duffy and asked if he had anything to say to Fox's objection.

"Indeed I do. I implied that my definition of incest was not the common one but included impermissible acts with a family member. Under the code what Ms. Dixon and her brother-in-law did would be enough to disbar him if he were a lawyer representing her in a matrimonial action."

"Mr. Duffy, rephrase your question eliminating the words 'incestuous relations.'"

He did, and Molly gave the predictable answer.

Q. The morning after your hotel tryst with Mr. Morrissey you showed up in his office. What was the reason for your visit?
A. He said if I wanted him to represent me I had to sign a retainer. I did sign a retainer, but I now know the real reason. He wanted to take my picture for future use.

Duffy could have asked the tagline to be stricken as it was not responsive to his question. But why? What was important was that she admitted what she did not have to. She became his client after they had had sex. Duffy conferred with Morrissey. When he returned to the podium, he said, "I have no further questions."

McGuire asked Fox if she wanted to examine Ms. Dixon on redirect. In a patronizing tone, he added, "You have a right to do so." Duffy controlled his smile and tapped Morrissey, motioning him to look glum.

Fox said, "Yes, just a few questions."

Q. In cross, you mentioned a telephone conversation you had with your former husband. What were the circumstances under which you called him?

A. My analyst asked me to call John. I had told her John had complained about Morrissey's bills. He said "Your greedy lawyer is trying to bankrupt me. When he's finished there'll be nothing left for you or me. Let's get this over with quickly. I said you could have a divorce. Why is this dragging on?" My analyst had a hunch. "Find out from John whether Morrissey charged for dinner at the Friars and the sex that followed." I called John. He got out Morrissey's bill, and sure enough he had. I asked John to send me a copy of the bill.

Q. I show you an affidavit purportedly sworn to by Peter Morrissey and a schedule of time charges. Are you able to identify the document?

A. Yes. It is a copy of the papers John sent me.

Fox offered the document in evidence and handed a copy to Duffy. "I have no objection," he said. "The document is crucial to the motion I intend to make at the close of the committee's case. I am sure, Mr. McGuire, you are familiar with the standard procedure in our profession to charge for preliminary consultations only after the client becomes a client. If Ms. Dixon had not become a client, Mr. Morrissey would have absorbed the expense. This document is important, because it establishes the encounter took place before Ms. Dixon was Mr. Morrissey's client. The code does not condemn the sexual practices of a lawyer except with a client and then only in matrimonial actions. Mr. Morrissey's charges, under the heading 'preliminary consultation,' establish that Ms. Dixon was not Mr. Morrissey's client at the time of the sexual encounter."

"I understand your argument as a general matter," McGuire said, "but you must admit the 'consultation' was unusual. The document is admitted."

Fox resumed her redirect.

Q. We will undoubtedly hear from Mr. Duffy about the preliminary consultation. He recorded five hours at $500 per. How long did the consultation last, including dinner, the aftermath in the hotel, and the cab ride?
A. Less than four hours. I was supposed to meet Mr. Morrissey at the Friars at six. He was at least fifteen minutes late. When I got home, it was slightly after ten.
Q. $385 is listed as expenses. What did you understand the expenses to be?

An inexperienced trial lawyer would have objected, contending that unless Ms. Dixon saw the bills, she lacked personal knowledge and her testimony would be a guess. Guesses were unreliable and inadmissible. Duffy only objected when the evidence might hurt. Since it appeared likely that the expenses covered dinner, the hotel room, and the cab fare, he made no objection. Molly testified to the obvious.

Fox conferred with Stern and said her redirect was over, and that the Grievance Committee rests. McGuire asked if Duffy wished to make a motion. He did.

"Under the code an attorney in a divorce action may not have sexual relations with his client unless they have had sexual relations before the client became his client. Ms. Dixon's testimony for purposes of the motion must be deemed true. She testified she became Mr. Morrissey's client the morning after. That means she wasn't his client when they had sexual relations. Ms. Dixon testified to only one sexual encounter. It occurred before she became Mr. Morrissey's client. According to the letter and spirit of the code, it was not violated."

"You're going too fast," McGuire said. "Mrs. Dixon came to see Mr. Morrissey in his office. She was seeking legal advice. Why shouldn't I conclude the attorney-client relationship began at that point? Aren't you attaching too much importance to a formality, the signing of a retainer?"

Duffy and Morrissey had anticipated McGuire's question. Morrissey had suggested that Duffy respond by contending that punitive rules should be strictly construed. Duffy adopted Morrissey's suggestion and added "strictly includes technically."

"Since Ms. Dixon was not *strictly* a client at the time she claims to have had sexual relations, what they did is a matter of complete indifference as far as the code is concerned."

McGuire leaned forward and stared at Duffy. "Are you asking me to consider as merely technical the fact that Mr. Morrissey charged for his time at dinner and for sex? A lawyer only has a right to charge a client for his time as a lawyer. Why doesn't the doctrine of nunc pro tunc make Mrs. Dixon his client at the time he billed for his time?"

"Every citizen, and that includes lawyers, has an obligation to observe the law. And the law, in turn, has an obligation. It must inform in plain, un-adjectival English the prohibited conduct. It is common practice for lawyers to charge for preliminary consultations only after a client becomes a client. By imposing a charge, the non-client, at the time of sexual intercourse, does not by an act of metamorphosis become a client at the time of sexual intercourse. She made that plain, since before she became a client, she had to sign a retainer. She did so the next morning. I recognize that there is a close line between the night before and the morning after. But whenever the law draws a line, those who fall outside the line, no matter how close they come, have not violated the law. Assuming, as we must, for purposes of my motion, that she and Mr. Morrissey had sexual relations on the night before she became his client, this proceeding must be dismissed."

McGuire shook his head no. "I have trouble accepting your basic premise that a rule designed to protect clients should be strictly or technically construed in favor of the lawyer. I am also troubled by charging for time and branding it 'non-lawyer-client time.'"

"Let's assume," Duffy said, "Ms. Dixon had not signed the retainer the next morning and had not become his client then Mr. Morrissey would not have violated the code. If I'm correct, then when she signed the retainer is a crucial fact. There is not a snippet of evidence that after Ms. Dixon became Mr. Morrissey's client, they had sex or even touched each other. The proceeding should be dismissed."

"I'm not sure I understand your point," McGuire said. "I'm confused. Mr. Morrissey invited Ms. Dixon to dinner and later that evening had sexual intercourse with her. A fact, you correctly state, must be assumed to be true for purposes of your motion. Suppose Mr. Morrissey, as do many lawyers, had not required a retainer as a condition of representing a client. What then? When would Ms. Dixon have become a client?"

Duffy stood up and started to speak when McGuire motioned him to be seated. "Save your answer for your reply. It's Ms. Fox's turn."

"When, under the law, does a person become a client?" she asked. "The answer to that question goes straight to the heart of Mr. Duffy's motion. Did Mr. Duffy address this critical issue? No. He danced around it. He said a 'preliminary consultation' does not a client make, and that what's necessary, indeed essential, is the signing of a retainer. Your Honor found his argument incomprehensible. In fact, Mr. Duffy's insistence on a technical condition being met before the attorney-client relationship begins flies in the face of four hundred years of common law jurisprudence. Mr. Duffy cited not a single authority in support of his bizarre theory. The reason: There is none. The law makes plain a client is a person who seeks advice and services from a lawyer—the very act engaged in by Molly Dixon when she first appeared in Mr. Morrissey's office. The relationship does not require the client to sign a retainer, agree to pay a fee, or perform any other formal act.

"In the leading case of *Goldstein v. SEC*, the Court of Appeals for the District of Columbia addressed this very question of when a client becomes a client. The court ruled: 'An attorney-client relationship, for example, can be formed without any signs of formal "employment." *See* Restatement (Third) of the Law Governing Lawyers. 'The client need not necessarily pay or agree to pay the lawyer.'"

Fox, mocking Duffy's approach, handed McGuire a copy of the decision in Goldstein and then turned to Duffy handing him a copy and saying as he took it from her, "I guess you overlooked the Goldstein decision and the Restatement of the Law Governing Attorneys. Otherwise you would have called them to the attention of the court. Isn't that an obligation of a lawyer? Or does he only have to do so if he has a signed retainer with the court?"

"Ms. Fox," McGuire said, "a personal attack on Mr. Duffy hurts, not helps, your case. Mr. Morrissey is the subject of this proceeding."

"I apologize to Mr. Duffy and the court. May I proceed?"

McGuire nodded.

"Morrissey's charges for legal services were incorporated in the judgment of divorce. In support of the charges, Mr. Morrissey submitted an affidavit affirming that the charges were necessary and appropriate in the course of his representation of Ms. Dixon. Attached to the affidavit was a detailed statement describing the legal work performed, and the precise amount of time devoted to each item. The first item called "preliminary consultation" listed the five hours spent by Mr. Morrissey at dinner and the additional time bedding down Ms. Dixon. He claimed his usual hourly rate of $500.00 for a total of $2,500.

"I've heard of lawyers' euphemisms for outrageous charges, but this one takes the cake. There's a word for those charging for sex, and it ain't lawyer."

"That's enough, Attorney Fox," McGuire warned. "You made your point without the tagline. I direct the parties to exchange briefs on Mr. Duffy's motion to dismiss. They are to be submitted to me by ten in the morning. Arguments will be heard promptly at two o'clock. If I deny the motion, which I am inclined to do, the hearing will continue the next day. Are there any questions? Hearing none, we stand in recess."

As Fox was collecting her papers, Duffy complimented her on her presentation. Fox, who had been under intense pressure, relaxed, and for the first time, smiled at Duffy. "That's praise from Caesar."

Encouraged by Fox's smile, Duffy asked, "Why did you pick Molly? Surely you had better witnesses."

"We don't pick our witnesses; the sleazy lawyer selects his victims. I wanted more than one to testify, but it's difficult, even in the age of women's lib, to persuade women to discuss their sex life. It's even more difficult when you tell them the discussion will be under oath and transcribed by a court reporter. You're right, of course, there were many victims. Only Molly was willing to testify. Off the record, several said he was good in bed."

"It's well known. Morrissey is a Casanova. He likes you. How about meeting him for dinner at the Friars?"

"He's not my type." But Fox said it with a smile.

13

In the cab on the way to Morrissey's office, Duffy called Joe Berman. "Listen Joe, we need a brief by tomorrow morning. There are two points and several subdivisions. First, the anti-sex rule doesn't apply to sex with a client before she becomes a client. As we discussed prior, that's an exception to the rule. So the sixty-four dollar question is: When does a client become a client? Fox read from *Goldstein v. SEC*. I didn't have a chance to read it, but Peter did. I'm putting him on the phone."

Peter took the cell. "Hi Joe. There's language in *Goldstein* that hurts but it's a securities case. Investment advisors have to register with the SEC if they have more than a hundred clients. The advisor managed investments for one corporation having thousands of stockholders. The issue was who is the client? The corporation, with whom the advisor had a formal agreement, or the thousands of stockholders who own the corporation with whom the advisor had no agreement? The court said the stockholders were the clients. Fox argues by extension that a client is a client even without an agreement."

"I don't get it," Joe said. "What does that case have to do with ours? If that's the best the committee can come up with, I'll bet there's lots of cases holding that if a lawyer requires a retainer before representing a client, the representation begins when the client signs. I'll dig to find support. Before I start you do require a signed retainer? Right? Any exceptions?"

"I never take on a client until I have a signed retainer. There are no exceptions. Bill and I discussed other legal points. Let me give them to you."

"Peter, we can save time if they're the ones I've already researched. First is intent. You had to know your action was in violation of law. If you had a reasonable belief that Molly was not your client then you didn't intend to violate the law."

"Great," Peter said. "Promise me if you ever get fed up with Duffy, you'll give me a holler."

Duffy asked for the phone. "The judge signaled he's going to deny the motion. You don't have to reinvent the wheel. We've written loads of briefs focusing on intent. Also on strict construction. McGuire hates that argument, so go easy on it. We don't want the brief to rise or fall on strict construction. Put it last, and make it short. Cut and paste from other briefs. We don't have a lot of time.

"There's a troublesome issue, and Fox milked it. It bothered McGuire. Morrissey billed for his time before she became a client. The egomaniac charged his hourly rate of five hundred for mostly having fun in bed. He didn't give her a discount for being a good lay. Fortunately for him he's not up for overcharging. See if you can find some support for the practice of billing later for initial interviews before the client becomes a client. Wait a minute Joe, Peter wants to talk."

Peter took back the phone. "Joe, there's another code provision that a lawyer can't insist on a night of fun and games as a condition for taking on a client. Molly's testimony can be construed that I asked for a quid pro quo. The charges against me make no reference to violating any rule other than divorce lawyers can't have sex with clients. Quote the committee's letter in full. In civil actions, we call what the committee is trying to do 'trial by ambush.' Hang on, Bill wants to talk."

Duffy said, "A defendant can't be tried for a crime not included in the indictment. That's Fifth Amendment stuff—due process. Look, I know this is not a criminal case, but it's penal in the sense that disbarment is a penalty. I don't care if we lose on this point, because we'll win after trial. McGuire, that dried-up prune, will owe me one. I'm off to Peter's office. Call me if you have questions. I'll get back to the office as soon as I can."

In Peter's office they agreed on Joyce, who was still waiting for her ex-husband to take her back, as their first witness. They outlined the testimony of each of the other four witnesses and then turned to the Fox's strategy.

"She will try to put into evidence her notes of the interviews of the twenty-five clients. It will be tough to keep them out. If they do get in, how do the notes stack up against live witnesses?"

"In jury cases," Duffy said, "notes can't compete with testimony. They're dry, no sex appeal. We don't have a jury. It's hard to tell how McGuire will react. I don't think he's going to base a decision on Fox's interpretation of what victims told her. He knows she's biased. I'll make sure he doesn't forget."

"Let's assume McGuire lets the notes in. I'll have to admit to having had many affairs. Perjury is a criminal offense. I don't want to commit a crime."

"Right," Duffy said. "Prosecutors go hard on witnesses who lie. As I advise my clients: always tell the truth. Also stay clean. In your case keep your fly zipped. I don't want a new offense added."

"Hold it," Peter said. "You're contradicting yourself. You said the committee can't add new charges."

"Wise guy! Why do I waste my time talking to you? Behave just for a few days. See you tomorrow at two."

In a few hours, Joe constructed his brief. By taking sections from other briefs and making a few refinements, a detailed and scholarly work was put together. Duffy strengthened the brief by adding facts, and then he turned to the law. The brief cited several Supreme Court decisions holding that a conviction cannot be obtained on charges not specified in the indictment. The brief argued that the Grievance Committee's charges were akin to an indictment, because a penalty was sought. Like an indictment the letter must put the defendant on notice of the charges he will have to face.

Duffy knew the argument was weak. The Fifth Amendment speaks of a criminal indictment. It was a large stretch to contend that the letter from the committee was the equivalent of an indictment. Yet a principle was at stake. Morrissey had a right to know the charges. They and they alone should lead to punishment. In preparing his argument, Duffy set aside a quote from a Supreme Court decision, *Stirone v. United States*. The part he anticipated reading precluded adding a new charge through trial testimony. Unfortunately, it referred only to criminal cases and a grand jury indictment.

Joe distinguished *Goldstein v. SEC* on the facts and the law. He found authorities going back four hundred years to Lord Coke that a client was one who receives legal advice from an attorney. The brief argued on the night before, whatever Morrissey was dispensing was not legal advice. It was another weak argument, but there was only so much he could do with this set of facts.

Duffy had the brief served simultaneously by hand to both Fox and McGuire promptly at 10:00 a.m. Peter and Duffy were huddled in Duffy's office anxiously awaiting Fox's brief. When it arrived Peter grabbed it and read it before turning it over to Duffy. He was surprised that Fox spent so much time reciting the facts drawn exclusively from Molly's direct testimony. It was unnecessary to discuss facts. Duffy had conceded for purposes of the motion the charge of sexual relations with Molly. *Assuming they're true why discuss them at all?* Fox probably wanted to pound them in to ensure McGuire wouldn't forget Molly's weeping and wailing. Peter turned to the legal arguments Fox had raised.

She argued that Dixon was a client the moment she entered Morrissey's office. The signing of the retainer was a formality. She quoted the passage read the day before from *Goldstein v. SEC*. Alternatively, she argued Morrissey coerced Dixon to have sex as a condition of representing her. She cited the provision of the code prohibiting such conduct. Anticipating Duffy's argument based on surprise, she pointed out that: "The entire section of the code regulating 'sexual relations' were contained in the charging letter. Morrissey was apprised of the claims against him. All he had to do was read. For Morrissey to claim surprise, as he has routinely done, is an attempt to shield his shameful conduct by closing his eyes."

She devoted several pages to the fees charged by Morrissey for dinner and sex before concluding that: "They underscore

Morrissey's evil character. For purposes of this proceeding, they constitute an admission Ms. Dixon was a client. If not at the time, then, in words favored by the court, nunc pro tunc."

Our brief is better, Peter thought, *but she'll win. There should be a prize for the best brief. Oh come on. This is not a law school exercise in moot court. This is real life. My pitiful life.*

14

Promptly at two o'clock, McGuire appeared. He thanked the parties for their excellent briefs. "Since it's your motion, Mr. Duffy, you're at bat."

Duffy began with a concession. His motion was grounded in law. "The facts, based on Ms. Dixon's testimony, incredible as they are, must be deemed to be true. Not only that, but all inferences supporting the committee's claim must be drawn in its favor." He cautioned that the presumption of truth applied only to the decision on the motion. If the motion was denied, Duffy would argue that the actual facts were very different from those testified to by Ms. Dixon.

Duffy stressed the seriousness of the proceeding and the possible adverse consequences. "A lawyer of thirty-five years standing may lose his right to earn his living in the only way he knows how. Further, his reputation will be ruined. In a very real sense, the Draconian relief sought by the committee will have an impact on Morrissey equivalent to a life sentence." For that reason, Duffy argued the rule must be strictly construed.

His argument on strict construction might be of interest to lawyers and judges, but probably it would be old hat even to them. Duffy did make an interesting point reflecting on the arbitrary nature of the rule.

"Let's assume a lawyer meets a woman at a cocktail party. She says she hates her husband and wants a divorce. He says it just so happens he specializes in matrimonial actions. They have sexual relations. A few days later, she comes to his office and signs a retainer. Ms. Fox may wish to disbar the lawyer, providing more fuel for Charles Dickens's low view of our profession, but I strongly doubt proceedings would be instituted.

"How different is my example from the case before you? There is only one difference. Morrissey met Ms. Dixon not at a cocktail party but in his office. Ms. Fox argues in her brief that the instant Ms. Dixon entered Mr. Morrissey's office, she became his client." He read from Fox's brief. "She cites no authority for her counterintuitive position." He pauses. "Mr. McGuire, I don't know about your practice, but the number of prospective clients who come to my office and promptly leave by far exceed the number of actual ones who sign retainers. Many times I reject a prospective client, because I cannot help. Other times I may have a conflict. Prospective clients may reject me. They may find my fees too high or perhaps take a dislike to me. A client becomes my client not when he or she walks in the door, but when a retainer is signed."

Duffy addressed a new point: Did Morrissey coerce Dixon into having sex as a condition of representing her? "I counted the number of lawyers listed in Martindale specializing in matrimonial action but stopped when the number reached fifty, and I hadn't finished with the letter J. Morrissey is one of the best matrimonial specialists, but there are many others, all good. Lots of them are women. If Ms. Dixon believed the hundreds and hundreds of male divorce lawyers would all want to have sex with her, an act she wished to avoid, she could have selected a female. New York is not a small town with one or two lawyers. Ms. Dixon didn't have to go to bed with Morrissey to secure legal representation. She didn't have to do anything she didn't want to do. And any lawyer with minimum experience could have handled Dixon's simple case. It was not a contested divorce."

Duffy turned to the importance of procedural due process. "Ms. Fox asks you to commit a procedural error when she seeks to add claims not specified in her letter. Procedure governs the turns and twists of a trial. Take a wrong path, and the parties may lose their way. Once a mistake is made, it is difficult to correct, as difficult as stuffing feathers back into a busted pillow after a wind storm. One inviolate procedural rule requires the prosecutor to obtain an indictment before a defendant can be charged with a crime. Once the case goes to trial, subtractions can be made but no additions. The rule is sacred and enshrined in the Fifth

Amendment. When called upon to vary the rule by compelling circumstances, the courts have unanimously refused."

Duffy read from a Supreme Court decision essentially supporting his argument but referencing only criminal cases.

"As you have noted, Mr. McGuire, there's a difference, between an indictment and the committee's charging letter. But the overriding principle remains the same: the criminal defendant and the lawyer facing disbarment are both entitled to notice of the charges leveled against them. Is it imposing too great of an obstacle on Ms. Fox to get her ducks in a row before the case begins? Is the prejudice to Peter Morrissey less meaningful, because he is facing disbarment, not jail time?"

Duffy discussed his distaste for the nibbling effect of a concession. "If you, Mr. McGuire, were to rule that the alleged coercion claim is properly before you, Ms. Fox would next want to put her skewed notes of interviews of Morrissey's clients in evidence or question him on matters pertaining to other clients. Let Ms. Fox nibble on the pinky, and she'll swallow the whole hand. I sympathize with her position. She has presented a very weak case and now seeks to bolster it with additional charges. In fairness you should not allow a variance between the issues pleaded and the issues tried."

McGuire looked straight at Duffy. "I have to weigh the arguments on whether coercion is in or out. I understand the distinction you make between New York and Peoria. That goes to the merits to be argued after trial. I'm not telegraphing how I am going to rule on the coercion claim because I haven't made up my mind. But," McGuire shifted from Duffy to Fox, "don't even think about introducing your notes into evidence or questioning Mr. Morrissey on any client other than Ms. Dixon."

Duffy exhaled. It no longer mattered how McGuire ruled on the motion. It was not likely that Morrissey would be disbarred on Dixon's testimony. Disbar a lawyer based on one sexual encounter testified to by a discredited witness? Never. Maybe a slap on the wrist but not disbarment. Nothing short of a parade of victims would justify the severe penalty of disbarment. Good lawyers know when to stop. Duffy thanked McGuire for his patience and sat down.

Fox began with a recitation of Dixon's testimony, but McGuire interrupted her after two sentences. "Ms. Fox, I'm interested in three legal issues. One, when does a client become a client? Two, was coercion fairly pleaded, and if so, can it exist in a major legal market when Molly Dixon has a choice of thousands of lawyers including women? Three, what is the effect on the rule if I were to find that Ms. Dixon seduced Mr. Morrissey? Mind you, I'm not saying I'm leaning toward that position. My question really goes to informed consent, something less than seduction. And please discuss a situation, perhaps not this one, in which the client seduces the lawyer."

Fox seemed to gain strength from McGuire's questions. They touched on heartfelt issues. She addressed the first: "There is no one act that initiates the attorney- client relationship. The signing of a retainer signals the start for many but not all. In this case the relationship began when Ms. Dixon disclosed, over dinner, confidential information about her case and her life. She reposed trust and confidence in Morrissey. He received her personal and intimate disclosures in his position as her attorney. He became her attorney at that moment not by pushing a retainer in front of her but by listening and questioning her."

Morrissey closed his eyes, put his hand over his mouth to hide his grimace, and thought, *She's right. Molly came to me for help. She confided in me. That marked the beginning of our relationship. Maybe today the world will end. Well, we knew we were going to lose the motion. I'd settle provided I can keep practicing.*

"Morrissey admitted as much," Fox continued. "He billed for his time on the night before she signed the retainer." Smoldering with outrage, she added, "Dinner took about two hours and their sojourn in the hotel about the same time. Morrissey billed five hours at five hundred dollars per for his 'consulting services.' He must have spent an extra hour ruminating on the events. I've heard of low-life, greedy lawyers doing just that." Now she turned her gaze to Molly but spoke to the judge.

"The lawyer-client relationship is a two-party affair. Molly testified that she wanted Morrissey to represent her. That's why she came to his office. So determined was she to obtain his services, she went to bed with him to seal the deal. This was not the situation described by Mr. Duffy, where a man at a cocktail party picks up a woman. Ms. Dixon came to see Morrissey for a purpose—to retain his legal services. He told her 'no sex, no services.' In an ironic twist, Mr. Duffy claims that the relationship began when Ms. Dixon signed a meaningless, boilerplate retainer binding not her but her husband to pay Morrissey's fees. He asks Your Honor to forget that Molly confided in Morrissey. And then made partial payment with her body. His contention would be funny if this were not a serious situation."

McGuire took notes and nodded his head. Fox's point had hit the target. Morrissey wrote a note to Duffy: "We lost that one. Worse. Momentum has shifted."

Fox turned to the second question, which she rephrased. "Was Morrissey on notice that he could not satisfy his sick craving for sex by imposing it as a condition of representing female clients? Our letter recited the entire rule. We did not limit its scope to matrimonial cases. Only a guilty mind could read it that way."

Fox handed McGuire and Duffy a copy of the letter. She read the no sex rule, the definition of sexual relations, and the one in matrimonial actions—prohibiting sex. "Nowhere in our letter does it state that a provision of the rule cited and quoted does not apply. The reason: our investigation showed Morrissey violated every section. Hence we quoted and invoked every single one."

"Hold it," McGuire said. "The anti-sex provision seeks to ban three activities. A lawyer can't demand sex as a condition of employment. A lawyer can't coerce sex or intimidate a client. A divorce lawyer can't have sex regardless of whether the client consents or even induces it. The one exception to all three bans is if the lawyer and client had an ongoing affair. In that case he can demand, coerce, and in the course of a matrimonial action, have sex with his client. Am I reading the rule correctly?"

"You are. Mr. Duffy, in his brief, pokes fun at the rule. He claims it's alright for a lawyer to coerce a client, provided he was coercing her before she became a client. He thinks it's funny. The code, however, was adopted by the Appellate Division. The legislative history shows that the court didn't want to play big brother and interfere with ongoing relationships. The rule represents a compromise. Only new relationships between a lawyer and a client are subject to regulation. I believe the exception is wrong. *No* lawyer should coerce, intimidate, or demand sex regardless of prior relations. We lack the power to change the code. Only the Appellate Division can do so. My job is to enforce the rules as adopted in accordance with their tenor."

Fox left unspoken that McGuire's task was to uphold the code. Duffy was pleased when McGuire referred to the rule as "anti-sex," a term he used again and again in his brief. Duffy knew, however, that his motion would be denied. Morrissey would be tried on every part of the rule. On the credit side, prospective testimony of other clients and Fox's notes were out the window. The case would rise or fall on Dixon's assertion alone.

"Addicts," Fox continued, "are generally thought to be dependent on substances. It is nearly impossible for lawyers hooked on alcohol or drugs to avoid detection. Sooner or later their drunken or drugged state prevents them from performing their duty. They are flushed out indirectly by their crazed actions, or blatant neglect. There is another addict, less known and studied, referred to by psychologists as a 'sex addict.' The code seeks to rid the law of their kind through the provisions under review. The rules should be construed to have a broad reach—to remove sex addicts from the practice of law. Mr. Morrissey represents only women. Why? Because he can charge more and be certain of getting paid? Yes, but he also craves his clients. He's a sex addict.

"He tries but can't seduce every client. Women are not monolithic. Some are strong. They look upon themselves as persons, not objects. They are offended by Morrissey's filthy ways, and tell him where to go. Many women, like Molly Dixon, are weak. Morrissey objectifies the weak to satisfy his insane lust. His victims are the very ones in need of protection.

"Ms. Dixon is not perfect. We saw in direct and again on cross that she is defenseless against attacks by sex-crazed men. The law can't protect her from her neighbor or her brother-in-law. The Appellate Division, however, can protect her from her lawyer. And that, Judge McGuire, is what this proceeding is about."

Fox's argument impressed Duffy. *A lawyer's office*, he thought, *is a sanctuary. Clients should be secure, served, not molested.* Duffy, however, was an advocate, first and foremost. His job was to defend Morrissey. In his years at the criminal bar, he had defended men a lot worse than Morrissey. When they were convicted, he didn't lose sleep. Would he lose sleep if Morrissey were disbarred? He thought not.

When Fox concluded her argument, it was Duffy's turn. "When I said the facts testified to by Ms. Dixon must be deemed true, but only for the purposes of the motion, I did not include the testimony of Ms. Fox. Where the devil does she come off calling Mr. Morrissey a 'sex addict'? Other than her ipse dixit, there is nothing in the record to support her defamatory remark. She is protected from an action at law only because her defamatory statement was made in the courtroom. Were she to repeat it in a non-privileged venue, we'd slap a defamation suit against her.

"I won't commit the same egregious wrong by testifying. Rather, I shall present the facts in conformity with the rules.

"The evidence in this case will show that Mr. Morrissey was seduced by Dixon, is not a sex addict but is a fine lawyer who serves his clients well. Can Ms. Fox counter what I have just said? She has closed her case without providing a scrap of evidence to support her fallacious argument that Morrissey is a sex addict. She has also failed to offer even a whiff of evidence that Mr. Morrissey failed to serve his clients well. If he did work hard for his clients, and the evidence will be overwhelming that he did, that is certainly a factor to consider in deciding on what penalty, if any, should be imposed.

"Attorney Fox suggests something sinister about Morrissey's limiting his representation to wives. First, there is no evidence to that effect. The decision to choose wives rests, not on prurient grounds but on economics. In most cases as I'm sure you know, the husband pays the legal expenses of both parties. He can, and usually does, instruct his attorney to limit his activities to essential tasks in order to keep his bill within reasonable bounds. He recognizes, at the end of the case, he will have to pay both lawyers. His own he can control; his wife's he cannot. She may urge her lawyer to leave no stone unturned in searching for wrongdoing or hidden assets. At the end of a case, the husband's lawyer may have to struggle to get paid. Not the wife's. Her fee is contained in the judgment of divorce, in an ordering paragraph requiring the husband to pay. It can be enforced like any other judgment. The evidence in the case will show successful divorce lawyers try to limit their representation to women. And highly successful lawyers succeed in doing just that."

Duffy turned to the argument on specificity. Did Fox discharge her responsibility by merely quoting the entire rule in the charging letter? "Morrissey knew he had sexual relations with Ms. Dixon but was stunned to hear her say he coerced her to have sex and demanded it as a 'condition' of representing her. There are words in the English language adequate to inform Mr. Morrissey of the committee's charge. For example: 'You are charged with demanding sex and coercing Ms. Dixon to provide sex. You also had sexual relations with her during the course of representing Ms. Dixon in a matrimonial action.'

"Defending a case should not turn into a guessing game. The additional charges dragged in, without fair notice, should be rejected."

Duffy moved on to the third and crucial point: Was Dixon a client at the time they had sexual relations? "Ms. Fox alluded to an exception in the anti-sex rule. The Appellate Division wanted to keep the Grievance Committee out of lawyers' bedrooms. In its wisdom the Appellate Division provided an exception for those who had had affairs before the attorney-client relationship began.

"Ms. Fox claims the exemption is wrongheaded. She would prohibit any and all encounters between lawyers and clients regardless of past history. She is not a justice sitting on the Appellate Division. She is employed by the Grievance Committee. Her extreme view on what the rule should prohibit reflects upon her bias. Prosecutors are public servants charged with enforcing the law as written. They should not possess, as Attorney Fox does, a personal agenda extending beyond the reaches of the law itself.

"The Appellate Division protects the privacy rights of attorneys. Yes, we lawyers possess those rights. If attorney and client have previously had a relationship, the disciplinary rules will not pry into the nature of a second encounter. Line drawing presents an arbitrary boundary for those who fall just outside or just inside. It should be obvious that if one is on the protected side of the line, it makes no difference how close the person is."

Duffy then rehashed his previous arguments that an attorney-client relationship begins the traditional way with the signing of a retainer. "It is at that point clients engage attorneys, and they assume their role."

When Duffy concluded his argument, McGuire called for a recess. "I will decide the motion when court resumes. We will stand in recess for one hour, that is, until 4:30.."

During the recess, Morrissey was gloomy. "I got kicked in the balls. I didn't realize I was a shit until Fox took me apart." Duffy was perturbed by his own plight. He had misjudged his friend and the case. He was sure McGuire would not dismiss the case. He was an establishment lawyer, a high-ranking member of the bar, the kind of lawyer who scorned divorce lawyers, personal injury lawyers, and probably criminal defense lawyers. Morrissey would get no sympathy from McGuire.

As anticipated McGuire denied the motion. "I hold Ms. Dixon was Mr. Morrissey's client the moment she entered his office. If she had refused to sign a retainer or hired another lawyer, their relationship would have ended. If the morning after, Ms. Dixon had decided on another lawyer and not returned to Mr. Morrissey's office, his activities the night before would still have violated the rule. I also rule that all three prongs of the rule are before me. This is not a criminal case but a proceeding to protect the public. The rule will be liberally construed. Not so liberally, however, to allow Ms. Fox to include other victims, assuming there are any.

No references direct or indirect can be made to any clients of Mr. Morrissey's except Ms. Dixon and clients testifying on his behalf. I have a low tolerance, Ms. Fox, for a lawyer who violates my ruling.

"Mr. Duffy, Ms. Fox's direct case is over. It is now time to hear yours. As far as I can tell, you're not planning to call Mr. Morrissey. You've named seven witnesses. Five are former clients, and two are experts. If that is your plan, you are taking a big risk. Without Morrissey's testimony it is likely I will disbar him. You've been warned. I'm calling a thirty-minute recess. When we reconvene I want you to disclose your final witness list."

McGuire's ruling had knocked the wind out of Morrissey. In McGuire's head disbarment was front and center. Morrissey had to testify.

Duffy cornered Morrissey. "The news is not all bad. Fox can't refer to other clients in crossing you. The best news of all: her notes are mashed potatoes. You, of course, will have to testify. Not about your Safe Horizon work. I prefer to have others toot your horn. Toot they will. You know the letters I referred to in my opening? We got them. Morgenthau rewrote his. It's weaker than the draft I wrote for him. I gave him a skewed version of the case. Although he hasn't much of a sense of humor, he made a wry remark: 'Morrissey is Robin Hood in a three-piece suit.' The letters from Safe Horizon and four victims are emotionally powerful."

When court resumed Duffy said, "Morrissey is eager to testify. The experts are necessary. I'm not sure whether we'll need all five former clients."

Fox rose to object. Before she could speak, McGuire motioned her to be seated. "Ms. Fox, you were on notice as to the five former clients. You've interviewed them. We have worked out a procedure to protect you as to the two expert witnesses. I'm probably responsible for the addition of Mr. Morrissey. Even if I had said nothing about my need for his testimony, under the rules of litigation, a party always has the right to testify. Court will resume tomorrow at ten." McGuire strolled out of the hearing room.

When the room was empty, Duffy said to Morrissey, "Why don't you write a draft of your testimony, and I'll review it?" He didn't have to tell Morrissey what to include—one of the benefits of having a lawyer for a client. Maybe the only benefit. Duffy tried not to dwell on his regret that he'd taken this case. He had other things to worry about now.

15

Duffy had planned to start with the experts, because he could control their testimony, even though what they had to say was dry. Now he needed witnesses to counteract Molly's emotional testimony, and the experts weren't up to that. So he went with the five former clients whom he had dubbed "the virgins." As he worked with each of them, Joyce Ryan emerged as the star. Tall, sexy, flirtatious, she would set the tone for the defense. Peter didn't coerce her. Nor did they have sex. She was divorced, and a final judgment entered. Judgments were rarely set aside and when they were, only for compelling reasons. Morrissey accomplished the difficult. He got the judgment reformed. True, Joyce was only one woman but testifying against Morrissey was only one woman.

In her own case, Morrissey had found Joyce a poor witness. The issue there was whether she had been tricked into agreeing to the financial terms of the divorce. Joyce couldn't keep her eye on the ball. She was consumed with guilt. When Peter had asked an unrelated question, out came: "It was my fault. I had an affair with the architect." She couldn't move on.

Morrissey solved the problem by hiring Joyce as a paid witness. "Look, Joyce," he said, "you were an actress. Suppose I hire you to play a role, yourself, and pay you Actor's Equity's minimum rate?"

Bingo. She played the role to the hilt. Peter told Duffy about his arrangement with Joyce. Duffy thought it crazy until he worked with her. Out of desperation he "hired" Joyce even though he was concerned about paying a fact witness. The amount was trivial, never more than $50 for a session. To Joyce the money was important. At the end of a session, she held out her hand and didn't leave until she was paid. Except for the exchange of money, Joyce was an ideal choice to start the defense.

Duffy called Fox and told her of his plan to begin with Joyce to be followed by Gloria Bienstock, Alice Burns, Margaret Gould, and Ruth Block. The experts would come last. "You can't claim surprise, because you interviewed each of my witnesses. If you pounce on one, I may drop a few weak sisters. I'm not telling you which ones. "

"What did you think of McGuire's decision?" Fox asked. "I'll bet you're sorry you made the motion."

"Sorry? Weren't you listening? That great jurist in the class of Justices Brandeis and Cardozo ruled you can eat your notes. I'll provide mustard or ketchup. Not both. Which would you prefer?"

"Oh, shut up. My boss was so pleased, he put me up for a raise."

"Get it finalized fast before the case is over."

When court reconvened Joyce was sitting between Duffy and Morrissey. McGuire greeted the lawyers and stared at Joyce. "You were to begin with your experts. I assume the woman sitting between you and Mr. Morrissey is a fact witness. Did you notify Ms. Fox of the change?" He sounded testy.

"Indeed, I alerted Ms. Fox. Joyce Ryan, as you can see, is a rose between two thorns. She will be our first witness." Duffy's answer pleased McGuire. He motioned to her to take the witness chair. Joyce sashayed to her seat and crossed her legs, exposing her thigh to McGuire. He noticed probably because she was dressed, on orders of Duffy, as if she were on a night out with her lover. Joyce oozed sex appeal, at least to middle-aged men. She smiled repeatedly at McGuire, who smiled back at her. *Good,* Duffy thought, *the old bastard is tempted by her charms, even briefly.*

Duffy asked preliminary questions. He established she was Morrissey's client in a matrimonial action. Joyce testified her divorce was her fault "because I had an affair with an architect hired to renovate our brownstone." She said her downfall was brought about by a diary she kept which referenced "each time the architect and I had sex." Her lawyer in the divorce action turned over her diary to Jim's lawyer claiming he was required to do so. Armed with her admission of several trysts with the architect, the divorce was automatic and followed by poor financial terms. Her friends told her she was stuck, and so did several lawyers. "Not Mr. Morrissey. He said he could help. 'Your lawyer was a pawn. He was in the pocket of Jim's lawyer, who employed him. You lacked independent counsel. I never would have handed over your diary.'

"Mr. Morrissey was so good. He won hands down. And he worked hard. It's not easy, so I've been told, to overturn a final judgment and get better terms. Mr. Morrissey did. I'm still divorced, but the financial terms are vastly improved. Almost every day, I thank God for Mr. Morrissey."

Joyce then crossed herself.

Duffy got to the point.

Q. Did you have sexual relations with Mr. Morrissey? Before you answer let me read the definition of sexual relations as contained in the Code of Professional Responsibility. As you will note, touching an intimate part is equivalent to sexual relations.

A. In my opinion touching isn't sexual relations. (McGuire tried unsuccessfully to hide his smile.) Mr. Morrissey never touched an intimate part on me, nor did I on him. We also didn't have intercourse.

Q. Forget sexual intercourse and touching, tell us about the occasions Mr. Morrissey flirted with you.

A. Well, he did flirt but only in the beginning. It wasn't anymore than other men did when I was young and pretty. Maybe he put his hand on my shoulder, but that was all. He stopped when I told him: "You're sweet but not my type." (She turned to McGuire.) Now Judge McGuire is my type. Oh, how I wish I were ten years younger and attractive. (McGuire told her to pay attention to Duffy, smiling as he spoke.)

Q. Did Mr. Morrissey ever tell you he would not represent you unless you had sex with him?

A. Of course not. We didn't have sex, and he represented me.

Q. Did Mr. Morrissey ever coerce you to have sex?

A. No. Mr. Morrissey used coercion on my ex to get me better terms than my first lawyer got.

Q. I show you a photograph of you and a handwritten statement signed by you. "You are the best." How did you come to write those words?

A. When I first became Mr. Morrissey's client, he took my picture. When the case was over, he asked me to write something about him and sign my name. I asked: "Would it be alright to say 'you are the best'?" He said, "How nice." So I wrote it and signed my name.

Duffy concluded his examination of Joyce. It was now Fox's turn.

Fox said she had interviewed Joyce and asked if Joyce remembered the occasion. When Joyce said yes, Fox asked, "Did you tell me the truth?" When Joyce again answered "yes," Fox, reading from her notes, asked if Morrissey had stroked her. Duffy had prepared Joyce for the question. "Yes, but not any intimate parts. He put his hand on my shoulder and held my hand. Nothing more than what many gentlemen do."

Fox persisted. How many times had Morrissey "stroked" Joyce? How many times did Joyce have to tell him to stop? "Mr. Morrissey was a persistent devil. It took a while for him to get the message, but when he did, he stopped."

Q. Did Mr. Morrissey suggest you and he spend a weekend together in a country inn in the Berkshires?

A. Yes, he did. Does the bar association define an offer to have sex as 'sexual relations'?

McGuire laughed, as did Duffy and Morrissey. Fox looked angry.

Q. Was one of your goals to get back with Jim, your husband?

A. Yes.

Q. Did you believe Jim would take you back if you had no more affairs?

A. Yes.

Q. Did you tell Mr. Morrissey of your resolve to abstain from sex?

A. Yes.

Q. Did Mr. Morrissey flirt with you before you told him of your resolve?
A. Yes.
Q. Did Mr. Morrissey proposition you after you told him of your resolve?
A. Yes.

Fox detected that Joyce's answers were stilted. Fox expected that Joyce would be thoroughly rehearsed. Yet, her testimony had a false ring. She had told Fox that Morrissey was a pest. Joyce had said she had been an actress, a fact that didn't find its way into Fox's notes. She recalled the statement and smelled a rat.

Q. Before you married Jim, you were an actress, is that correct?
A. Yes, but I had only small parts.
Q. The thrust of your testimony is different from what you said when we first met. How many times have you met with Mr. Duffy prior to today?

The question was outside the range of Duffy's preparation. He had advised that unanticipated questions should be answered in the fewest possible words and honestly. Joyce answered "three sessions." Still unsure where she was going but convinced that something was wrong, Fox continued:

Q. How long, approximately, did each session last?
A. Oh, about two hours.
Q. What was the reason you were willing to spend at least six hours plus travel time on a case in which you had no interest?
Joyce thought again about Duffy's advice. Then, she answered.
A. I was paid for my time.

Duffy turned pale; McGuire lowered his eyes; Fox cracked a smile. When further questioned Joyce explained: "I'm an active member of Actors Equity. Although I haven't acted for many years, I still pay my union dues. Although my role today is important, I'm getting minimum pay, the same rate I got for rehearsals."

Q. On any other occasion, did you receive compensation for testifying?

A. Yes. In my action to change the divorce judgment, Mr. Morrissey paid me the same amount.

"I move to strike Ms. Ryan's testimony," Fox said. "Fact witnesses are not allowed to be compensated." McGuire asked Duffy to respond.

"I agree to Ms. Fox's motion as it pertains to Ms. Ryan's testimony on cross." Duffy hoped McGuire would smile, but he did not. "I know of no rule barring payment to fact witnesses," Duffy said. "Excessive payment affects credibility. Ms. Ryan was paid fifty dollars per rehearsal lasting two hours and one hundred dollars for her testimony today. May I ask Ms. Ryan several questions in the nature of a voir dire?" McGuire nodded and said, "Go ahead."

Q. Who suggested that you be paid for testifying?

A. You.

Q. Would you have testified without compensation?

A. Yes, but I liked the idea of being treated as a professional.

Q. How would your testimony have differed if at all if I had not offered to compensate you?

A. How could it differ? I'm under oath to tell the truth. That's what I did.

"Thank you, Judge McGuire. I have no further questions."

"I'll take Ms. Fox's motion under advisement and rule on it at the end of the case. If any other witnesses, fact or expert, are being compensated, I instruct you, Mr. Duffy, to make that point known before you begin direct. We'll now adjourn for lunch. Court will resume at two o'clock.

Duffy realized he had been too cute. Joyce was his best fact witness. The pitiful few dollars she was getting had damaged her testimony. He had underestimated Fox in thinking she would not inquire. *Trials,* he mused, *are like the tide. They ebb and flow. Right now for poor Morrissey, it was ebbing.*

16

Gloria Bienstock was next. Duffy's first question was whether she was being paid. She answered no. McGuire reprimanded Duffy. "I asked you to make known when a witness is being paid and the amount. I'm not interested that a fact witness is not being paid. That's the usual procedure. Proceed."

Gloria told how she fell in love with Betty and out of love with Eric. She mentioned Betty's name frequently. Said they were married in Massachusetts and living very happily in New York. Duffy read the definition of sexual relations and asked if she and Morrissey had a relationship. Gloria answered: "Betty and I touch a lot. We're very loving. Mr. Morrissey never touched me nor I him. Betty and I thought that he was kind of attractive. If we liked guys, we could go for him."

Why can't witnesses limit their answers to the questions asked, Duffy mused. Duffy wanted Gloria's sexuality back in the closet. *Too late now.* He asked how well Morrissey served her. "Mr. Morrissey was so understanding, kind, and skillful. Although I was at fault, he pinned the tail on Eric. I got the divorce and excellent financial terms."

McGuire asked if her relationship with Betty was concealed from her husband. "Oh, no. Eric met Betty several times and knew we were in love. What I didn't know was that Eric was carrying on with another woman. Mr. Morrissey found that out."

McGuire asked whether the judge presiding over the divorce knew she wanted to marry Betty. "Yes, that was alleged in Eric's counterclaim. When Eric's lawyer tried to raise it, the judge scolded the lawyer and told him not to go there. I remember his words. 'You threaten to sling divorce cases deeper into the mud than these sordid procedures have ever sunk. You will not do that in my courtroom.' Betty and I discussed the judge's narrow-minded view of same sex love. I wanted to write a letter to him, but Mr. Morrissey told me not to."

"Sorry to have interrupted you," McGuire said. "Please continue, Mr. Duffy." Duffy showed Gloria her photograph and the inscription. He asked whether she had written it and signed the photo. She said yes to both.

On cross Fox asked when she disclosed to Morrissey her love for Betty. "At our very first meeting. Almost as soon as we met. It's the most important thing in my life. I'm proud of my love for Betty and will never, never hide it. "

Fox's question and Gloria's answer destroyed whatever little value Gloria's testimony added. In her final brief, Fox would argue Morrissey knew he had no chance. The only advantage derived from Gloria's testimony was that Morrissey served a client well without regard to sexual favors. The adequacy of Morrissey's services were, however, not at issue.

Duffy could now see that Gloria's testimony was a waste. Joyce's too. He had played the best cards he had, and so far, had no chance for a winning hand. *No need to spell it out to Morrissey.*

Over lunch the two men picked at their food and had nothing to say until Alice Burns, the next witness, ran into them and sat down. She was bursting with news. Nicholas, her husband, told her that his former teaching assistant and lover had obtained a tenure-track position at Portland State in Oregon. They were separating for good. He wanted Alice to come back. "What pleasure it gave me to tell him: 'You can't treat me as detritus one day and gold the next.' I'm going to keep him dangling but not too long. I don't want him to find someone else. My Nicholas is no Lord Warburton. Why do I waste literary references on you? You've probably never heard of Henry James."

"Warburton remained constant in his love for Isabel Archer," Peter said. "She should have married him."

"No, you're wrong. Had Isabel chosen Lord Warburton, the novel would have lacked tension and suspense. The work is a masterpiece, because Isabel made the wrong decision. I'm not a character in a novel. I'll make the right decision and go back to Nicholas. He'll have to suffer for a while and then beg. Why am I telling you this? How's the case going? You don't have to answer. I can see by the way you were eating or rather nibbling on your sandwiches. Stop worrying. I'm ebullient. I'll turn the case around."

Duffy touched on the essentials. When asked if she and Morrissey had sexual relations, she smiled. "That's the most improbable thing I could imagine. I know you have to ask the question." She also denied that Morrissey had flirted. "Too ridiculous" was her answer. She said she refused to have a photo taken. At the end Morrissey again tried to take Alice's photo. Again she refused. "I glanced at all the photos on the wall. Disgusting. I hate billboards."

Alice's testimony on direct was straightforward. "Morrissey," she said, "did a good job. He did not touch me, nor did he flirt." Her demeanor was ice cold. Although she made no gaffes, it was clear she looked down on Morrissey.

On cross Fox referred to Alice as Professor Burns and delved into her background and professional career. Fox referred to Alice's marriage as collegial, as her husband was also a professor of English literature. Fox also established that Alice was attracted to a man's mind. To Fox's question as to whether Morrissey was an intellectual, Alice replied, "Your code defines sexual relations as touching erotic areas. If you also define an intellectual as one who occasionally reads a good book, then Mr. Morrissey is an intellectual. Using a rational definition, he is not."

Trial was adjourned for the day. McGuire said he had some pressing matters. They would skip a day and meet the next day. Duffy regarded it as a bad sign. McGuire had lost interest in the case. So far the defense had flopped. An actress, a lesbian, and a frosty intellectual. Duffy wished he had not been required to produce a witness list. He saw nothing to be gained from Margaret Gould, the aloof heiress, or Ruth Block, the depressed wife of a swindler. Not calling them, however, would amount to a concession that they were even weaker than the ones who testified. Perhaps McGuire would think they were paid too. He had no alternative but to call them.

He hadn't wanted Morrissey to testify, but on the present state of the record, Morrissey's testimony would be crucial.

Two days later Ruth Block was on the stand. She looked miserable, hunched over, and her face was in a persistent frown. Her voice halting.. As soon as she began to speak, Duffy knew it was a mistake. After all she had gone through, Duffy knew he was scraping the bottom of the barrel.

She cried at the mention of her husband. She cried even more at his conviction and jail sentence for the swindle of their friends, charities, and family. She cried so much that McGuire called a recess to enable her to compose herself. She denied having sexual relations with Morrissey and said he had never touched her.

When Duffy's direct was over, Fox declined to cross-examine. McGuire thanked her for her forbearance. Fox scored points with the judge; Duffy had lost more ground.

Duffy, a usually pumped-up trial lawyer, was deflated. What he had thought would be a blazing victory now looked like an ignominious defeat. He had been there before. Sometimes the tide changed, but he doubted it would this time.

Margaret Gould, the last of the client-witnesses, testified that she didn't have sexual relations with Morrissey and added "or any relationship with him." She said that he did a good job, but that she wasn't "sure of his ethics." Duffy was surprised. He didn't want to leave the issue of ethics for Fox to unravel. As coolly as he could, he asked if she believed Morrissey overcharged her.

A. Yes. You see I paid Anthony's legal expenses, since he doesn't have a bob. Morrissey said Anthony's lawyer's fee would be $50,000, and that he earned it. When I asked what his fee was, he said, "Also fifty thousand."

Q. Did you ask Mr. Morrissey to explain how Anthony's lawyer earned his fee, and if so, what did he say?

A. Anthony agreed to a divorce if I hand over $10 million to him. Morrissey persuaded his lawyer to reduce Anthony's demand to $1 million. Morrissey threatened an annulment action by claiming that Anthony had defrauded me by concealing his bisexuality. If it succeeded Anthony would get nothing. Morrissey also promised the lawyer a handsome fee if an agreement was reached. I assumed Morrissey believed he was entitled to the same fee.

Q. In dealings with other professionals, what opinion, if any, have you formed as to their charges?

A. Being a well-known, wealthy woman, I'm generally overcharged. I resent it.

Duffy thought the "ethics" was laid to rest. Fox, however, raised it again in cross. She asked:

Q. In addition to overcharging, you complained that Morrissey concocted a false claim that Anthony was gay?

A. Anthony is not gay. I told that to Morrissey when he made the accusation, but Morrissey sold the claim to Anthony's lawyer who sold it to Anthony.

On redirect, Duffy asked:

Q. Did you form the impression that Anthony, with whom you had been married for only two years, had an "ethics" problem, demanding $10 million?

A. Yes. He showed his true colors.

Q. Did you tell Mr. Morrissey in substance that Anthony's demand amounted to a holdup?

A. I said extortion. I had to eat my words. The extortion took the form of legal fees. First, to Anthony's lawyer and then to Morrissey.

Q. During the last six months of your marriage to Anthony, how many times did you have sexual relations?

A. We didn't.

Q. Whose decision was it not to indulge, yours or Anthony's.

A. Anthony's.

Q. Were you advised by Mr. Morrissey that, if you approved, he planned to hire a private investigator to explore whether Anthony was presently engaged or had been engaged in sex with a man?

A. Yes, and I approved. I knew the investigator, if honest, would turn up no evidence.

Q. Were you informed what the investigator found?

A. Yes. He manufactured evidence and concluded Anthony was gay. The investigator's report was based not on eyewitness evidence, confessions, or other reliable evidence but solely on surmise.

Duffy thanked the witness and told McGuire he had no further questions. Margaret was excused and, with her head held high, she raced out of the courtroom.

Margaret's testimony hurt the case and wounded Morrissey. It was always a bad tactic to turn on your own witness. It was worse for a former client to attack a lawyer's ethics, especially in a disciplinary proceeding. Morrissey looked sleazy on two counts: he overcharged and asserted a claim his client believed was false. *It's a good thing*, thought Duffy, *that neither being a sleazebag nor overcharging is grounds for disbarment. If they were there would hardly be a lawyer standing, except, of course, McGuire and guys like him.*

McGuire said the hearing would resume again on Monday. He asked Duffy whom he planned to call. When Duffy said Peter Morrissey, McGuire nodded. "It's predicted to be a hot weekend. I hope you have a cool retreat. I'll see you on Monday at ten."

17

Morrissey needed a break, and so did Duffy. "We've been fighting our own war," Morrissey said. "We need R and R. Let's go to my beach home in Amagansett. But we won't speak a word about the case. We'll catch a jitney on Saturday around noon to avoid the traffic and return on Sunday in the afternoon. It's my treat."

"Sounds good. A day away from thinking about McGuire and Fox will help my elevated blood pressure. One modification. Let's hire a car to take us back on Sunday. We'll sit in the backseat and review your testimony."

At the jitney stop on Lexington Avenue across from Bloomingdale's, the two men made an odd-looking couple. Peter was dressed in a blazer, pressed grey slacks, a natty sport shirt, and black loafers. Duffy wore khakis, a golf shirt, sneakers, and a baseball hat bearing the New York Mets logo.

All the way to the East End, the two loquacious men barely spoke. On his iPad Morrissey alternated between reading the *Times* and playing a computer chess game. Duffy slept.

At Morrissey's home they changed into bathing suits and went for a walk on the beach. In contrast to Duffy's demeanor on the jitney, he was expansive. He talked about his wife, Maryanne. "We were divorced less than a year when we got back together again. The divorce was my fault. I was in New York Hospital recovering from a bout of cellulitis. A middle-aged, unattractive Irish nurse came into my room—you know how Irish women are either beautiful or plain—this one was plain. She was a frequent visitor. Taking my temperature every hour. This time, in addition to my temperature, she was armed with a wash basin, cloth, and towel. She offered to wash me as I was attached to tubes dripping antibiotics. At first I suspected nothing. But soon her real intention became clear. She disconnected the IV and locked the door. I should have pushed her away, but instead I encouraged her. I couldn't drink, was depressed, and could think of nothing but myself. Maryanne had left her magazine or book, I forget which. She knocked on the door, astonished it was locked and demanded to be admitted. I was miserable. I promised and promised. Maryanne refused to forgive. We got divorced. I persisted. A year after the divorce, we remarried. We spent our second honeymoon on Martha's Vineyard. The beaches there are like yours on the East End. After she died about three years ago, I knew I could never be that lucky again. I haven't thought about remarriage."

Duffy's confession inspired Morrissey to open up. "Unlike you, I had no intervening circumstance to blame for my infidelity. I too promised. Joan forgave. I broke my promise. Joan forgave a second time. When it happened again and again, we had the marriage annulled. My uncontrollable lust cost me a wonderful wife. Now it's going to cost me my license. Sorry, we're not to bring up the case."

That night they dined at Nick and Toni's, an upscale East Hampton restaurant. Peter was well-known, and they were seated at a prominent table near the entrance. Arthur Grossman, a New York lawyer, stopped at Morrissey's table and was introduced to Duffy. Grossman knew Duffy by reputation. "Hey Peter, what are you doing hanging with a criminal defense lawyer?"

"We have a case together," Peter said.

"I hope you're not the subject. I know your vice is women. But that's not a crime is it, Duffy?"

Grossman laughed, but he laughed alone.

They ate and drank a lot. Peter called John Hayes, a retired police officer, to drive them home. "Too many DWI accidents around here. We'll pick up my car in the morning. John has agreed to drive us into the city."

The next day they went for a swim in the ocean. Hayes arrived about noon, and the three set off for the city. "John," Peter said, "Mr. Duffy and I will be discussing confidential legal matters. As you know from your police work, the privilege is lost if our conversation is heard by a third party. Please wear these ear plugs."

After a long review, Duffy said, "Peter, too many rehearsals can make the performance dull. You don't want to throw your best pitches in the bullpen. Open your iPad; I'll take a nap."

When they reached Duffy's brownstone, he thanked Morrissey and said, "I feel the tide shifting. See you tomorrow."

18

Duffy began his examination of Morrissey on a high note. He wanted Peter to be upbeat and have a head of steam when they hit troubled waters. He also wanted McGuire to take notice of Peter's accomplishments, saying, "I'd like to place on the record your many accomplishments. Too much has been made of an aberrational act." Duffy asked Peter not to be modest.

He graduated from Fordham Law School. He began as a night student working during the day as a paralegal. After his first year, Peter ranked fifth in his class and was named to the *Law Review*. He was granted a scholarship and switched, in his second year, to a day student. He graduated with high honors and was hired by the law firm of Cahill, Gordon, & Reindel, one of the most prestigious New York firms.

He worked on briefs and assisted partners at trial, but his big break came with a case of his own, a divorce action in which he represented John Keegan, a leading industrialist. Matrimonial actions were undertaken by Cahill only for good clients. Keegan was the CEO of one of the largest mining conglomerates in the world and one of the firm's prized clients.

Duffy knew that McGuire was a partner at Sullivan & Cromwell, another top-drawer firm. At the mention of the Cahill firm, McGuire's face lightened. Perhaps he was looking for some common ground with Morrissey, as a fellow big-firm lawyer. Duffy hoped he was seeing a shift in McGuire's attitude and was playing it for all it was worth.

Duffy added questions digging into the nitty-gritty of the Keegan divorce. In question and answer form, Morrissey told the story of Keegan's divorce:

Keegan's first wife had died. His second, Joanne, twenty years younger, hated him, showed it by tormenting him, and made no effort to conceal her contempt. In the presence of business associates, friends, and relatives, she humiliated her husband. "He has all the bad traits of a money-grubbing businessman. He's immoral, unethical, and without any decent principles. He takes advantage of widows and orphans. He has none of the admirable traits of a Joseph Pulitzer or an Andrew Carnegie."

There was no aspect of Keegan's life she didn't make fun of. She said "I don't know whether I married a man or a eunuch" so often that it became her mantra.

Before marrying Keegan and Joanne had entered into a pre-nuptial agreement, providing for a small payment to Joanne if Keegan divorced her for cause. Keegan wanted the divorce, and the powers at Cahill were obliged to help. Since Joanne had not had an affair, adultery was out. The only remaining ground was "cruel and inhuman treatment requiring proof of physical injury inflicted by one spouse upon another."

Peter proposed a variant. Hate words and insults uttered in the presence of family, friends, and business associates could rise to the level of mental torture and cause physical injury. He persuaded the partners to take a chance on his theory and they, in turn, assigned the case to him.

Under Morrissey's direction Keegan's high-profile trial lasted three weeks and resulted in the judge finding Joanne's conduct cruel and inhuman. The decision was unprecedented, and a high-water mark in matrimonial law. Keegan got his divorce, and his wife got the pittance in alimony that had been spelled out in their prenuptial agreement, and Morrissey's career was launched.

Keegan threw a celebratory dinner for Peter at the Down-town Athletic Club, housed in a thirty-eight story skyscraper at West Street in the city's financial district, a hangout for lawyers, businessmen, and financiers. It was the club where the Heisman Trophy was awarded annually to the outstanding college football player. Looking now in McGuire's direction, Morrissey said, "In major New York law firms, once you milk a purple cow, you're the guy who milks purple cows. I got all the divorce actions."

After being at Cahill only five years, Morrissey headed the firm's newly formed divorce practice. But before very long, he understood that the firm was uneasy about his specialty, considering it "undignified." Morrissey felt he was ostracized and not fairly compensated. He was confronted with a choice: leave the security of a large firm and run the risk of running his own shop or abandon divorce cases and find a new niche at Cahill. Morrissey chose the former. With the firm's consent, Morrissey took his cases with him and started his own one-man firm.

Cahill and other establishment firms referred divorce actions to Peter, and his practice grew along with his reputation. He was looked upon as 'the dean' of the matrimonial bar, named chair of the New York State and co-chair of the American Bar Association committees on matrimonial actions. He was called upon by Governor Patterson to revise the state's divorce law. In 2010 the legislature passed and the governor signed the bill drafted by Morrissey. New York became the fiftieth state to adopt non-fault divorce. He received the pen used by the governor and a letter of thanks. Duffy introduced the letter into evidence.

Morrissey wrote the seminal article on the new law which was published in the *Fordham Law Review* and was repeatedly cited in decisions by New York courts. Duffy asked McGuire to take judicial notice of the decisions. When McGuire agreed, he handed him a file containing them.

In 2006, Morrissey was named Fordham Alumnus of the Year, appointed an adjunct professor at Fordham, and taught a course in matrimonial law. He donated his salary to the law school. The Practicing Law Institute and the County Bar Association called on Peter to teach courses on continuing legal education to lawyers. He lectured at many bar associations throughout the country.

Duffy had succeeded in portraying his client as a lawyer who, through commitment and intelligence, had risen to the top of the matrimonial bar. Rather than get into Peter's public service work, as he had told McGuire he would do, Duffy decided it should come in later on through the mouths of others..

Q. By any standards you have had a highly successful legal career. Unfortunately, we must now digress into the dark area that brings us to this proceeding. When and where did you first meet the complainant in this proceeding, Ms. Molly Dixon?

A. She came to my office in March 2008. She said she had been referred by a former client, Sally Whitmore, a friend of her sister's. She wanted a divorce but was unwilling to state a ground. It was a very busy phone day. There were constant interruptions. I told Molly, I needed to know the grounds for divorce in order to decide whether I could be of help. She refused to talk. On a quiet day, I would have offered her a cold drink or coffee, but this was anything but. I suggested we meet at the end of the day at my club. She smiled when I mentioned the Friars. "I'll go home and change. I'll look nice. You won't be embarrassed in front of all the theatrical stars."

Q. Ms. Dixon has testified extensively about the dinner. Please begin by telling us about the change if any in Molly's appearance and the drinks she testified you forced upon her.

A. I was late and failed to recognize Molly, since she had changed so dramatically. In my office she was plainly dressed. At my club, she wore a sleek, low-cut white blouse, a tight black skirt, and high boots. Her manner had also changed. In my office, she was shy, confused, reticent. At the club she approached me—as I have already said I didn't recognize her—and took my arm and announced she wanted a drink. She headed to the bar, but I steered her upstairs to an almost empty dining room. It was only 6:30; the room would eventually be full. I suggested we have a drink at the table and discuss her case. We both ordered martinis. She drained her drink and signaled for a second. I told her one was enough. As dinner was served, she asked for wine.

Q. Molly testified that you encouraged her to drink. What did you do in that respect?

A. I discouraged her from drinking. I told the waiter not to bring her a second martini and refused to order wine.

Duffy showed Morrissey a copy of the bill covering that night's dinner. Morrissey identified it, and the bill was received in evidence. It showed charges for dinner and two martinis but no charge for wine. Molly's testimony that Morrissey forced her to drink several glasses of wine was refuted. Her credibility was tarnished. Duffy was ready to confront the circumstances leading up to the sexual encounter.

Q. At dinner did Molly disclose the reason she was seeking a divorce, and if so, what did she say?

A. She and her husband had not had sexual intercourse for several years. "My marriage is dead," she said. "I try my best to arouse him but without success." She discussed her efforts and then graphically illustrated them. She took my finger and licked it. "That's what I do to his penis. I even do more kissing and licking around erogenous zones all to no avail. Is there something wrong with me or John?"

"You and John may need a sex therapist or a surrogate. Have you sought help?"

"What's the difference," she said, "between a therapist and a surrogate?"

I said a therapist talks to you about your problem; a surrogate will physically engage you.

"I want a surrogate. Not talk but action." She placed her hand on my knee and massaged my thigh. "You're so experienced and macho. Why don't you serve as my surrogate? Please say yes."

Q. Were you aware of the rule prohibiting an attorney from having sexual relations with his client during the course of a matrimonial action?

A. Yes, I was. I told Molly that the canons of ethics bar an attorney from having sexual relations with a client during the course of a matrimonial action. I added there was no exception for an attorney-surrogate. She laughed. "How silly! We're grownups. Whose business is it but ours?" Her hand then grazed my penis. "Besides, you're not my attorney, at least not yet. I haven't agreed to you."

I have a weakness for women. It doesn't rule my life. It's not like I'm addicted. But if a woman is provocative, I'm hooked. Molly was not merely provocative, she openly solicited me. I said, "OK, you're not my client. I won't represent you." I placed my hand on her thigh. We left without finishing dinner and checked into a nearby hotel. I anticipate your next question. Yes, we had sex.

On the way home, Molly asked if I was serious when I said I wouldn't represent her. "Please do. I have confidence in you." I asked her to return to my office the next day and sign a retainer. She did. I said, "No sex until the case is over."

Q. Did you have sexual relations with Molly during the time you were representing her? Before answering I refer you to the extended definition of sex as contained in the rule?

A. I did not, nor did I have sex with Ms. Dixon at any other time.

Q. What is that *weakness* you earlier referred to?

A. I'm hypersexual, or so a psychotherapist has told me. I have a high level of attraction to women. I can and do control my desire. Sex is important to me, but it does not rule my life. Molly didn't just flirt. She openly propositioned me. In retrospect I should have said no.

Duffy wanted the record to reflect that Molly was the only client with whom Peter had had sex. Peter was prepared to testify that way. They both knew it was false. Duffy rationalized it by saying: "In every successful man's life lies a criminal act. Morrissey's false testimony will be his one act." Before he asked the question, Duffy glanced at Fox. She was looking for her notes on the twenty five former clients she had interviewed. Duffy had thought McGuire's ruling keeping references to Fox's notes out of the case and prohibiting her from calling other clients gave him leeway to have Morrissey claim Molly was the only client with whom he had had relations. He stared at Fox and had second thoughts. He had underestimated the Fox before. He had not anticipated that she would expose Joyce Ryan as a paid witness. Suppose the Fox argued that Peter's denial of sex with other clients opened the door to contradictory evidence? Morrissey's defense would collapse. Too risky. Better not ask and, after the case was closed, argue that Molly was the only one. Duffy stepped back and returned to a different subject.

Q. How long did Molly's divorce action take?

A. I negotiated a separation agreement, including financial terms. They lived apart and after a year, the divorce was automatic. It took several months for the parties to agree on the terms of the separation agreement. She was an active client for about two months and inactive for twelve.

Q. Did you have sexual relations with her during the active period?

A. No. I had advised her not to have an affair until she was legally divorced. It would provide a ground to set aside the separation agreement and permit her husband to bring an action for divorce. If we had indulged, I would have been doing her a disservice.

Morrissey took out his handkerchief and wiped his brow. He was relieved that Duffy had not asked about other clients. He knew he had agreed to deny he had had sex with others but feared he would not be able to do so when the question was posed.

Q. Same question for the inactive period.

A. Same answer.

Q. What contact did you have with Molly after her divorce became final?

A. She called me and said: "Congratulate me. My divorce is final. How about we celebrate at the Friars?" I said no. It's easy for me to say no over the telephone.

Q. Prior to this proceeding and after the telephone call you just testified to, what contact, if any, did you have with Molly?

A. None.

Duffy questioned Peter about his reasons for representing women exclusively. Peter said the preference was dictated by economics. "A woman's legal expenses, at the end of the case, are generally shifted to her ex-husband and incorporated in the divorce judgment. Collection is certain. For that reason most divorce specialists, if given the choice, choose the wife, unless the husband is prominent. I have, however, represented husbands.

Duffy was now ready to resurrect the five defense witnesses.

Q. Whose idea was it to pay Joyce Ryan a fee measured by Actor's Equity standards?

A. I guess I had a hand in that. I told you how difficult it was to prepare Joyce for an evidentiary hearing on her claim that she was tricked into agreeing to a divorce. No matter how hard I tried, she always volunteered that she had sinned. She should not have had an affair with the architect. She deserved the little she got. I reminded her that Jim was running around, or so she believed, and of her statement that she would have been faithful if he had not ignored her. She retained her composure but then regressed. I was about to give up, when I had an idea.

Joyce had been an aspiring actress before her marriage. "From now on," I said, "you're an actress playing the role of 'Joyce Ryan,' a woman deceived by her husband throughout their marriage and then tricked into a phony divorce. I'll pay you the minimum rate set by Actor's Equity, provided you perform the way you outlined your case to me." She agreed. No more crying. No more self-condemnation. Jim's lawyer took her deposition. She was fine. All told I paid her $500.

You had a similar problem. Joyce was unable to focus on the issues. In answer to questions about her relationship with me, she kept bringing up the architect. She was consumed with guilt. I told you about my arrangement with Joyce. You followed my practice. It seemed to both of us a harmless way to get a distracted witness to testify truthfully.

McGuire smiled. Peter and Duffy had survived Joyce's revelation.

Duffy was now ready to refute Margaret Gould's charge that Peter had trumped up the claim that Anthony was gay.

Q. Margaret Gould testified that you concocted a claim about her husband's sexuality. What evidence, if any, did you have on Anthony's sexual proclivities?

A. Male sexuality comes in all different forms. Some men are asexual. Others are hypersexual. Still others are bisexual. Margaret showed me a photograph of Anthony. He looked effeminate. I asked to see more photographs. One was a group shot. Anthony was in the center, Margaret on one side, and a dashing, young man on the other with his arm around Anthony. Margaret identified the man as a young Italian fashion designer. "He's clever, talented, and witty. Anthony and I both like him."

Margaret admitted her marriage had been a mistake. "Anthony was only after my money. An adventurer, nothing more. Now that I want a divorce, he has turned into an extortionist. Can you image, he expects I'll pay ten million to get rid of him."

I told her my suspicion that Anthony was gay. "If we can prove you were defrauded, your marriage will be annulled. Anthony will get nothing. The downside: There will be lots of publicity. This is the kind of case the tabloids love. Regardless of your decision whether to bring an annulment action, I suggest we find out whether there is a basis in fact. I urge that we hire a private investigator. If you decide not to pursue an annulment action, I can use the information in my negotiations. I'll threaten an annulment action unless Anthony reduces his demand."

Margaret was livid. She attacked me. Threatened to fire me if I ever again said Anthony was gay. Eventually, she calmed down. "If the investigator finds no evidence," I said, "the matter ends. You have nothing to lose."

"Except of course, my pride. I thought I married a homosexual. Only a hard-up old woman would harbor that thought. Even if we obtain convincing evidence, I won't have a spotlight turned on me. I don't want the world to know what an idiot I am. I'd sooner pay ten million than make myself a laughingstock."

I said that faced with a lawsuit, in which he gets nothing if he loses, Anthony might be amenable to a modest settlement. Think of it as a crowbar to use against a mule to get him to move. She agreed and authorized me to hire an investigator. "All small minds think artistic people are gay. I know lots who are not. He'll find nothing. I'll have another bill to pay. A waste of time and my money."

Women are loath to admit their husbands or lovers are bisexuals. They think of it as a shabby reflection on their own sexuality.

The detective found evidence that the Italian designer was gay and that he and Anthony had spent time together, sans Margaret, in her homes in Newport and Palm Beach.

Duffy showed Morrissey the detective's report, and it was received in evidence. Duffy then asked how he came to ask for a fee of $50,000. "Unlike the Republican-dominated congress, I believe in taxing the rich. Very often my fees are reduced, because neither party can afford to pay. When one with deep pockets comes along, I make up for undercharges. Margaret's net worth was over five hundred million, all of which she had inherited. Through my acumen her husband's ten-million-dollar demand was reduced to one million. My fee is 0.625 percent of what I saved her. Under contingent fee practice, my fee was a tiny fraction of what a contingent-fee lawyer would have sought. Of course, it was not contingent, so I guess the analogy is a bad one, but I saw no reason to go easy on her."

Q. Alice Burns, Ruth Block and Gloria Bienstock testified that they did not have sexual relations with you. Why didn't you make an attempt to seduce them?
A. I like women. Perhaps too much. It's a weakness, I blame it for destroying my marriage. I draw the line, however, at my clients. They're off limits. I refuse to allow sex to destroy my legal career. Unfortunately, as was the case with Molly, I was too weak to resist. She propositioned me. I asked you to call Joyce, Alice, Ruth, Margaret, and Gloria to testify. They were reserved, dignified, and didn't proposition me; nor did they act in a sexually provocative manner. I wanted Judge McGuire to see, first hand, the distinction between the behavior of Molly and that of Joyce, Alice, Ruth, Margaret, and Gloria.

Morrissey's testimony created the impression that the affair with Molly was his only transgression. By indirection he did what would have been a disaster if he had directly claimed Molly was his only client with whom he had had sexual relations. Duffy grimaced. It could backfire. The inference drawn from "I draw a line" was too big a risk for too little gain. Morrissey snuck it in. If only the Fox would leave it alone, he would argue Peter had observed the code except for Molly. *Do you disbar an attorney because, on only one occasion, he had sex with a client? A client who actively solicited him?* Lisa, he feared, would not leave it alone. Duffy knew he'd better come up with a defense against a frontal attack.

Fox knew Morrissey had had sex with many other clients. In light of McGuire's ruling that only Molly was before the court, she pondered how and whether Morrissey's testimony had changed the rules. She wrote down "I draw the line at my clients." She would use that as a wedge to get Morrissey to say that there were no other client-affairs, or that there were. It didn't matter which way he went. He was trapped. Fox felt her heartbeat quicken as she contemplated her cross, and as she listened to Duffy and Morrissey.

Q. You identified womanizing as a weakness. What efforts have you made to reform?

A. After the complaint in this proceeding was served, I attended a session of Sex Addicts Anonymous. It holds meetings on Sunday nights at a church on Ninetieth and Fifth.

Q. If you believed you were not a sex addict, why did you attend SAA?

A. I had an analyst's opinion that I was not a sex addict. I wanted to test his opinion with lay people who have the affliction.

Q. What did you learn?

A. As the new man, I was asked to speak first. I revealed my strong attraction toward women. One fellow laughed and said he wished that was his problem. Others confided that their sickness was worlds apart from mine. After the second meeting, the leader, Philip Gross, asked me not to attend further meetings. 'Your ailment,' he said, 'assuming it is an ailment, is unrelated to sex addiction as I know it. Your attendance is confusing the others. I wish you good luck in the action before the bar association."

"Mr. Referee," Duffy said. "Mr. Gross is one of our experts. He is a recovering sex addict and will testify as to the nature of the illness and how to contain it. I prefer that he put meat on the barebones introduced by Mr. Morrissey. I want to talk with Mr. Morrissey before deciding whether to close my direct."

McGuire agreed to a fifteen-minute recess.

"Your testimony impressed McGuire," Duffy said. "But it was risky to add the bit about drawing the line at clients. God only knows what the Fox will do with it and what McGuire will let her do."

"As soon as I said it, I wanted to retract. Of course, I couldn't. If she goes into others, I'll just say 'I neither admit nor deny having affairs with others.' How do you think McGuire will react?"

"He'll be annoyed. He'll think you tried to slip one past him. It's too bad. He liked your Cahill, Gordon connection."

When the hearing resumed, Duffy said his direct was concluded. It was now Fox's turn.

Lisa read each accusation made by Dixon followed by the question of whether her testimony was, in substance, accurate. Each time Morrissey answered no, but with each accusation, he squirmed. His answers became less and less audible. At one point McGuire asked him to speak up. In response Fox's voice rose until McGuire cautioned her "to tone it down. I'm not deaf."

Fox asked whether Morrissey chose dinner at the Friars as a first step in his plan to seduce Molly. "I dine regularly at my club. There's a large table reserved for members who have no dinner companion. I'm not married and often sit at the community table. I also take clients there for lunch or dinner. The dining room is quiet and conducive to personal discussions. The food is good, and the prices are reasonable."

Q. Was Peggy Dolan one of your clients?

"Object," Duffy said. "I ask for an offer of proof. I'm sure Ms. Fox recalls your ruling prohibiting the addition of new charges. I can't, however, conceive of any reason for bringing up Ms. Dolan other than to add a new alleged victim. You, Mr. Referee, have cautioned Ms. Fox about the consequences of attempting to add clients."

"I also don't understand why you're introducing a new person " McGuire asked. "Surely you remember my ruling. What's your purpose in bringing Peggy Dolan into the case?"

"I interviewed twenty-five former clients," the Fox said. "I turned my notes over to Mr. Duffy. Only six claimed they didn't have sex with Morrissey. Mr. Duffy called five but not the sixth, Peggy Dolan. I'd like to know the reason she was not called."

"Ms. Fox has attempted to summarize her notes," Duffy said. "They are not in evidence and have no place in the record of this case. The notes are plainly hearsay and represent the warped opinion of an opinionated prosecutor. I move her statement to be stricken from the record."

In an angry voice, Fox complained about Duffy's personal attack. McGuire told the attorneys to calm down. "I'll strike Ms. Fox's comment about her notes. She may ask one question as to why Ms. Dolan was not called, but that's all. Do you understand my ruling?" McGuire stared angrily at Fox. She nodded, relieved she had told McGuire that nineteen out of twenty-five clients interviewed had had sex with Morrissey, even though her remark was stricken from the record, it was not expunged from McGuire's memory. She had laid a foundation for questioning Morrissey on his half truth of "I draw the line at my clients." His line, Fox chuckled to herself, was drawn in sand, not etched in stone. She continued to construct her foundation.

Q. Why didn't the defense call Peggy Dolan?

The reason, of course, was that Morrissey and Duffy had smelled a rat. Morrissey remembered having sex with Peggy and thought Fox's notes were intentionally false in order to set a trap. Morrissey avoided answering the question and said Duffy was in charge of the case. He suggested Fox should address the question to Duffy. Lisa didn't care about the answer. She knew she had no right to question Duffy. Fox wanted to prepare McGuire for what was coming. She sensed McGuire's curiosity was aroused when he asked, "Let me in on the secret, Mr. Duffy. Why didn't you call Ms. Dolan?"

"Judge McGuire, I interviewed the five witnesses called. I didn't speak with Peggy Dolan. Now, if you think five witnesses are not enough, you can reopen the case, and I'll call the sixth."

McGuire did not credit Duffy's answer. The other witnesses had been terrible. Could Dolan have been worse? His suspicions were aroused. "Please continue with your cross but no more questions about Peggy Dolan."

> Q. You testified that Molly called you once her case was over and asked for a date. She testified on cross and was not examined about the call. Why was she not given a chance to respond?

McGuire interrupted. "I'll answer for Mr. Morrissey. That was Mr. Duffy's decision. I'm not going to ask Mr. Duffy to explain his decision but will allow you to call Ms. Dixon as a rebuttal witness and inquire about the call. There is a risk. If she denies the call, I will authorize a subpoena to the telephone company to get the records of her calls. How much longer is your cross? The hour draws late."

"Not much more, Judge McGuire."

The stress, built up like boiling water in a tea kettle, had turned to steam. Morrissey felt relaxed. He had withstood the blows. This was the best time to spring a trap. Lisa's timing was exquisite.

> Q. I wrote down your answer, so I wouldn't forget it. You testified: "I like women. Perhaps too much. It's a weakness. I blame it for destroying my marriage. I draw the line, however, at my clients. They're off limits. I refuse to allow sex to destroy my legal career." Did I correctly write down your testimony?

Morrissey started to perspire, the steam returning to the kettle. "That sounds about right."

Q. Did you mean to imply Molly was the only client with whom you had sex?

"Here we go again," Duffy said. "She's asking about the very area you ruled was constitutionally protected. Ms. Fox, finding the front door locked, is trying to enter through the back door. I object." Then, in an attempt to rescue Peter, Duffy added, "I didn't infer anything either way. Did you, Mr. McGuire?"

Ignoring Duffy's enquiry for the moment, McGuire said, "It's an interesting evidentiary question. Did Mr. Morrissey open either the front or back door when he said: 'I draw the line at my clients'? Contrary to you, Mr. Duffy, I inferred his affair with Ms. Dixon was the only one. Not that that would excuse him, but it would be a fact going to the penalty. I don't have to disbar Mr. Morrissey. I can fine him and/or suspend him from practice for a period of time. I can even order Mr. Morrissey to offer his services to Legal Aid, and through that agency, represent poor women seeking divorce. I can also impose no penalty. There's a lot I can do. Getting back to the objection, I rule the question is fair cross in view of Mr. Morrissey's earlier answer. Please answer the question."

Morrissey answered, "I didn't mean to imply one way or the other."

Fox, sniffing blood, continued:

Q. Is that line drawn in sand or etched in stone?
A. Neither. It's an imaginary line.
Q. Have you imagined that line for purposes of this hearing?
I withdraw the question. How many clients have you had sex with?

Duffy barely got out "I object" before McGuire ruled. "You may refuse to answer the question but if you do, your attorney may not argue that Molly Dixon was the only one."

Fox had made her point. Molly Dixon was joined by at least nineteen others. Peter gave the answer he had prepared during the recess preceding cross. "I admit to an affair with Ms. Dixon. As to any other client, I neither admit nor deny."

Fox said her cross was over. McGuire adjourned the trial until the following morning. "We'll start with the experts, followed by Ms. Fox's rebuttal witnesses. She said she had two, Ms. Dixon's psychiatrist and Ms. Dixon. Goodnight to all."

Outside the court house while they were hailing a cab, Duffy accused Peter of self-destruction. "'I draw the line.' Where did you get that from? There's a lot in the record that you flirted with Joyce and Margaret. If clients were off limits, why were you flirting?"

"You prepared me for a direct question about other clients to which I was to say that Molly was the only one. You said McGuire couldn't/wouldn't touch me if Molly were the only victim. But you didn't ask the question. I thought I could slip it past the Fox."

"For Christ's sake, Peter, she interviewed twenty-five of your clients. She knew you tried to put the make on almost all of them. That's why I thought better than to ask the question. I shouldn't have put the thought in your mind. It hurt, but we're still alive."

The finger pointing continued until Duffy said, "No more recriminations. It's not over until the fat lady sings. The tide is out but maybe it will start to flow in our direction. Stay upbeat. Smile. Take that loser's look off your face." Just then an empty cab pulled up. Safely inside the cab, Morrissey again raised the issue of settlement. "I'm in the wrong. Why don't I accept the punishment and be done with it? This game of cat and mouse is torture. The Fox has her fangs in me."

"Peter, you may be ready to lose," Duffy said, "but I'm not. The big issue is penalty. McGuire will welcome a settlement. We've come this far. Let's give our experts a chance."

What else could he do? Jesus, he had made a mess of things. It was a wonder he hadn't been caught before now.

19

Duffy introduced Philip Gross to Judge McGuire. "He's that rare expert who's appearing without compensation. Mr. Morrissey has voluntarily agreed to make a contribution of five thousand dollars to Sex Addicts Anonymous. Mr. Gross is affiliated with that organization."

McGuire did not grasp the difference between paying Gross or contributing to his charity, but other than rubbing his chin, he let the matter pass.

Gross wore the same outfit he had on in Duffy's office: a blue suit, blue shirt, and a red tie. His testimony was also substantially the same except, told in a question and answer format, was more dramatic. Phillip's tale awakened a frightening image for the four men in the courtroom. All had stared, at one time or another, at a *Playboy* centerfold. They had seen pornographic movies, read filthy books, and paid for sex. The difference between them and Gross was one of degree.

McGuire, although he showed no outward sign, was hit hard. He was a good customer of a service providing what was euphemistically called an 'escort service.' He rationalized by claiming his wife was unimaginative and cold. He knew his rationale was false; he rarely gave his wife a chance. *I'm not a sex addict*, he thought. *I like alcohol. I drink vodka and wine almost every day. I'm not an alcoholic anymore than I'm a sex addict. I empathize with Gross. Do my feelings extend to Morrissey? Well, maybe a little.* It showed. When early in Gross's testimony, Fox rose to object, McGuire silenced her with a wave of his hand. He wanted to hear Gross and would not brook an interruption.

Morrissey wondered if he was alone in thinking that Gross's testimony had changed the atmosphere. Sympathy for an abnormal proclivity and the will necessary to overcome it replaced self-righteousness. The realization that we are all afflicted seemed to keep fidgeting to a minimum as Gross spun his sad tale.

Richard Stern, Fox's boss, had been silent throughout the hearing. Occasionally, he wrote a note to Fox or whispered in her ear, but during Gross's testimony, Peter noticed his demeanor had changed. Emotion seemed to creep in. Maybe he knows a thing or two about lust.

The stage was now set for a light to be turned onto Morrissey's affliction.

Q. When did you meet Mr. Morrissey, and what were the circumstances?.
A. He showed up at a Sunday meeting of SAA. As the new man, he was called upon to tell his story.
Q. What was his story?

"Object hearsay," Fox said.

Without waiting for a response from Duffy, McGuire overruled the objection. "The testimony is introduced not for the truth, although I don't exclude the possibility that what Mr. Morrissey told the assembled group was true, but rather for the fact that that was what Mr. Morrissey said. You would have made a stronger objection if you had suggested relevancy." McGuire's ruling was made with a smile to Gross. Duffy took heart. Was McGuire warming to the defense?

A. He said he was a lawyer specializing in divorce cases. His clients were almost all women. The Canons of Professional Conduct prohibit sexual relations between a lawyer and his client in divorce actions. The rule, Morrissey said, reflected a weakness on the part of a woman off balanced by the life-changing experience of divorce.
He also discussed his sexual proclivity: Mr. Morrissey finds it difficult to curb his desire to have sexual relations with any woman who shows an inclination to have sex with him. He said he had been informally diagnosed by a friend, a psychologist, as hypersexual.

Knowing of the rule and his weakness, he tries to exercise control when he is with his clients. One openly propositioned him. He succumbed. Several years later she complained to the bar association and he is facing disbarment.

Q. What was the reaction, if any, to Peter's story?

A. When Peter finished his story, I asked for comments. One man laughingly said: "Lawyers regularly screw their clients out of lots of money. That's fine. But if a lawyer makes love, he can be kicked out of the profession. No wonder there are so many lawyer jokes." Another asked whether force or coercion was used? When Peter answered "only on me," the group laughed again.

Q. What, if anything, did you say to Peter?

A. At the end of the meeting, I talked to Mr. Morrissey. I told him he was welcome to come to our meetings, but I didn't see the point. Our group is addicted to pornography, not sex. Most of us were released from our fantasy world by having a satisfactory sexual relationship. We view having sex as a catharsis, as a healthful activity, as the road to normality. Peter's lust for sex with women was plainly different from the group's affliction. He stuck out like a sore thumb.

A good trial lawyer knows when to stop. Duffy smiled at the witness, nodded to McGuire, and turned to Lisa. "Your witness, Attorney Fox."

Fox asked for a two-hour recess, reminding McGuire that he had earlier ruled that a recess would be called after the direct of each of the two experts. McGuire said yes.

When court resumed Fox read portions of Molly Dixon's testimony accusing Morrissey of taking advantage of her. Duffy had, through Gross, retold Morrissey's side. Now it was Fox's turn to remind McGuire that there was another side. She was eager to balance the scales. Fox followed each section with a question as to how the group would have reacted if Molly Dixon had told her story. Duffy had prepared Gross for Fox's likely cross. "I don't know, but I'm sure the reaction would have been different. It's wrong to coerce a woman; it's not wrong to have sex with a woman who invites you to make love to her. I suppose that in some seductions there is an element of coercion preceding consent."

Duffy wanted to turn the case away from a violation of the code to a "he says, she says" contest. Gross's answer made him appear neutral. Duffy believed that a jury perceived no witness as neutral. The closest a witness can come is "neutral for" or "neutral against." Duffy believed that Gross came across as neutral for Morrissey. Duffy hoped his view on seduction would be considered.

As he considered his next moves, Duffy weighed the credibility of Peter and Molly. Peter's remark about line drawing would hurt. On the other side, Molly had denied having an affair with Charlie Monk and then had to recant. Molly's testimony about being induced to drink wine was contradicted by the bill. And then there was the passionate session with her sister's husband, which McGuire viewed as bearing on credibility. Both were tarnished, but Duffy believed Peter had an edge.

Fox turned to the principal point in her cross, one pointed to by McGuire. Gross's testimony was not relevant. She would like to have it stricken. Any testimony that diverted attention from the absolute nature of the violation served only Morrissey's interest.

Q. Do you hold to the view that a lawyer who tricks his client into having a sexual relationship is upholding the best standards of the legal profession?
A. I'm not an expert on legal ethics, but deception is always wrong.
Q. Do you believe that a woman facing divorce may be in a weakened state and easily seduced?
A. I don't know any women undergoing divorce well enough to answer your question.
Q. Do you recognize that clients repose trust and confidence in their lawyers?
A. I suppose they do. I've never been a client.

Fox then moved to strike Gross's testimony. "Mr. Gross has no personal knowledge of the facts and lacks expertise upon which to express an opinion. Also, I agree with Your Honor, his testimony is irrelevant. I move to strike Mr. Gross's testimony."

McGuire said he shared Fox's doubts as to relevancy but not expertise. "I have no doubt that Mr. Gross is an expert. He has empirical knowledge on sex addiction. My problem is what sex addiction has to do with our proceeding." McGuire turned to Duffy, "Tell me why his testimony is relevant or material to the issues. I dislike striking testimony, as I can always ignore it."

"Ms. Fox called Mr. Morrissey a sex addict." Duffy then read a passage from the record in which Fox said just that. "Mr. Gross is certainly an expert on the subject of sex addiction. I wonder if Ms. Fox is willing to stipulate that Mr. Morrissey is not a sex addict."

"Certainly not!" she said a little too loudly.

"Motion denied, Attorney Fox. Mr. Morrissey is charged with having sexual relations with his client. Strictly speaking, I should strike all references by Ms. Fox to sex addiction and grant her motion. The trouble is that the issue may surface on appeal. It's only fair to Mr. Morrissey to have a full record, anticipating all arguments that may be raised before me or on appeal."

On redirect Duffy read from Morrissey's testimony. Imitating Fox's tone of voice, he mockingly asked Gross, "How would the group have reacted if Morrissey had told the story as he believed it?" Gross answered, "Exactly as they did. What you have read is what Morrissey told us."

Duffy said no further questions. McGuire excused the witness. He then addressed the lawyers. "I instruct Mr. Duffy to call his next expert witness. When the direct is concluded, we will then adjourn. Ms. Fox, you will have an overnight and then some time to prepare for cross. We will resume tomorrow at eleven instead of ten. Today, court will remain in session until direct is concluded."

20

Max Wolfe, a neuropsychologist, was an experienced witness. His task was to impress judges and juries with his erudition. Duffy, as the conductor of a virtuoso, learned through experience to give Wolfe his head. To establish his credentials as an expert on neuropsychology, Duffy led the witness through his academic background and teaching affiliations, his professional associations, his publications, and his appearances as an expert witness. Duffy moved "to certify Wolfe as an expert on human behavior." The motion was granted without objection.

Q. What role does the brain play in our everyday activities?
A. The brain weighs only three pounds and consists of eighty to one hundred and twenty billion ions. From nothing else radiates the sensations of joy and grief, the need to laugh and cry. The brain enables humans to see, feel, hear, and taste. It also controls memory, knowledge, personality, and predilections. It determines our ethical and moral values.
The brain enables some people to achieve excellence in the arts and science. It causes others to murder and plunder. We have identified the part of the brain, the cerebral cortex, that regulates executive function, such as self-control, the lack of which leads to substance addiction. The same area, especially the frontal lobes, controls personality aberrations such as depression or sex addiction. Addiction can be treated clinically, provided the addiction is not severe. The treatment consists of medication to relieve the cravings and therapy to increase willpower.
Despite many years of autopsies, X-rays, and magnetic resonance imaging, how the brain's billions of cells perform their many functions remains a mystery.
Q. Mr. Philip Gross testified about his struggle with sex addiction and those of others in Sex Addicts Anonymous. You were present during his direct and cross. Is sex addiction

recognized as a mental disorder by the American Psychiatric Association?

A. The diagnostic manual of the association does not recognize sex addiction. I believe it is a serious omission. An obsession with pornography, a life lived in a shadowy fantasy world, is a serious disorder. If the governors of the APA heard Mr. Gross's testimony, I believe they would change their minds.

Q. Have you had an opportunity to meet with Mr. Morrissey, and if so, were you able to form an opinion as to whether Mr. Morrissey suffers from an addiction to sex?

A. We had a long session with much give and take. Based on what I learned, I believe I am able to form an opinion as to whether Mr. Morrissey is a sex addict.

Q. What is your opinion?

A. I divide sex addiction into two parts: those who are preoccupied with pornography and other forms of sexual escapism, and those who lead highly active sex lives. Mr. Morrissey reads soft porn magazines such as *Playboy* and *Penthouse* but only in his spare time and then rarely. Many men do; most are normal. Mr. Morrissey doesn't read hard porn or see Triple X-rated movies. A problem arises when pornography becomes as addictive to a person as liquor or drugs are to an alcoholic or drug addict. An occasional foray into the world of pornography is no more harmful than a drink before dinner.

Sex addicts, such as those in Mr. Gross's group, rely on self-masturbation to achieve satiation. From what he said, Mr. Morrissey does not self-masturbate. If sex addiction is defined as a dependency on pornography and masturbation, Mr. Morrissey is not a sex addict.

That begins—not ends—my analysis. The sex drive is primeval and remains as strong in modern times as in ancient history. Since the earliest stages of evolution, the propagation of the species has depended on the desire of males and females to copulate. Sexual awareness begins at puberty. A typical teenage male satisfies it by engaging in self-masturbation. As boys mature into young adults, they seek relationships with consenting women as a means of fulfilling their sex drive. Some young men engage frequently in sex, others less frequently or not at all. The range of normality extends from hypersexual to asexual.

A strong urge for sex is not necessarily a weakness. Tiger Woods was unfairly criticized for being a hypersexual. His problem was not over-indulging in sex but being unfaithful to his wife and family. The press referred to him as a 'sex addict;' the psychiatric profession did not.

Mr. Morrissey admits to a strong attraction to women. He seeks frequent encounters with women. Is one who over-indulges in sex a sex addict? Is that a form of mental illness? An obsession? Sexual intercourse, for the male, requires physical strength, which, as is well known, cannot be incessantly repeated. Put simply, the hypersexual male cannot binge or overdose on sex as say an addict hooked on drugs or alcohol. Further, there is the all-important role of the brain. In my professional judgment, a desire that cannot become an all-day occurrence is not an addiction. A strong attraction to women falls into that category.

The brain controls emotions as well as behavior. It recognizes that endless repetition of the sexual act is beyond the ability of man. To accommodate reality, the brain sends signals producing a feeling of satisfaction and a temporary end to more sexual activity.

Mr. Morrissey is at the high end of the sexual range. He is, however, not a sex addict. For reasons I have already discussed, no man who craves women is a sex addict.

Q. I ask you to assume that the bar association has a rule prohibiting a lawyer representing a woman in a matrimonial action from having sexual relations with his client. Is a divorce specialist who is hypersexual able to comply with the rule?

A. The sexual appetite of the hypersexual can be brought under control with much greater ease than an obese person can control his diet or an alcoholic or drug addict restrain his input of alcohol or drugs. Why? The hypersexual male is not a compulsive obsessive. He is not an addict. Not being addicted, he doesn't lose control.

Q. Under what circumstances, if any, can a hypersexual lawyer aware of the bar association rule be unable to resist having sexual intercourse with a client?

A. The hypersexual lawyer is likely to abandon his self-control if he is propositioned by a client. With clients who do not
solicit him, he is no more likely to seek sex than other lawyers. The hypersexual lawyer may flirt more than others. It is
a way of testing the waters. How the client reacts to a sexual
advance is under the control of the client. If she accepts the
invitation, the lawyer is faced with a conflict. Does he honor
his professional duty or serve his sexual craving? It's problematic. It cannot be answered as a general proposition. It
depends on the lawyer's level of self-control.

Q. Do you have an opinion as to Mr. Morrissey's level of self-
control?

A. Yes, I do. I asked Mr. Morrissey a series of questions about
priorities in his life. He was adamant. 'Work comes first.' In
the event of a conflict between a social engagement and work,
an event which frequently occurs, Mr. Morrissey cancels his
date and tends to business. Mr. Morrissey's work ethic is part
of his cerebral code. As such, the brain mandates duty over
pleasure. Based on my knowledge of the controlling power
of the brain, I have no hesitation in expressing the opinion
that Mr. Morrissey can and will respect the rule except under
unusual circumstances, such as an open invitation to have
sex.

Duffy concluded his direct of the doctor, satisfied that he had
squeezed every ounce from him and more. He took a deep breath
and sank into his chair as he contemplated the Fox's cross-examination. She would have had plenty of time to prepare her cross,
scheduled for the next morning at eleven. But Lisa requested
permission to ask one question before court was adjourned. Her
request was granted.

Q. Dr. Wolfe, you are a distinguished neuropsychologist. You
have published many articles in learned periodicals, are a
chaired professor of neurology at New York University and

have testified as an expert in lots of cases. I'll bet your fees are high. What is your fee in this case?

A. My fee is the standard one I charge in all cases, a minimum of $5,000. If my time exceeds twenty hours, I charge $250 for each additional hour.

Fox thanked the court. She said she hoped to complete her cross by the lunch break. McGuire adjourned court until eleven o'clock.

Lisa's question had invoked a rule of litigation. Once cross begins Duffy is prohibited from discussing Wolfe's testimony with him. Fox's action reflected distrust of Wolfe and Duffy. It also showed she saw flaws in Wolfe's direct and did not want to give Duffy a chance to correct them. Duffy had no choice but to observe the rule notwithstanding that it had been artificially invoked. He said to Wolfe, "Be sure to arrive promptly at eleven" and nothing else although he had a lot else to say.

The next morning, with the principal actors in their seats, Lisa's eyes were aglow. She sat on the edge of her chair eager to begin her cross. Wolfe appeared calm and ready to use what he believed to be his superior intelligence to fend off the anticipated assault. He was used to slaying lawyers. Duffy sat slumped in his chair, his hand resting on his cheek. He knew that Wolfe was vulnerable, but Duffy had to believe he was up to the job. Wasn't he?

When McGuire took his seat, he asked Fox to begin. Before she reached the podium, she launched right into her examination. Still smarting from being caught talking to Molly during a break in cross, she asked:

Q. From the time court was adjourned up to the moment you arrived here today, did you have occasion to talk with Mr. Duffy on any subject whatsoever?

A. Yes. Mr. Duffy cautioned me to arrive promptly at 11:00 a.m. We had no further conversation.

Fox turned to Duffy and stared. He rose and said, "Dr. Wolfe has expressed the extent of our conversation." If Lisa were disappointed in the response, she showed no outward sign.

Q. Dr. Wolfe, you expressed an opinion that a hypersexual divorce lawyer was not a threat to female clients. Have you conducted a study on hypersexual divorce lawyers and their relations with female clients?

A. I assume by study you mean a statistical study. As rephrased, I will answer your question. I have not conducted a statistical study, nor do I know of one on the narrow ground you propose. In my judgment no such study would ever be commissioned.

Q. I'm sorry, Dr. Wolfe, for my narrow question. I accept your refinement. Have you conducted any studies on hypersexual men?

A. No, and to my knowledge, neither has anybody else. The reason is that a sample group would be impossible to gather. There's no lodestar to measure normality. Some men claim to engage on a daily basis. They may exaggerate their activity in order to identify with a trait they assume macho men possess. Then again others may be reluctant to disclose their sexual activity. While there is no taboo about talking about sex, many prefer to keep their sex life private. A reliable study cannot proceed without an established norm as to how often the average man engages in sex.

A study may isolate causes of diseases and help in avoiding or overcoming them. Hypersexuality is not a disease; it is a human condition within the range of normality. There is no reason to treat it, and hence, no need for a study. There's another pragmatic reason. Studies are expensive. They are supported by corporations or governmental agencies. I doubt if a sponsor could be found to bear the costs of a study on hypersexual males. It's not a hot-button subject needing medical or psychological treatment.

Q. What percent of the male population in this country is hypersexual?

A. I don't know. Nor does anybody else. It all goes back to the absence of a statistical study.

Q. Can you provide a range? Is it 10 percent or 50 percent or somewhere in between?

A. Any answer would be a guess. I'm under oath and would rather not guess.

Q. You have published thirty-two articles, appeared as an expert in hundreds of cases. Surely at least one article or an opinion expressed in a court of law involved hypersexuality. Am I correct?

A. No, you are not. I have not published any articles on hypersexuality. Nor, for that matter, am I familiar with any scholarly articles on that subject. Such articles are based on statistical studies. The absence of such studies precludes articles.

Q. In the absence of studies or articles, is it fair to state that the opinion you have expressed in this case, that a hypersexual lawyer can control his obsessive sexual craving for women who are his clients through the exercise of self-control, is unique to you?

A. No. My opinion was based on patterns within the brain. Other neuropsychologists, if asked the same series of questions, would express the same opinion.

So far Morrissey was upbeat. He believed Fox was making a mistake to cross an expert in his field. It leads to longwinded answers, invariably enhancing the expert and revealing the naiveté of the lawyer. Wolfe's opinion, that Morrissey posed no threat to women clients—with the exception of those who propositioned him—was so far, untouched. Peter wondered how and when the Fox would get there. He had no doubt she would.

Q. You have testified in hundreds of cases. How many times have you expressed an opinion in a court of law on male sexuality?

A. This case is my first.

Q. Let's put to one side your court appearances. In the course of your private practice, have you treated any male hypersexuals?

A. No.

Q. Other than Mr. Morrissey, do you know any other hypersexuals?

A. No.

Q. I apologize for asking you this question, but I must. Are you hypersexual?

A. No.

Q. You have already testified that you have not testified as to hypersexuality. Have you testified on other aspects of male sexuality?

A. I can't recall any.

Q. I ask you to assume that there are two divorce specialists of approximately equal ability. One is hypersexual, and one has an average sex drive, which one would you advise a woman to retain?

A. I would tell her that the sexual proclivities of the lawyer are immaterial. She should select the one she feels more comfortable with.

Q. I googled you. You have two married daughters. Is Google correct?

A. Yes.

Q. If one of your daughters were to seek a divorce, would you alert her if she had selected a divorce lawyer you knew to be hypersexual?

A. No. Both my daughters are strong-willed and secure. It is unthinkable that they could be taken advantage of.

Q. I ask you to assume that a woman is not like your daughters but weak and insecure. Would you advise her to avoid a divorce lawyer who was hypersexual?

A. No. I'd advise her not to proposition the lawyer.

Q. What concerns, if any, do you have about a hypersexual lawyer representing women in divorce actions?

A. None. My concern resides with the client. Conduct yourself in a businesslike manner, and you have nothing to fear.

Morrissey was stunned and trying not to show it. *Why didn't Duffy retain a psychologist specializing in sex problems? Why hadn't Duffy asked about his experience? What the hell was he thinking? This case has been a disaster from start to finish.*

Duffy was mortified. And furious. Not with himself but with Wolfe. He should have recommended someone who knows what he's talking about. *No. The buck stops with me. I should have plumbed.*

Peter and Duffy stared into space as Fox continued the slaughter. How much worse could it get?

Q. Are you familiar with the term "professional witness"?
A. Yes.
Q. What does it mean to you?
A. A person who derives a substantial part of his income from testifying.
Q. Are you a professional witness?
A. Of course not.
Q. Over the past five years, what part of your income has been derived from witness fees?
A. I don't know.
Q. Is there someone in your employ, a bookkeeper, an accountant who would know.
A. Yes, my accountant would know.

"Judge McGuire, I request a short adjournment to allow Dr. Wolfe to call his accountant and obtain the information." Before McGuire could rule Wolfe interposed. "My financial records are private. I will not disclose them."

McGuire summoned the lawyers to the bench for a conference. "I can't compel Dr. Wolfe to disclose the requested information. But if he refuses to do so, I will strike his testimony."

Lisa was pleased with McGuire's ruling. She had hit a sore spot. She did not want to overplay her hand and decided to make a magnanimous offer, one that would earn her brownie points. "I don't need the absolute numbers. The percentage of litigation fees to income over the past five years will suffice."

McGuire thanked Fox for the concession. Duffy consulted with Wolfe and said the compromise was agreeable.

The answer came within the hour. 15 to 25 percent of his income came from being a witness.

Q. Over the past five years, how many clients who have sought your expert opinion have you turned down?

A. The lawyers who enlist my service know whether I can help. It is a self-selecting process. It works so well that I have never had to turn down a client.

Q. Dr. Wolfe, if the Grievance Committee's budget could afford your fee, would you have been willing to testify on our behalf? (Fox didn't care how Wolfe answered. She had made her point. His gun was for hire.)

A. The answer is no. If I cannot help, I don't take the assignment. I accepted this case because I believe it's wrong to blame the lawyer for having sexual relations with a client who solicited him. The more I got involved, the more convinced I became of the merits of the defense. I would not have agreed to appear for the Grievance Committee, because I do not believe in its case.

Lisa was too smart to challenge Wolfe's answer. He was attacking the law, a poor position for an expert to be in.

Q. You expressed an opinion to the effect that "Mr. Morrissey's adherence to duty would create a pattern in his brain restraining him from engaging in sexual relations with clients, except perhaps ones who solicited him." Have I correctly paraphrased your testimony?

A. Our sensory worlds—seeing, hearing, touching—are controlled by sensory receptors responsible...

McGuire interrupted. With a touch of impatience, he said, "My notes on your opinion reflect pretty much what Ms. Fox said. The question can be answered yes or no. Alternatively, we can ask the court reporter to read your testimony. What I won't allow is new testimony. What's it going to be?" Wolfe had no choice but to answer. "Ms. Fox's restatement of part of my opinion is essentially correct."

Q. In forming your opinion that Mr. Morrissey did not pose a threat to female clients, did you ask him how many clients he had had sexual intercourse with?

A. No.

Q. Were you instructed by Mr. Duffy not to make an inquiry?

A. Yes.

Q. Based on your experience as a paid witness, did you understand that if you had refused to follow Mr. Duffy's direction, you would not have been retained?

A. Since I had agreed that my opinion would be based solely on science, I don't know or care what Mr. Duffy would have done if I had declined to follow the instruction. I hasten to add…

"No, no, no," McGuire said. "Don't add. Just answer the question. You will have an opportunity on redirect to add to any of your testimony. As it now stands, you believe that Mr. Morrissey's prior conduct is immaterial as to how he will act in the future. Please go on, Ms. Fox."

Q. But for Attorney Duffy's instruction, would you have inquired?

A. No. I based my opinion on Mr. Morrissey's sense of duty as registered in his brain.

Q. I ask you to assume that a student you were mentoring was given the assignment of determining the propensity of hypersexual lawyers to have sexual intercourse with their clients. I ask you to further assume the student failed to ask the lawyers whether and how frequently they had sexual intercourse with their clients. Would you give that student a failing grade?

A. No. I would not punish the student for pursuing a strictly scientific approach.

Q. Would you mark down a student who did both: asked about facts as well as developed a theory?

A. Yes, I would.

Q. Would you anticipate that a hypersexual lawyer devoted to duty would flirt with his clients?

A. 'Flirt' is a highly subjective term. Some men have a warm personality regardless of whether they are hypersexual. They may tend to engage in harmless flirtations. To answer your question, I would have to know more about the lawyer.

Q. You are familiar with Mr. Morrissey. Would you expect his brain patterns to prevent him from flirting with clients?

A. No. The brain would not alter his personality in a harmless way. It would, however, prevent him from having affairs.

Q. Because you followed Mr. Duffy's direction, you have no factual basis to test your brain theory. Is that correct? Please answer yes or no.

A. I cannot answer yes or no. I put my trust in science.

"I have finished my cross," Fox said.

"OK, Mr. Duffy. Do you wish redirect?" When Duffy said he did, McGuire called a recess. Since cross was over, Duffy talked freely with Wolfe. When court reconvened, Duffy attempted to staunch the bleeding.

Q. In cross you wanted to add to your answer. Judge McGuire asked you to wait for redirect. We are there. You testified that I instructed you not to inquire into whether Mr. Morrissey had had affairs with clients. But for my instruction would you have made such an inquiry?

A. No.

Q. What is your reason for excluding such information?

A. I opined that Mr. Morrissey's self-control would prevail in every situation except one: a client propositioning him. So, if Mr. Morrissey said there were prior sexual encounters, I would have had to determine whether the client solicited sex. In making such a determination, I'd probably have to interview each of the clients. This issue can be highly contentious as we see from this very case. I believe such extended inquiry would be a waste of time and lead to unreliable conclusions.

Duffy thought that to pursue the critical issue any further would be counterproductive. He ended his redirect by thanking Dr. Wolfe (although he wished to murder him) and added, "I have no further questions. The defense rests."

"We'll begin tomorrow," McGuire said, "with Ms. Fox's rebuttal case.

I thank you all for an interesting and informative session."

At the end of the day, for the first time since the trial began, Duffy and Morrissey went their separate ways. Peter went back to his office and reviewed pending cases with his lawyers. All noticed he was impatient, preoccupied, and irritable. Several asked how the case was going. "Duffy's doing a wonderful job. He's killing the other side. As good as Duffy is, there are times I wish I were representing myself. It's tough for me sitting on the sidelines in my own case. It will be over in a few days."

Peter called his niece. He tried to sound upbeat, but he knew it was hard for him to conceal his despair. When she invited Peter to dinner, he turned her down. "I'm tired. I'll have room service bring my dinner and get to sleep early."

When Peter left his office, he did not go back to the Pierre. Instead, he headed for Central Park. He walked along the park until he reached Lincoln Center. He stopped at Gabriel's, one of his favorite restaurants. Peter told the maître d' that he was alone and would like to take his dinner at the bar.

After dinner he walked home, oblivious to his surroundings, the city, the smells, the weather. He was physically and mentally exhausted. He went directly to bed. With thoughts of *I don't care whether I win or lose*, his anxiety diminished, and he was surprised that he slept so well.

21

Molly Dixon made her second appearance, this time as a rebuttal witness. Fox did not rehash Molly's direct. She realized that would only irritate McGuire. Molly's psychiatrist, Helen Baker, the second rebuttal witness, would do the job more effectively.

Q. You testified that in addition to two martinis, one for each of you, Mr. Morrissey ordered a bottle of wine and poured several glasses for you. The bill reflects two martinis but no charge for wine? Are you sure you had wine with dinner?

A. Absolutely. When I said one martini was enough and declined wine, Mr. Morrissey told me it was Argentinean night at the club. A bottle of Argentinean Medoc was complimentary. He said it was splendid wine and urged me to try it.

Q. What was your reason for not telling me that the wine was complimentary, so that it could have been included in your direct testimony?

A. Mr. Morrissey had insisted that I drink wine. I had no idea that he was going to deny we had wine.

Q. After your divorce, did you have occasion to call Mr. Morrissey?

A. Yes. About a year after the divorce became final, my ex-husband failed to meet an alimony payment. I was too embarrassed to speak with Mr. Morrissey, so I left word with his secretary, Gina. She called back. Said Mr. Morrissey had talked to my husband's lawyer. It was an oversight, and a check would be delivered by hand. It was.

Q. On direct you said that you had no communication with Mr. Morrissey after the case was over. Do you consider a call to Mr. Morrissey's secretary a call to him?

A. No. I do not.

On that note Fox concluded her examination of Dixon. It was short and sweet but carried a sting. After Morrissey's direct it appeared Molly had lied about the wine. Now, Morrissey was the liar, twice. From Molly's telephone call, an inference was drawn that she wanted another sexual encounter. It was explained as a pure business call. Fox smiled at Duffy as she turned Molly over to him.

Duffy was furious that Morrissey may have lied to him. Before getting up to address Molly, he whispered a question to Peter. "Was there an Argentinean night?" Peter said wine distributors hold promotional events at the Friars. "It is possible that Molly is correct. Let's check." Duffy feigned a personal matter and asked for a short recess, during which Peter called his club. Yes, there was a wine promotion on that night. And his secretary Gina recalled Molly's call. Returning to the courtroom, Duffy decided to use his examination to get some ammunition for the psychiatrist, Helen Baker.

Q. What was your reason for seeking psychiatric help?
A. I was lonely and painfully depressed.
Q. I take it that loneliness and depression took a long time to set in as you didn't see Dr. Baker until a year after your divorce became final. Am I correct that you waited a year before seeking help?
A. Yes.
Q. Did you tell Dr. Baker all about your sexual relations with Peter?
A. Yes.
Q. Who suggested that you file a complaint with the Grievance Committee?
A. Dr. Baker.
Q. Did Dr. Baker assist you in preparing the complaint?
A. Well, it wasn't a complaint. It was a letter. Yes, she helped me.
Duffy marked the letter as an exhibit and showed it to Molly. When she identified the letter, Duffy asked:
Q. Isn't it a fact that Dr. Baker did more than assist you? She drafted the letter? You signed what Dr. Baker wrote?
A. I signed it but would not have if I had believed it was not true.

Q. Did you show the letter to a lawyer before delivering it to the Grievance Committee?

A. No.

Q. Did you pay Dr. Baker for writing the letter?

A. No. My ex-husband's health insurer pays her bills.

Q. Did you show the letter to your ex-husband before filing it?

A. No.

Q. Same question to the health insurer?

A. Same answer.

Q. Are you still under Dr. Baker's care?

A. Yes.

Q. Were you forthcoming in your sessions with Dr. Baker?

A. Yes.

Duffy concluded his cross of Molly. Fox called Dr. Baker.

Lisa reviewed Dr. Baker's credentials and then began the substantive examination. The doctor said Molly was severely depressed and heaped blame on herself for what she viewed as a "failed life." Molly suffered from denial, causing her to suppress events that implicated others. Months passed before she was able to discuss her "tragic affair" with Morrissey. Consistent with other sad events of her life, she blamed herself. "I shouldn't have agreed to meet him for dinner. It sounded like a date. I was wary of his intentions from the moment we met in his office. Upon being introduced he kissed me, not on the lips, but close. He held my hand and patted it. There were several telephone calls, which interrupted our meeting. I should have said no to dinner and just waited for the calls to end."

Dr. Baker accused Morrissey of being a hunter, single-minded in his intentions. "Men who suffer from an excess of testosterone or an inflated or deflated ego have to prove themselves over and over again. To insure the likelihood of success, they target the weak and ill prepared. The victim—depressed, dependent, and isolated—sees her lawyer as a sympathetic person, someone who listens to her. Poor Molly. She is all of the above. She wears a bull's-eye on her chest."

Dr. Baker discussed the two other men who took advantage of Molly, her neighbor and her brother-in-law. "They're not professionals. Just sleazes. We punish only professionals. They're under a duty not to take advantage of their clients."

Dr. Baker turned to psychologists who have affairs with their clients. "They're mainly men. Eager to gratify their hunger by taking advantage of those entrusted to their care. Their abuse of trust causes severe trauma. I know firsthand, because one of my specialties is the treatment of the victims."

Dr. Baker described the no-nonsense handling of offending psychologists. "They're booted out of the profession and prohibited from returning." Moreover, she said, "Civil actions are brought against them. Juries have awarded large sums as compensatory damages. Egregious situations give rise to criminal actions. Ejection from the profession and civil and criminal actions serve as deterrents. The American Psychiatric Association reports that the number of violators has substantially declined. I sit on its committee that reviews charges. An admission, such as the one made by Morrissey that he had sexual relations with Molly Dixon, would result in automatic expulsion. Although sexual exploitation by therapists has received major attention, the legal profession has a similar problem, but for some reason, it remains a dirty little secret.

Q. You have testified that you have treated victims of sexual exploitation. Aside from Ms. Dixon were any of them the victims of lawyers?

A. Yes.

Q. What conditions, if any, have these victims had in common with Ms. Dixon?

A. Women are not monolithic. Some are not troubled by the affair. Others may react immediately. Some, like Molly, repress the assault for several years before seeking help. A year or two is not unusual. Those women who are adversely affected suffer from depression. If there are other causes— and there usually are—these women may become suicidal. The affected women consider that they have been battered and tormented mentally comparable to the physical and mental harm caused to rape victims. There are many articles in psychological journals recounting the trauma of victims by those who, occupying positions of trust, abuse their duty.

Q. Dr. Wolfe was called as an expert witness for the defense. He testified that prior conduct was not indicative of whether a lawyer would likely become sexually involved with clients in the future. Do you have an opinion on the materiality of prior offenses?

A. Yes, I do. Statistical studies reported in the literature concerning sexually exploitive therapists reflect those who have engaged in prior abuse are more likely to repeat. The point is made in an article by Bates and Brodsky.

Q. I show you an article entitled "National Study of Therapist-Client Sex" by Bates and Brodsky. Is this the article you made reference to?

A. Yes. May I read from the article at page 141?

Fox handed copies to McGuire and Duffy, and Baker began: "The best single predictor of exploitation in therapy is a therapist who has exploited another patient in the past."

"Do I understand you correctly," McGuire said, "that among therapists, there's a one-strike rule. One affair and a therapist is barred from practice?"

"Not always. The therapist may be allowed to teach, engage in research, or hold an administrative position. The prohibition is against treating patients."

"Do you see any problem," McGuire continued, "if, as a punishment or protection after a repeated violation, the therapist's practice is limited to males?"

"Yes, I do. The violation caused by libido trumping rules of proper conduct would go unpunished. The deterrent effect would be lost. A severe punishment is required to deter others."

Q What do you see as different in the role of a divorce lawyer vis-à-vis his client and that of a therapist and his patient?

A. They are each concerned with different aspects of a woman's life. In both instances, however, the lawyer and the psychologist assume the role of professional counselors and should act as respectful advisors, not predators.

Fox asked Dr. Baker what she was charging for her testifying. When Baker said: "I view my appearance as rendering a public service. I'm not charging a fee," Fox said her direct was concluded.

As Duffy rose to commence his cross, McGuire signaled him to remain seated. "It is after four. I allowed extra time to Ms. Fox to prepare for cross of your expert and will extend the same courtesy to you. We'll begin tomorrow at eleven and wrap up the case by the end of the day. At least that is my hope."

As they left the hearing room, Morrissey was dejected. He mumbled to Duffy, "The damn shrink's testimony was persuasive. It was based on experience and not on a cockamamie theory of brain patterns."

Duffy agreed Baker was a good witness but spotted a weakness. "She's not seeking compensation. You get what you pay for. I'll bet Baker didn't do her homework. I don't care how much experience she has, this case is particular to you. McGuire is not going to decide on general principles."

But Duffy felt like crap too. There was a chance he could save Peter's ass, but it was slender and getting thinner by the hour.

22

Morrissey and Duffy read the Bates and Brodsky article and reviewed Wolfe's testimony. When the hearing resumed, Duffy started tentatively with Dr. Baker, sticking his toe in the water before plunging in.

Q. I gathered from your testimony that you relied on your experience relating to abuse by therapists. Am I correct?
A. No, you are not. I relied on my experience, of course, but Ms. Dixon is my patient. I combined what she told me with the many other cases dealing with abuse. Her case fit within the general pattern. A woman in trouble seeks help from a therapist, or in this case, from a lawyer. The professional who takes advantage of her to satisfy his corrupt and perverted psyche reveals a nature incompatible with the fiduciary position he occupies. He will do it again and again unless the penalty imposed makes repetition impossible.
Q. You learned Ms. Dixon's side of the story directly from her. Did you ask to interview Mr. Morrissey?
A. No, I did not. Nor, may I add, did I see any necessity to do so. As I said in answer to your first question, the pattern of abuse was clearly and unmistakably present.
Q. Well, I guess judges are not nearly as perspicacious as therapists. Judges insist on hearing both sides before judging. Let's put to one side interviewing Mr. Morrissey. Were you aware he testified under oath that Molly Dixon seduced him?
A. Yes. Ms. Fox summarized his testimony. We both believed it was a pack of lies.

Duffy could have moved to strike "we both believed etc." but why? At some point McGuire would recognize Baker had crossed the line between expert witness and advocate. Furthermore, Duffy liked her answer. She had not read the testimony but accepted the Fox's take.

> Q. In your vast experience, have you come across a situation in which the patient seduces the therapist?
> A. Yes. They are rare. It is my belief that even in those situations, the therapist creates the atmosphere leading the patient to seek solace in his arms.

McGuire interrupted. "Was the therapist seduced by the patient booted out of the profession?"

"No, Judge McGuire, the therapist was fined and warned that a second occurrence, even one in which he was seduced, would lead to expulsion. I was on the panel. The therapist was handsome. He resembled Cary Grant."

McGuire said, "Please continue, Mr. Duffy."

> Q. In the case of the good-looking therapist, did the panel hear both sides, the therapist and the patient?
> A. Yes. The patient admitted she wanted to make love with him. She didn't file a complaint. You want to know who did? Her husband.
> Q. In the law admissions take many different forms. Would you say that a patient who demonstrated on her therapist's finger the many tricks she uses to arouse her husband's penis was admitting she wanted to make love to her therapist?
> A. It would all depend upon whether the therapist asked the patient to demonstrate, or whether the patient initiated the act. Molly told me about the finger nonsense. Morrissey insisted on it. Otherwise he would not represent her. While she was demonstrating—under coercion I should add—Morrissey's other hand was under the table stroking Molly's thigh.
> Q. To reach that conclusion, you would have to know both sides of the controversy. Did you read Mr. Morrissey's testimony as recorded in the trial record of this case? (Duffy gave thought to adding, "answer the question yes or no." McGuire,

Duffy sensed, was agitated by Baker's long-winded answers. *Better to let her go on and perhaps dig her own grave.*
A. There was no need for me to read Morrissey's testimony. Molly told me he insisted on a demonstration. I believe her, and Ms. Fox told me what Morrissey said. A typical response from a typical predator.

"Dr. Baker, you could have and should have answered the question 'yes or no,'" McGuire interrupted. "I recorded your answer as no. I know you want to help Ms. Dixon, but the polemics aren't helping. I will decide on the record. Non-responsive answers will not influence me. Carry on, Mr. Duffy."

Q. You know, of course, that your patient had an affair with her next-door neighbor. They met solely as lovers. Do you believe Ms. Dixon encouraged the act that followed?
A. No. She was again taken advantage of. She was recently divorced and assaulted by Morrissey. She was in no condition to give her consent.
Q. Do you know whether the affair with neighbor Charlie Monk took place before or after the sexual encounter with Mr. Morrissey?
A. It occurred after. No, I spoke too soon. It occurred before. I have my notes of sessions with Ms. Dixon. I'd like to consult them.

"I'm sorry Dr. Baker," McGuire said. "You should be prepared before you testify. No, I've changed my mind. You testified Morrissey's assault paved the way for the neighbor. I think timing is important. Please check your notes. We'll take a thirty-minute recess."

After the recess Dr. Baker said the affair occurred before Molly met Morrissey. She apologized for her error but added: "The neighbor was not a professional, so his conduct is not sanctioned. Morrissey is a professional. He had no right to take advantage of Molly."

Dr. Baker was so eager to stick a dagger into Morrissey, she ignored McGuire's advice. The weapon hit a target, but it was not Morrissey.

Q. Ms. Dixon had a passionate session with her brother-in-law. Was that Mr. Morrissey's fault?

A. It's not a question of one act causing another. Molly was vulnerable. All three took advantage of her.

Q. I take it you didn't speak with either Mr. Monk or the brother-in-law. Am I correct?

A. Yes, you are. There was no reason to speak with them. I knew what their response would be. "It was the victim's fault. Her sweater was too tight; her skirt too short."

Q. How many other men has Ms. Dixon carried on with either before or after she met Mr. Morrissey?

A. You must know, Mr. Duffy, what a patient tells her therapist is privileged. The one exception comes if the patient confides an intent to inflict bodily harm on another. Then the analyst has a duty to inform the authorities. I say you should know, because you defended a psychologist who failed to make the required report. Despite your talents the psychologist was convicted.

Duffy remembered the case. It had sent a chill through the analytic society. Was she attempting to flatter, or was it a dig? There was a touch of sarcasm. In either event it wouldn't sit well with McGuire.

Q. I'm not interested in names, just numbers. How many, Dr. Baker?

"Objection," Fox said too loud.

"I'll sustain the objection. It really doesn't matter, Mr. Duffy. If Ms. Dixon had twenty affairs, that wouldn't excuse Mr. Morrissey. It might, however, go to the penalty. Privileges in criminal cases are protected, and no inference can be drawn from the claim. In civil actions a claim of privilege may be sustained but an inference will be drawn. But it doesn't matter. We have to decide on Mr. Morrissey's conduct, not Ms. Dixon's.

Q. Dr. Wolfe was called as an expert witness. Did you determine that his opinions were invalid based on Ms. Fox's summary?

A. Apparently Dr. Wolfe said Mr. Morrissey was not likely to repeat his assault on clients, because his brain would restrain him. It's an interesting theory but refuted time and again by recurrence after recurrence. Bad habits more strongly influence conduct than the ethereal willpower. Ms. Fox told me Wolfe was a hired gun. I checked with others and heard the same thing. It's a shame professionals misuse their expertise for profit rather than to assist a court in arriving at a just decision.

Q. Did you read Dr. Wolfe's testimony, yes or no?

A. I didn't have to. His opinion is for sale.

Duffy looked at McGuire, who showed his frustration by shaking his head. Duffy let the matter rest. "My cross is concluded," he said.

When McGuire asked whether there were any more witnesses, Lisa said no, and Duffy said he planned to offer seven letters in the nature of character evidence as he had mentioned in his opening statement.

"In that case," McGuire said, "the evidentiary phase on the merits is over. After I resolve the disputed facts, I will reach the issue of penalty. I will consider at that time whether the letters will be helpful. This is a serious proceeding holding dire consequences for Mr. Morrissey. If I find against him, it would be my inclination to allow Mr. Morrissey to make as complete a record as he wished. I therefore request that you hand copies of the letters to Ms. Fox as soon as possible. I want her to have an opportunity to respond."

Duffy found them in his briefcase and turned a set over to Lisa.

McGuire thanked both attorneys for their superb conduct of the case. "I know a lot about trial work as I was active in the field when I was young. I do not believe that I could have done a better job."

McGuire instructed the parties to exchange briefs in two weeks. And he requested that they concentrate on the facts. "After I have reviewed the briefs, we will meet again for oral argument, but it will differ from the usual. Instead of arguments I will ask questions about areas which give me pause. There will be no formal argument unless I change my mind. I'll alert you only if there's a change."

As Peter left the courtroom, a future loomed before him that he had not contemplated until today. He needed a vacation, a change of scenery. He also needed to find a place to spend his retirement years, because they might be forced on him in two weeks. In the meantime he just needed to get away from all this stress. The prospect of his career ending had turned Peter's thoughts toward his final years. Who would care for him when he could no longer care for himself?

That night he decided he would go to Miami, which several friends had told him about, and he had always avoided. The next morning he booked a flight and a hotel and left at the end of the day. He read a guidebook on the plane and looked forward to the warm climate, the sea, and the international flavor of the city. Miami was a vibrant city, or so he had heard. There were excellent restaurants and nightclubs, an opera and ballet company and frequent appearances from the Cleveland Symphony Orchestra. It seemed like a good place to visit and maybe a good place to live.

Peter spent the two weeks between the exchange of briefs and oral argument in South Beach, in a revitalized section of what used to be an old-folks home populated by blue-haired widows hobbling around on walkers. The old folks were gone. South Beach was a swinging, beautiful, young people's playground.

Peter stayed at Canyon Ranch, a new hotel and spa. He adopted a healthful routine. Every morning he took long walks on the beach. He swam laps in the hotel's Olympic-sized pool, had a massage, and then ate his first of two healthy meals of the day. The hotel had a special spa menu featuring low cholesterol and low fat foods. After a nap, with the help of a cab driver, he toured South Beach and the neighboring towns. After a week of touring, he engaged a real estate broker and looked at condos. The supply was plentiful, and the market was soft. He liked Aventura by the Sea, an upscale retirement complex for independent living fifteen minutes from South Beach; it was coupled with a fully staffed hospital for what was styled "end of life care." Although he was too anxious about the disbarment hearing to serve his psychosexual needs, he was well aware of the abundance of women at Aventura. A good hunting ground. The time, however, was not right to purchase an apartment. Peter put Aventura on hold.

When he boarded the plane for New York, Peter's mind and body were in good shape. He had lost five pounds and found it easy to smile. He was happy. His mood changed as soon as his plane touched down at JFK. He became tense and agitated. His fate would be decided in the next few days.

23

The committee's brief repeated Molly's direct testimony, and in summarizing Dr. Baker's testimony, repeated it all over again. "Molly had nothing to gain by testifying falsely," the brief argued, "and a lot to lose by deceiving her therapist." When the brief turned to Morrissey and Duffy, it oozed vitriol, claiming that they "lied through their teeth" to conceal the full extent of Morrissey's unlawful behavior.

"Morrissey," the brief said, "denied plying Molly with gin and wine. It was she who wanted more, and he, who cautioned restraint. His complicit lawyer flaunted what he knew or should have known was a misleading Friar's Club bill. When the truth came out, Morrissey did not recant, nor did his lawyer withdraw the deceptive document."

The brief excoriated Morrissey for producing and Duffy for extolling the evidentiary value of the inscription on Molly's photograph and asked: "Is it likely that a lawyer who has made a career out of representing crooks, failed to ask Morrissey how the writing came into being? When the truth emerged that Morrissey was the author, once again these two lawyers remained silent. Morrissey should be punished for violating rule ten of the code and punished severely for his additional offense, perjury."

"Damn," Duffy said, "the Fox has nailed us to the cross. Why weren't you square with me? 'Look what she wrote on her photo. Here's the bill. See no wine.'

"Bill, I can't remember whether two years ago, I had a glass of wine. You asked for the bill and for Molly's photo. Did I know that wine was complimentary that night? I didn't think about it. As far as Molly's inscription is concerned, she signed it. How can she attack something she signed?

"Bullshit! You should have told me the words were yours, and I should have known. Trauma was the giveaway. She barely knows what the word means. You use booze as an elixir d'amour. It's part of your modus operandi. Candy is nice, but liquor is quicker. McGuire can figure that out. We're stuck."

"What's next? Can we still make a deal?"

"Yes and no. The time to deal is when you're ahead. Berman did a great job on our brief. It hit Molly and Baker hard. Let's wait for the argument and hope McGuire jumpstarts settlement. Judges welcome settlements as they save them from writing a decision. We may be surprised, but don't get your hopes up. McGuire's an old-fashioned guy. He doesn't like personal attacks. There's a chance the Fox's vituperative brief will backfire."

Although the hearing room was air conditioned, on the day of the final argument, Morrissey's shirt was soaked with perspiration. The tension was heightened by McGuire's late appearance. When he arrived he looked only at Lisa. "You're up first. Don't read anything into my questions. I will ask the same questions to Mr. Duffy with a one hundred and eighty degree spin. Ready? If I were to find that Ms. Dixon propositioned Mr. Morrissey, would disbarment be the appropriate penalty?"

"Your honor," Fox said, "the Appellate Division in its wisdom adopted a rule requiring disbarment. And the rule is a wise one. A woman may be emotionally shocked by divorce. She may see it as rejection of herself as a companion, a lover, a mate. To regain confidence, she may seek solace in the arms of another. The law cannot protect her from men who take advantage of her weakened condition, but it can and does protect her from her lawyer. This safety net should not be ripped apart because of sympathy. Morrissey showed his true colors. He is a menace to women. His name should be stricken from the list of lawyers.

"I recognize that women differ. Many treat divorce as a release from bonds that strangle. They revel in their newfound freedom. Several testified in this proceeding. They are not in need of protection from lawyers who are sexual predators. They are able to take care of themselves. Molly is representative of a different genre. I do not seek disbarment to vindicate the assault on Molly but to protect the Mollies to come."

"Your answer gives rise to my next question," the referee said.

"Would it be permissible for me, within the framework of the code, to craft a remedy that would allow Mr. Morrissey to remain a lawyer, but at the same time, protect women? Suppose I were to bar him from representing women in matrimonial actions? Please, once again, do not read more into my questions than what they are intended to do—that is to provoke comments. Would such a remedy satisfy the Grievance Committee?"

Sophisticated lawyers never disagree straight-out with a judge. Rather, after saying how wise his suggestion is, they offer a reason why the judge's "brilliant" suggestion should not apply to the case at hand. A typical response might be: "What a Solomonic solution! The only problem is one of enforcement. Mr. Morrissey, if left to practice as a lawyer, may also serve his obsession in an indirect manner. He will still come in contact with women in divorce proceedings and, as he has done in the past, bring shame upon the profession."

Fox was neither sophisticated, nor did she dissemble. If she thought the other party was wrong, she said so. She was principled, and her principles ruled her life.

"The rules do not allow second chances. Sexual predators are punished. And the punishment is more than a slap on the wrist. Lawyers are held to a standard higher than the ordinary man. They are fiduciaries in their dealings with their clients. When they violate the rules, the punishment must be real, not only because the erring fiduciary deserves it but to set an example for all members of the bar. I oppose any penalty other than disbarment."

Duffy thought about McGuire's proposal. Morrissey had built a lucrative practice representing wives. Referring attorneys would demand a reason for the switch. "Say Peter, why are you willing to represent husbands and saying no to wives?" The truth would hurt business. His practice would most likely wither and die.

If McGuire was disappointed in Fox's response, he made no sign. He continued his questioning. "In matters other than divorce, lawyers are not barred from consensual relations provided they have not applied coercion, intimidation, or undue influence. Only in matrimonial actions are consensual relations punished. Are there any authorities or law review articles providing reasons for tolerance of consensual sexual relations in all areas except matrimonial?"

"Yes, the provisions governing sexual relations are part of the ABA Model Code. They represent a consensus of bar associations throughout the country. The Appellate Division lifted our rule directly from the model code. Almost all fifty states have adopted this very provision. By enacting without change the model code provision, the states have placed their imprimatur on the no-sex rule in matrimonial actions.

"In other actions, as Your Honor has noted, the draftsmen of the code have relaxed the rule, but even there, sex between a lawyer and a client is discouraged. In a report written to explain the very point raised by Your Honor, the draftsmen of the rule warn that sexual relations raise a potential conflict of interest. The discussion is quoted in full in my brief. I will read a part:

"Even if a sexual relationship is consensual... conflict of interest problems...make such relationships dangerous. If the couple breaks up or has a fight during the lawyer-client relationship, [it] may seriously affect the representation—perhaps so seriously that the jilted lover files a grievance claim or a legal malpractice claim. Therefore, if a lawyer's lover needs legal help, the safest course is to find another lawyer for the sexual partner, especially if the couple is not married or has a rocky marriage."

"I read that section in your brief," McGuire said and then added, "I even read the entire background to the model rule. I interpreted the advice to protect lawyers, not clients. My question remains unanswered: Is there any explanation for the different treatment depending on the nature of the action?"

"Yes there is." Undaunted, Fox added, "That, too, is quoted in two separate sections of my brief. I'm sure Your Honor read my brief carefully, but to be sure I will read the relevant part

"As discussed in the commentary, the rule does not prohibit dating, drinking, dancing, or dinner. But sexual attractions and emotional passions are hard to control—Hollywood tries to teach us this every day—and if sexual relations ensue, it will be no defense for an attorney to say: 'It was supposed to be just a friendship. I didn't mean for it to go this far.' Nor will it be any defense for the lawyer to say, 'It was the client's idea.' The rule says that a lawyer must not begin sexual relations with any domestic relations client, no matter whose idea it was. No sex means no sex."

"Ms. Fox," McGuire said, "I read your brief and the report of the Milonas Committee recommending the no-sex rule. My issue is: the Appellate Division did not enact the commentary. Is the rule as enacted as absolute as the commentary, or is there wiggle room?"

"Legislative history is the Rosetta Stone in resolving ambiguous rules. Here the rule is clear on its face. There is no need to look to legislative history to interpret the no-sex rule. But if you were in doubt, the commentary makes it explicit: sex, even sex induced by the client, is prohibited. This case is a clear example of conduct prohibited by law. There is no need to interpret. It is clear on its face. I cannot conceive how it could be plainer. There is absolutely no wiggle room."

"The law," McGuire said, "as Shakespeare's Portia spoke, must temper justice with mercy. Assume a lawyer in the course of representing a woman in a matrimonial action coerces, intimidates, and deceives her into having sex with him. Suppose the same circumstances, but that the lawyer is seduced by the client. Is it your position that a judge must impose the same punishment on both?"

"The rule's focus is on the attorney's conduct, not the client's. When two lawyers have sexual relations with their clients under the different circumstances posited by Your Honor, the punishment should be the same."

McGuire asked Fox other probing questions, but his attempt to wring a concession failed. Lisa was unwavering. Only disbarment. Any lesser punishment would be appealed by the committee.

Judges despised being reversed, even ones appointed for a special proceeding. McGuire did not want to disbar Morrissey but knew his decision could be appealed by either side up to the Appellate Division. The only way out was through a settlement. Fox would not give an inch. McGuire intuited that Richard Stern, Fox's superior, might be flexible. At the right opportunity, he would call on Stern.

It was now Duffy's turn to be questioned. Before beginning McGuire granted a thirty-minute recess. Morrissey and Duffy huddled. Duffy proposed that they build on McGuire's suggestion of limiting Morrissey's practice to men into a settlement proposal. "Could you live with it? It's better to survive in a limited way than risk disbarment."

Morrissey initially thought the proposal was unworkable. "In New York a divorce lawyer specializing in representing wives can't turn on a dime and switch sides. At least I can't. The husbands' divorce bar hates me. They would detect I was wounded, sense blood, and attack. It would effectively end my career."

"You have no choice. Even if McGuire accepts your version of the facts, you're doomed. Either McGuire, or if he refuses, the Appellate Division may disbar you. It's better to take a different tack than to capsize and drown. Give it a shot. I'm far from certain we can persuade Fox to accept anything less than disbarment, but I'll try to steer the questioning toward a settlement."

"In about two weeks," Peter said, "I'm scheduled to discuss the proposed change in the divorce law at the City Bar Association. I'm thinking of declining the honor. But if we settle on terms barring me from representing women, perhaps I could make a virtue out of necessity."

Peter decided to try his newly created strategy on Duffy. "The new law allows for no-fault divorces, but it comes at a cost to the better-healed party, generally the husband. Alimony, which made it attractive to represent wives, is out along with fault. Instead, a new concept maintenance is imposed at two different stages: before the judgment of divorce is granted and after. Suppose I say that it will be more challenging to represent the husband than the wife. I'll add that a conflict of interest may be present by lawyers who represent both husbands and wives. For example, an interpretation of maintenance pushed by a lawyer in representing a husband may come back to haunt him when representing the wife in a different case."

"Peter, I think you're on to something," Duffy said, "Conflict is the lawyer's trump card. It provides the best reason for turning down a case. I only represent the accused. Conflicts arise between co-conspirators. No lawyer will represent both. Suppose one wants to make a deal and rat on the other? That happens a lot. What's the lawyer's advice who represents both? 'Turn against my other client to spare your hide?' I choose the one with the deepest pockets. The ones I turn down believe I have done so for ethical reasons. Potential conflict provides an easy passage to representing only husbands. But let's talk about my answers to McGuire's questions."

Peter stayed with his thought. "One more addition before we get back to business. I'm thinking about throwing a dinner for lawyers who have referred cases to me and others who might. How about the Fox? Do you think she would refer husbands? Maybe I should invite her to the dinner?"

"Very funny, Morrissey, but the case is not settled. I'll work hard to get McGuire to impose settlement on the Fox. I've heard judges say: 'If you don't accept settlement, I'll write a decision that you cannot reverse on appeal.' The threat works. I'll put it in McGuire's bonnet."

When court resumed, McGuire's first question was the other side of the one he asked Fox. "If I were to accept Ms. Dixon's testimony as corroborated by Dr. Baker, what do you believe the remedy should be?"

Duffy deflected it. Remedy was his weakest point. He would try to turn the case into an evidentiary dispute where he had a chance. "In all trials the evidence is crucial. Otherwise what's the purpose of having a trial? The testimony of the two parties in this case, the only ones who were present, are poles apart. It is a classic case of 'he said, she said.' Neither you, nor I, or even Ms. Fox will ever know what was said at dinner at the Friars and how the affair progressed from there. Why? We were not there.

"I believe my client, but I also believe that he and Molly have been bitten by the verisimilitude bug. It emits poison that makes each believe he or she is telling the truth by tempering what happened by the way they want it to have happened. This is not a new phenomenon or one peculiar to Peter or Molly. It strikes all of us. I see it all the time in my practice.

"Some years ago, I collected old newspapers covering the Civil War. The papers, printed on high quality rag more than one hundred and fifty years ago, were better preserved than yesterday's *Times*. I purchased newspapers from southern and northern editions covering the same battles. The reporters, who had no animus to deceive, recounted versions as different as Peter's and Molly's. How could professional journalists, eyewitnesses to the same event, write two dissimilar descriptions of a battle? The answer: they saw and reported what they wanted to see and were blind to the other side. I chalked it up to verisimilitude. I have come to believe that truth is relative, and absolute truth is a rarity.

"We once believed the Earth was flat. Then Copernicus and Galileo persuaded us otherwise. We believed the sun revolved around the Earth. As you know, Mr. Referee, I could go on and on. Yesterday's truths are today's falsehoods. But let's come back to our hearing.

"We will never know this side of heaven what happened over dinner at the Friar's. And yet the Grievance Committee lawyer would hang Mr. Morrissey regardless of what happened. Isn't it better? Doesn't it make more sense, in the words of the Gilbert and Sullivan operetta, 'to make the punishment fit the crime?'

"You implicitly suggested a fair resolution. 'Bar Morrissey from representing women.' I like it. Assuming about-to-be-divorced women need protection from this *ogre* Morrissey, your proposal provides the necessary protection. It also guarantees that if Molly seduced Peter the way she seduced her neighbor and brother-in-law and God only knows how many others, Peter will not be punished for an offense that most men would be tempted to commit.

"I've heard judges who favored a settlement sometimes induce agreement by threatening to write a decision that neither side would like and would be appeal- proof.

"If, Mr. McGuire, you want the case settled, I have a suggestion to sweeten the pot, and thereby, make it more agreeable to the committee." By referring to the committee, Duffy sought to anoint Stern, chief counsel, to lead the negotiations. Duffy smiled at both Fox and Stern. Fox made no response. Stern smiled back.

"Well, we're all together in one room," McGuire said. "Ms. Fox and Mr. Stern and Messrs. Duffy and Morrissey and no one else. So let's begin. Let's go off the record. Our discussion is confidential.

"Settlement discussions will not be fruitful if one side is irrevocably opposed. Let me make this clear: *I want the case settled*." McGuire issued the very threat Duffy had suggested. "If it is not, I'll write a decision that will stand up on appeal. I have no doubt I can do that. Mr. Stern, you are the head of the office. You have sat quietly throughout the proceeding. Now it's your turn. Is your office prepared to negotiate?"

Stern, who was present throughout the trial, felt the pressure. He took McGuire's threat at face value. In this case he was the judge and jury. If McGuire found that Peter was telling the truth and Molly's testimony was fabricated, his findings could not be set aside except for egregious error. Morrissey's version was reinforced by Dixon's other peccadilloes, and a finding for him, would be well within McGuire's discretion. Would the Appellate Division disbar Morrissey if McGuire found that Morrissey was seduced? Stern thought it unlikely. He asked for a short recess so that he could consult with Fox. When court resumed he said: "We are always prepared to discuss settlement and reach an agreement that's in the best interest of the public. Far from being intransigent, at my first meeting with Mr. Duffy, I proposed a settlement. I asked him to get back to me. I thought he would. So certain were Ms. Fox and I that the case would be settled that we put it on the back burner.

In my next contact with Mr. Duffy, I asked to adjourn the hearing to allow time to negotiate. He refused. Following Ms. Fox's strong answers to your questions, we got the first indication that Duffy and Morrissey are willing to settle."

"Let's have an end to finger pointing," McGuire said. "Mr. Duffy, you mentioned 'sweetening the pot.' Let's hear from you."

"Mr. Morrissey has twenty-three pending cases. All of his clients are women. He cannot, consistent with his professional obligations, abandon his clients. He will agree, however, to assign responsibility to lawyers in his employ. He will supervise and strategize with them. He will not meet with female clients either alone or with others. He will limit further matters to representing men. He will provide the committee with a list of pending cases. As he adds new cases, he will supplement the schedule. This agreement will remain in effect for ten years. After that Mr. Morrissey will no longer be under any restriction. I analogize this part of the settlement to probation, which always has a time limit. No one is ever sentenced to probation for life.

"Safe Horizon performs support services for women abused by domestic violence. Mr. Morrissey will donate twenty-five thousand dollars to the organization. I analogize his contribution to a fine. Mr. Morrissey has a long history with Safe Horizon. It has been his major outside interest for over thirty five years. He supports Safe Horizon with money but also with his time and attention.

"In my opening I spoke about his work on behalf of abused women. I said if penalty became an issue I would offer letters attesting to his dedicated services. Penalty will be resolved by the proposed settlement. If not, the submission will bear on that issue. I request to place in the record seven letters. As instructed by you, copies have been given to Ms. Fox. One is from Robert Morgenthau. Another is from the executive head of Safe Horizon. The remaining five are from victims. They provide a snapshot of the dedicated activities performed by Mr. Morrissey."

McGuire read the letters and admitted them on the limited issue of penalty in the event settlement was not reached. "It would be harsh," Duffy said, "to disbar a lawyer who has helped poor women for over thirty-five years for an offense that lasted a few hours."

"Well, Mr. Stern," McGuire said. "What do you think of Mr. Duffy's proposal?"

Stern asked for a recess. When court resumed Fox remained seated, and Stern took the podium. "A settlement proposal must pass four steps. My office must recommend it; Your Honor must approve; the six-member panel appointing you must approve; and finally the Appellate Division must approve. The committee approves, provided the restrictions on Mr. Morrissey's practice are implemented immediately. He must also alert the other attorneys in his office to the terms of the proposed settlement. The ten years will run from the time the agreement is approved by the Appellate Division. Mr. Morrissey will have sixty days after approval to make his contribution to Safe Horizon."

Duffy nodded his approval. McGuire congratulated the parties for the expert manner in which the proceedings were conducted. He made a point of smiling at Lisa. She did not smile back. Her arms were crossed, and her face emitted an angry look.

Since the day the deal was agreed to was Friday, McGuire wished the participants a well-deserved, restful weekend. Recalling what he thought was a witticism from his early years as a lawyer, he said: "Settlements are like a box of eggs. If they sit around too long, they start to give off an odor. Get the agreement to me by Wednesday. Good afternoon, lady and gentlemen."

Peter emerged from the hearing room in high spirits. The case was over; his career alive. "I'm a lucky man," he said to himself over and over. Lucky but changed. Life before would not resume. Life after was going to look different. Everything about it would be different, including him.

Lisa held her tongue until they were out of earshot. When she was alone with Stern, she called him a "weak-livered sissy." Two weeks after the settlement became final, Lisa resigned from the staff of the Grievance Committee.

24

Morrissey was too busy to have the 'restful weekend' suggested by McGuire.

He spent Saturday and Sunday in his office mapping out his future. He reviewed his pending cases and reassigned them to one of his five lawyers, all of whom were men. Many years ago Peter had employed a female associate. She left after two years, threatening to sue him for sexual harassment. Peter had paid a lot to prevent a suit. To avoid a reoccurrence, he hired only males.

Morrissey spent Sunday afternoon reviewing his bar association lecture. With his labors done, he had an early dinner and went to sleep. Purged from his brain were all images of the Fox, Molly, McGuire, Duffy, his clients who had testified, and the experts. The trial was flushed down the toilet.

He smiled at himself while shaving and mumbled, "You buried your past. How many guys get the chance to start all over? I won't miss my female clients. My hot-shot male clients will have friends who have friends. They'll be young and attractive. Maybe I'll develop taste? No more worries about the canons of ethics. If my clients don't provide leads, I'll go on cruises. I won't travel alone. I've got bachelor friends. We'll find women. I'll also spend more time with my niece and her family. Families provide warmth. Perhaps, I'll try marriage again. Marry a woman with a family. The possibilities are endless. Hey, you know what? I'm free." Peter eagerly awaited what he hoped would become a new life, different from the old…and better.

On Monday he met with his staff. All were "associates," a euphemism for attorneys who were employees, not partners. In most firms an associate could aspire to become a partner. Not in Peter's firm. He was upfront about his policy. He told all prospective hires that as long as they worked hard and the firm thrived, they could expect to be well compensated, but they would not make partner.

Peter's no-partner decision was based partly on his own experience at Cahill, Gordon and scuttlebutt from other lawyers. Partners spent too much time wrestling over the division of the spoils. This was especially true around year's end, when bonuses and next year's draws were determined. The squabbling lasted for several weeks into the New Year. When the splits were released in mid-January, the battle was renewed. Bruised egos created ill will as partners argued why their share should be more than others.

One firm, having hundreds of partners, sought to deflate the conflagration by assigning one partner to make all compensation decisions and forbidding any partner from disclosing his share. *They're not partners*, Morrissey thought, *only the guy making the decision is. Why dissemble and call it a partnership? Its monarchal rule over a bunch of serfs who hold a meaningless and powerless title.*

Morrissey encouraged his associates to go out on their own. When they left his employ and started their own practice, Peter referred cases to them and provided start-up loans.

The associates harbored no rancor. The door was always open for them to leave with Peter's blessing. While waiting to make the transition to their own practice, the lawyers received generous salaries and bonuses. They considered it fair that Peter retained the profits. After all, he was the rainmaker, and unlike many rainmakers, he worked hard. They were loyal and respected him.

Morrissey was now faced with a difficult office task. He had to inform his lawyers about the trial and the restrictions limiting future cases. To insure support and prevent a mass exodus, both matters had to be presented in a positive light. Peter decided to deemphasize the problem areas by distributing an outline of his upcoming lecture, with a request for advice and assistance. Attention would focus on the lecture, not the shift to representing men. The disbarment trial would be discussed as a footnote. He would proclaim the men-only practice as an exciting new chapter for the firm.

On Monday morning Peter and his five associates were seated in the firm's conference room. Peter began by assigning the firm's twenty-three cases to one, or where the case was complicated, two lawyers. The assignments followed the responsibility over cases assumed by the staff during the disbarment hearing.

After assigning each case, its status was reviewed with emphasis on the tactics and strategy designed to achieve the best possible result. "We're part of a team," Peter said. "Discuss and consult freely with each other, and don't forget to come to me."

Peter next turned to the trial and settlement.

"In an off-hand remark, Duffy said I will not meet with our female clients in existing cases nor accept new cases representing wives. The committee didn't ask for that, but since Duffy said it, I'm bound. It's really for my own protection." Laughing, he said, "Women find me too attractive! As you know, the code frowns on fraternizing with clients. You'll just have to tell clients who want to see me that I'm otherwise engaged, but that you will discuss their case with me. If a client is insistent or in case of emergency, to hell with what Duffy said, my loyalty to the client comes first."

The young lawyers nodded knowingly; none, however, smiled. Among themselves all condemned Peter's lecherous behavior but none had the temerity to speak up.

Peter made a note to add an exception to the "no meeting with client clause" in the settlement agreement. In an emergency he could meet with a female client.

"We would have won hands down," Peter continued with a statement he knew was not entirely true, "if the case had gone to decision. The committee's case was full of holes."

To exonerate himself, he tore into Molly. Saving face was more important than telling the truth. "Molly Dixon seduced me. She also had sexual relations with her brother-in-law, a neighbor, and God only knows how many others. After her divorce case was over, she called and asked to see me again. I refused. She got back at me by filing a complaint. I've learned my lesson. No cavorting with female clients. The hearing was expensive, so fellas, be careful. No sex with a client.

"I agreed to the settlement, because the terms imposed were, in light of the change in the law, exactly what I had planned for the firm. I believe a good divorce lawyer should not work both sides of the street. A point successfully urged on behalf of a husband might come back to haunt you in another case where you are representing the wife. Better to avoid potential conflicts by limiting the practice to either husbands or wives. I had previously chosen wives. Their side was more challenging. Now that New York has agreed to join the other forty-nine states in adopting no-fault divorce, the husband's side has sex appeal."

"I don't get it," Joel Bernstein said. "We've got no friends on the other side of the street. We know how to handle wives, but husbands carry different baggage. Wouldn't it make more sense to move slowly? Take both wives and husbands. Test the waters and then decide on a future course. An abrupt shift away from wives carries the risk that we will lose our client base and not be able to replace it."

"Joel, I don't disagree with you but we have no choice. I can't renegotiate a done deal. Suppose in my address to the lawyers assembled at the bar association, I say: 'in order to avoid even the appearance of a conflict, it's better practice for an attorney to represent either husbands or wives.' Then I drop the bomb. Formerly, I represented only wives. Now my practice will be limited to husbands. Duffy said conflict is a lawyer's trump card. It gets you out of all kinds of messes. Lawyers should avoid conflicts. We're going one step further and avoiding even the appearance of a conflict."

"How do we get our message across to the firms feeding us clients?" Henry Greene added. "What do we do if they send us wives? How do we get them to change?"

"It's a problem. Suppose before addressing the lawyers at large, I reward the guys who have fed us cases by inviting them to a private dinner at the Friars. During dinner I'll tell them of my change and ask for their support. Then we'll all march forth to the bar association, where they will see me in a starring role. At the lecture I'll discuss conflicts. To avoid them I'll let the audience know that I will represent only husbands."

"We always looked upon the husband's side as dull," John Harvest said. "Typically, the wife sues. The husband's at fault. We dig and find the evidence. The meat and potatoes are on her side. It's also less lucriferous representing the husband."

Everyone laughed except John. "What does 'lucriferous' mean?" Joel asked.

"Don't you know? I thought my cellmates were literate. It means 'profitable.'"

"So, why not say 'profitable,' which we all know?" Joel asked. "You're a show-off."

Rushing to John's defense, Peter said, "You'll see. Representing husbands will be more 'lucriferous' than wives. The new law eliminates fault and substitutes the husband's income as the critical issue. His lawyer bears the laboring oar; the wife's lawyer has a passive role. You know all about that. You got copies of my law review article and read it. Right?"

All nodded, and several pulled out their copies. "We'll discuss my article and the law a little later. Let's stay on point. This meeting is about how we'll operate. Any questions?"

"Peter, we're ducks out of water," Mark Fitzer said. "We're not corporate lawyers. We've got no experience in valuing speculative compensation arrangements. What's a stock option worth? How do you value a hedge fund guru's contingent fee based on say twenty percent of the profits? How certain are bonuses for investment bankers? In the past we relied on the husband's sworn net worth statement, usually prepared by an accountant. Now we'll have to value speculative forms of compensation. We're neophytes. We're bound to make mistakes."

"Don't worry. If we represent a fat-cat investment banker, we'll hire financial experts. Our client will also help."

"Suppose we don't get the husbands?" Sam Doughty asked. "The faucet is turned off for wives. How do you know we'll get work?"

"Within a year I predict our docket will be full. I will devote one hundred and ten percent of my time building our new practice. I expect you to handle the old, and give me the time to develop the new."

His lawyers all had copies of Peter's article on the change in New York's divorce law, published the prior month in the *Fordham*

Law Review and copies of his lecture notes. Peter held up the bound version of the law review and then quickly put it down. He thought about that day in Dr. Wolfe's office when Wolfe had handed him a copy of the journal containing his article. He was as much an egomaniac as Max Wolfe. *They can skip my article. They provided comments on the draft. No sense commenting on what's already published. I'll direct the meeting toward my lecture notes.*

"Let's skip the article and focus on the lecture," Peter said. "It, I hope, will produce *lucriferous* business for us." Peter smiled warmly on John Harvest. "Let's begin by examining the tactics of our opponent, the wife. What advantages would you seek if, under the new law, you were representing a wife? Then we'll switch to how we can protect the husband. I'm taking notes."

The lawyers discussed tactics to the advantage of the wife and then how to refute the stratagems. As they talked over the ploys, a sense of excitement engulfed the room, along with a feeling of camaraderie, similar to what occurs when close friends embark on a new and difficult adventure. Peter delighted in the discussion, not because it added to his knowledge (he was well aware of the problems the husband's lawyer would face), but because his lawyers enthusiastically embraced their new role as attorneys for the husband. He felt sure there would be no defections.

"Since we'll be beating up on women, should we hire a woman lawyer?" asked Peter. "According to Duffy we can't represent women, but we sure as hell can hire them. It will help our image to have a female attack dog."

"I know a smart woman lawyer who's looking for a job," said Arnold. "Tough as nails. She has nothing but scorn for the dependent female. And Peter, you won't have any problems with her. She's a lesbian." There were hoots and howls.

"None of that," said Peter, "we're a politically correct firm. I'm a member of a committee to legalize same sex marriages. Bring her around."

Joel commented that the lecture was dry. Peter should add spice by discussing the extreme situations pleaded in contested divorces. "When a marriage is dead, the parties can't say the truth:

They hate each other. That's not a ground for divorce. Remember the guy who said he despised the tuna fish casserole his wife fed him three times a week? And her winning reply: 'His doctor said given his weak heart and high blood pressure, red meat was out. The jerk only wanted steak and hamburgers. I fed him tuna fish to save his life.' Divorce denied."

"How about the wife," John said, "who claimed her husband had not talked to her in five years, leaving Post-it notes all over the house? I remember his devastating reply: 'Post-it? She hid. Notes were the only way I could communicate. I'd have preferred to speak, but I couldn't find her.' Divorce denied."

"How about the husband," Henry said, "who claimed his wife never bathed? The body odor was suffocating. She was very fat. When she came to the office, I thought she stank, but she was our client so I chalked it off to the power of suggestion. If only the judge had sat close enough to sniff her, we might have lost that case. Instead, the judge bought the wife's defense: 'I bathed every day. Use deodorant and splash Chanel No. 5 all over me. If only my husband would have come close, his olfactory senses, assuming they're working, would show how sweet I smell.' Divorce denied."

"Then after the funny stuff," John said, "you can segue into the new law and say all three divorces would now be granted. Look, you've a good catch phrase. If one party hates the other, why should the law force them to stay married? With our amended divorce law, New York has entered the twenty-first century."

Peter agreed to add humor and show how contrived attempts had boomeranged. "It will be great to try divorce actions on the merits," he said. "It will be a whole new day in New York."

On the morning of the lecture, Peter was exuberant. Out with the wife, in with the commander in chief. He'd lose his locked-in sex mates. Fox had been mostly right. Rejected by their husbands, they were weak, thrilled by his sexual advance and happy to comply. They looked upon him as Moses leading them to the Promised Land. If, along the way, there was a stop for hanky-panky, it was a pleasant interlude.

Other women had to be wooed. He had neither the time nor the patience. Seducing a non-client was hard work. Hard work? Who was he kidding? He had had no success whatsoever with women other than his clients. His stable of male clients might, however, provide leads to willing females. Some of his male clients would be having affairs. *Perhaps, they'll fix me up? I'll have stature and cachet. A lawyer representing a tycoon in a divorce case.* He laughed at himself. *Better check the code to see if it proscribes against using clients as pimps.*

Was he a new man or the same old operator up to new tricks?

The Friars has a reputation for serving comfort food, unhealthy, but delicious. That, together with drinks, all on Morrissey, provided an inducement too good to be turned down. Although none of the lawyers who referred cases to Morrissey were divorce specialists, almost all attended the pre-lecture dinner. He was determined to win them over. He spared no expense.

Before dinner, Peter gave a snapshot of the new divorce law. He mentioned his role and that Governor Patterson had given him the pen, when in 2010, he had signed the bill. Peter discussed the importance of a solid grasp of business and finance. "The dispute will center on the party earning the dough, usually the husband. In determining the amount the husband should pay, the court will need lots of help, since there are no precedents. I want to avoid urging a point in one case where I'm representing the husband and attacking it in another where I'm on the side of the wife. To avoid even the appearance of a conflict, I will only accept new cases on behalf of husbands."

The purpose of the dinner was twofold. Peter wanted to remind lawyers who had referred clients to him that he was the top matrimonial lawyer. He also needed to explain his change from representing wives in a way that would cast no suspicion on the true reason. Satisfied that he had achieved both goals, Peter thanked the group for their past kindness in referring their clients. "I hope you have heard no complaints," Peter said somewhat nervously, "and that we will continue to do business. I also hope that you will come to the lecture. It's a quick and easy way to become familiar with the new law. Don't think, however, that after the lecture you'll know enough to handle a divorce. You won't. Your clients will still need me. You will, though, acquire a heads-up on the new law. As for getting to Forty-Fourth Street, I've hired a bus to take us there. If anyone is kosher, ask the waiter to serve you fish."

Justin Cooper, the president of the City Bar Association, waited until last-minute arrivals were seated, and the lecture hall was quiet. He introduced himself, then Peter. Cooper anointed Peter "the dean of the matrimonial bar." He commended Morrissey for his dedicated service in getting New York to join the rest of the country in changing "our restrictive divorce law to no-fault." "Peter Morrissey," Cooper said, "was the principal draftsman and advocate of the change. He represents the best in our profession: a paradigm of a lawyer who devotes substantial time for the benefit of the public. We are privileged to have him address us. I trust the large turnout reflects interest in the change in the law and not unrest in marital relations."

Peter thought it a paradox that the head of the organization, which several months earlier was seeking to disbar him, was holding him out as an exemplar of the bar. He guessed that the head of the bar association didn't talk to the tail or whatever part of the body politic the Grievance Committee represented.

The audience clapped as Peter strode to the podium. He thanked Cooper for the wonderful introduction. He added that there were others who "fought with me in the trenches, including the members of the Association's Committee on Matrimonial Law to bring about the change that made New York, the last state in the country to eliminate fault and provide an escape hatch for parties to an unhappy marriage." Peter named each member of the committee and then launched into his talk.

He began on the light note suggested by his staff. He recited the contrived attempts by one spouse to obtain a divorce contested by the other on the ground of cruel and inhuman treatment. The audience laughed at the stories of tuna fish casseroles, the Post-it notes, and the wife's body odor. "I understand why you find these circumstances amusing, but they were a cause of unhappiness. All three marriages had irretrievably broken down. One spouse, unwilling to end the marriage, was able to hold the other captive. Those marriages, suffused with hate, will now be ended, but under circumstances which, unless lawyers and judges are careful, may come at a Draconian cost."

Lecturers delighted in a forum populated by their colleagues as it presented an opportunity to broadcast their expertise. Professionals often had conflicts and needed to refer business. The lecturer hoped he would be kept in mind. There was also a secondary reason: to feed his own ego. The stage was set for Morrissey to shine. He made full use of his opportunity.

"Under the new law, fault is irrelevant. If a marriage is dead, a divorce is granted. The focus will be on maintenance, a new concept replacing alimony. It is designed to enable a spouse with no outside income, married to one with earnings, to survive during the divorce proceedings, and for a reasonable time thereafter.

"In discussing maintenance I intend to depart from the politically correct terms, 'moneyed spouse' and 'non-moneyed spouse'. In fact, the moneyed spouse is generally the husband. There, I said it. During my lecture tonight, for purposes of clarity, I'll reference the parties in the roles they usually occupy."

Peter launched into PowerPoint presentations to illustrate formulas applicable to temporary maintenance. He discussed discretionary factors which might be weighed in setting final maintenance. He lectured on the intricacies of other financial components of a divorce, equitable distribution, and child support. Then he made his striking announcement.

"Conflicts may arise if a lawyer represents husbands and wives in different divorce actions. An argument advanced for a wife in one case may hurt a position taken on behalf of the husband in another case. The law is new. There are few precedents. Pitfalls exist that can turn a law designed to help unhappy couples gain release into a trap that destroys future happiness.

"I've departed from protocol by avoiding euphemisms and referring to the parties as husband and wife. I'm going to make another such statement. From now on to avoid even the appearance of a conflict, I foreswear representing wives and will accept, as clients, only husbands." With that he was done.

The audience clapped. In side discussions many thought Morrissey's decision to represent husbands was freely arrived at and made for ethical reasons. No one in the audience knew the truth, except for Lisa Fox. She sat in a back row and left as soon as the lecture was over.

There were questions from the more than two hundred people in attendance; none Morrissey could not easily answer. The impression, which many times was all that remained from lectures of this sort, was that Morrissey was an experienced divorce lawyer. Wealthy men, contemplating divorce, giving all the pitfalls existing under a new law, would be wise to retain him.

Peter was now in that state of happy tiredness, reached when a stressful event ends well. He took a deep breath as he exited the building, raised his head high, and strode briskly toward his apartment in the Pierre. He knew he did the best he could. Would he get clients? Only time would tell. Meanwhile the winding down of the old would keep him in sauerkraut. Why sauerkraut? He hadn't tasted sauerkraut since he was a young boy, when he was able to digest a hotdog on a bun with mustard and sauerkraut. The reference triggered a recollection of his youth. *Who would have thought that this scrawny kid whose face was covered with pimples and who slept in a small, badly furnished room in a row house in Flatbush would someday be lecturing lawyers and living in an apartment in the sky on Fifth Avenue and Sixty-First Street? Not me.*

As he continued up Fifth, Morrissey's life passed before him. Through hard work and luck, he had achieved many attributes of a successful lawyer. *Yes, I'm proud of myself*, he thought, *but I have no one to be proud of me. Soon I'll be in my elegant apartment all alone. What will have to happen for that to change?*

Referrals flowed to Peter. The early cases kick-started Morrissey's new practice. Two received prominent attention in the trade paper for lawyers, the *New York Law Journal*. Both were featured on the front page, upper right-hand corner. Peter's name was prominently mentioned, and a comment from him was included in a box alongside the article.

In the first case, Peter's client, William Kahn, after he married, enrolled in medical school, became a doctor, and after a long internship and residency, a neurosurgeon. While in medical school, his wife, Joan, supported them by working as a nurse. After William finished his training, he joined the staff of New York Hospital and soon the Kahns started a family. Joan quit her job, raised the couple's three children, and managed their two homes. Kahn's practice thrived. At the time of the divorce, some fifteen years later, he was the chief neurosurgeon at his hospital. His annual compensation exceeded $2 million.

The divorce was uncontested. Joint custody of the children was agreed to, and their support was imposed solely on William.

Joan was awarded temporary maintenance of $15,000 per month. At the conclusion of the divorce, temporary maintenance would end, replaced by final maintenance. Joan sought final maintenance of $15,000 per month. It, like temporary maintenance, was based on 35 percent of William's net income.

Joan also sought, under the doctrine of equitable distribution, 50 percent of all assets acquired during their marriage. The assets included the New York co-op, the country home in Connecticut, William's IRA, their bank accounts, and William's medical license. The license gave rise to a hotly contested controversy and a precedent-setting resolution.

The law was on Joan's side. Courts had ruled that law degrees, MBAs and medical degrees obtained by one spouse during a marriage were assets of the marriage, particularly where one spouse worked to support the family while the other went to school.

Peter did not dispute that Joan's sweat equity enabled William to become a neurosurgeon. He did contest her claim to a 50 percent interest in William's license computed as 50 percent of his earnings and an award of final maintenance based on 35 percent of William's earnings.

The case gained prominence because of Peter's successful argument opposing both final maintenance and a share of William's medical license. "It is important," Peter argued, "for the new law to be construed fairly, justly, and equitably. Joan's claim to share twice in William's earnings, once through final maintenance and again by sharing in his medical practice amounts to 'double dipping,' an inequitable and unfair practice. William gets the privilege of working, while Joan enjoys the fruits of his labor not once but twice."

Peter argued that William's excellent work made his license exceptionally valuable. The value, over and above what an average neurosurgeon earned, should belong solely to William. Peter offered evidence that the average neurosurgeon earned about $1million per year. He urged that Joan be awarded 50 percent of the average earnings of neurosurgeons or $500,000 per year, but only if William continued to work and earned at least $1 million annually. Peter opposed final maintenance. "Final maintenance is discretionary. In this case it should not be awarded."

The court agreed. The judge awarded Joan $500,000 per year for ten years or until William retired, whichever occurred earlier, provided William's earnings equaled or exceeded $1 million. The judge awarded Joan not a penny in final maintenance. "It is inequitable to allow Joan to share twice in William's earnings," the judge ruled.

The court divided the real estate, brokerage accounts, bank accounts, and William's IRA equally between the parties.

In the second case, a young investment banker, Robert Sylvester, earned $500,000 in the year he sought a divorce. Abe Klein, the wife's lawyer, argued that $500,000 was close to the minimal salary paid to professionals at Goldman Sachs, Sylvester's employer. "He's a hotshot. His earnings will at least double over the next five years. I'm being conservative in asking for final maintenance to rise by only $100,000 per year." In support Klein read from a Goldman SEC filing reflecting average compensation for professionals in excess of $1.5 million.

The judge accepted the wife's argument and fixed final maintenance based on a percentage of Sylvester's earnings, assuming it would rise $100,000 per year.

Morrissey urged protection for Sylvester, if his future turned out to be less rosy than predicted by the court.

"Lawyers make bad prophets. Since judges were lawyers before being elevated to the bench, they, too, are not immune from this weakness. Compensation at Goldman is not fantastical. It does not move, like a ratchet, as Mr. Klein urges, in only one direction, upwards. It is not unheard of for bonuses to get slashed and professionals fired. Adversity happens even in the storybook culture of Goldman Sachs. Robert Sylvester needs protection. My snapper clause, inserted in the final judgment, will protect him. It states that in the event of a substantial adverse change in Sylvester's earning, final maintenance can be adjusted or even eliminated."

"Mr. Morrissey, what does 'substantial' mean," the judge asked. "Ten percent, twenty percent? What?"

"At this time there's no need for quantification. It may not happen. If it does, I have every confidence that when the change occurs, we'll know whether it is 'substantial.'"

The snapper clause was inserted into the judgment. When the following year, Sylvester was fired and remained unemployed for a year, the judge cancelled Sylvester's maintenance payment "unless and until his circumstances change." In his decision the judge urged that snapper clauses be inserted in future judgments. He praised Peter for his perspicacity.

The lecture and Morrissey's success in the Kahn and Sylvester cases established him as the go-to lawyer for rich husbands. Within three years he had a full book of business, all men, all rich and all parties to a divorce.

His successful practice had a downside. Peter could not relate to his clients or they to him. Most clients were a lot younger and worked in finance. They ran hedge funds and were partners in investment banking firms, while others were officers in large corporations and still others were high-tech entrepreneurs. Their incomes were in the stratosphere, and so were their noses. They talked a different language and dressed in casual clothes. In an effort to understand his new clients, Peter read the *Wall Street Journal.* He also tried to dress down but felt uncomfortable in sweaters and slacks and reverted back to his standard dress of suits, shirts, and ties. In the old days, his female clients worshiped him; his new clients barely tolerated him. Peter was a petty nuisance whose task was to comb the knots out of their tangled personal affairs. He was a hired hand, on their payroll, certainly not someone to socialize with.

His female clients had filled a void. They were his family and his lovers. With his apartment empty but his office full of women, Peter was never lonely. In between meetings he gazed at his former clients' photographs. It helped him to recall tender moments.

After the disbarment action, the photos were removed, stored in a corner of his file room, and eventually, shredded and dumped. Hanging in their place were framed cartoon prints originally published by *Punch* magazine, satirizing lawyers and judges. Peter thought they were smart, appropriate, upscale. One client's comment, probably summed up the opinion of others: "Where did you get that shit hanging on the wall? What a collection of chestnuts. You know there's such a thing as art."

Peter's sex life suffered. He had trouble meeting women. He was too old in the eyes of young women and those his own age looked upon him with suspicion. "Why wasn't he married? Was he gay? Asexual? A pervert?" Most refused to give him a chance. The few who did, insisted on being wooed. They asked to be taken to dinner, the theater, and museum openings. Peter lacked patience. He wanted only to make love, but his too-obvious behavior was a turnoff. The women he encountered now were worldly, independent, and strong willed. They refused to fall for the ploy his former clients had found irresistible: "Let's elope for the weekend to a nearby country inn. The restaurant is renowned and the scenery magnificent. We can take long walks and get to know each other. " He did have some success, but on those few occasions, Peter was overwrought and anxious. They were not fulfilling encounters.

Peter was depressed. He sought help from Stanley Ginsberg, a psychoanalyst. Ginsberg told Peter he was burned out. He needed a change of scenery. Peter recalled the two weeks he had spent in Miami three years earlier during the hiatus in the disbarment hearing. In particular he had fond recollections of Aventrua by the Sea. He was due for a vacation. *The complex is not far from the airport in Fort Lauderdale. It's easy to go back and forth.* He could spend two weeks there and two weeks in NY. With the Internet, a laptop, and a cell phone, he could stay in touch. He was certain that Adventura would raise his spirits. If it didn't, he'd still have gotten some sun during a gloomy time of the year.

Morrissey's visit confirmed his earlier opinion that Aventura was right for him. There were many women and very few men. He watched dozens of possible female candidates swimming and splashing in the pool, relaxing on lounge chairs—some in bikinis—others, in tight-fitting outfits exercising in the gym. Notices on a bulletin board in the lobby described current activities: tai chi, yoga, water classes, lectures, dances, book clubs, and discussion groups. Peter saw himself in the center of the activities. A fox in a chicken coop.

As lust dominated his daydreams, one fear emerged. As he aged his potency diminished. He railed against the unfairness. Other addicts could feed their passions until death. He analogized his frustration to that of an alcoholic surrounded by bottles he could not open. He thought about Viagra and Cialis, but the possible side effects were frightening. He dismissed the most publicized—an an erection lasting four hours—as promotional. Other advertised effects—memory loss, hearing and vision impairment, numbness in arms or legs, diarrhea, dizziness—seemed too high a price to pay for a few moments of pleasure. And, his doctor told him, the drug doesn't always work.

Peter's cousin, Henry Fields, was a medical researcher for a pharmaceutical company. He was part of a team working on a break-through erectile-dysfunction medicine. Henry described his new project. "It's in the experimental stage. The code name is 'Iron Mike.' Unlike Viagra or Cialis, our product comes with a guarantee.

If it doesn't perk up your pecker, you'll get your money back. No questions asked. Based on our preliminary study, we don't anticipate any returns. There's a risk: it might kill you. I'm not kidding. It can affect the left ventricular chamber of your heart. That chamber pumps blood to all the vital organs without which one can't live. A healthy chamber will flush about fifty-five percent of the accumulated blood. You must have a normal ejection fraction to get into the program. "That's the bad news. The good news: Iron Mike will not have any of the side effects reported by users of Viagra or Cialis.

"We're in the experimental stage. Our guinea pigs get echocardiograms once a month. If their ejection faction falls below forty percent, they're out of the program. I know you're a libertine right out of Chaucer's Canterbury Tales. I can get you into the program."

Peter asked if his ejection fraction dropped below forty whether the drug had long-term harmful effects. Henry assured him that once off the drug and taking heart medicine, the ejection fraction, within a month or two, would return to normal. "There are no ill effects from a temporarily lowered ejection fraction. You'll have no symptoms. Only the echo will know."

"I don't need the drug in New York," Peter said. "I might as well be living in a monastery. I'm planning to spend part of the winter in Southern Florida. I'll have lots of fun. I'll return to New York every two weeks or so. Is there a program in Miami?"

"We have only one clinic, and it's in the city. We don't care where you live as long as you get tested every month, If, for some reason, you're unwilling to come home, call me. I'll arrange for you to have an echo in Miami."

Morrissey passed the examination at the drug company's clinic. His cousin gave him four pills and cautioned: "Take a pill when you have a twinkle in your eye. No more than one every two weeks. Pace your sexual activities. Be sure to hit the pause button. You may feel like a young man, but you're not. Potency reaches its highest point shortly after you take the pill and then slowly declines. Don't be tempted to overdose. Better to delay an encounter. Keep in touch. And Peter, happy fucking."

25

Morrissey rented a furnished penthouse in Aventura, with views of the Intracoastal waterway and Miami's famed South Beach. The glow returned to Peter's cheeks and elation replaced depression. He spent the first week acquiring a new wardrobe and enjoying the surroundings. He swam in the pool, used the weight machines, and enrolled in the bridge, chess, and drama clubs. He attended lectures, musicals, and movies. Peter was a model resident: happy, involved, and active. He was ready for his first conquest.

Peter was a rarity, an unattached male. He was popular with the women. When he smiled and greeted a woman, she invariably smiled back. One in particular caught his eye: Edy Farnsworth. He was attracted to her; she appeared not to notice him. When they met face to face, she turned away. Peter confronted her. "You don't know me. Yet you make a conscious effort to avoid me. What's wrong?"

"You remind me of my brother, only you're worse. He had to call attention to himself. Here, no one can fail to notice you. Yet you go around smiling at every woman and putting yourself in the center of every conversation. Why can't you give other people a chance to shine? Why are you on stage with a spotlight on you? Were you in show business?"

"Unless you consider a lawyer an actor. I'll make an effort to hide my head under a bale of hay if you will pay a modicum of attention to me. Although I've never been on a real stage, you, however, were a Broadway star, or so I've heard."

"Nonsense, I had leads at Bryn Mawr but only bits in Off-Broadway shows. Did some shots for ad agencies, but I got married, had four children, and took my bows at home." She smiled at Peter and added, "If you retreat from encounters, not always but occasionally, I'll be your friend. Do we have a deal?" Peter nodded yes and offered her his arm.

Edy was tall and slim, her big blue eyes set off by a thick head of closely cropped white hair. She was aloof, but Peter spotted that hidden deep down, she had a capacity for warmth and attachment. As they walked she asked Peter what he specialized in. When he said divorce law, she rattled off the terms of her divorce. "Everything was split down the middle. We had two homes. One in Canaan, Connecticut and our apartment in Adventura. James, a psychiatrist, whose office was in our Canaan home, purchased my interest offset by his interest in Adventura. He wanted Canaan, claiming a move might disrupt his patients. I knew the real reason but could not prove it. James was having affairs with his patients. A spare bedroom, a few steps from his office, was his lair. I found signs but no hard evidence.

"He claimed we lived off his earnings, while I was miserly in preserving my inheritance. He argued my inheritance was reserved for use during our retirement. We spent his money; he saved nothing. As part of the divorce, he wanted half of my inheritance. The judge denied his claim."

Peter asked innocently, "Isn't it against the law for a psychiatrist to have sexual relations with his patients?"

"Indeed it is. Analysts have been severely punished. Some have been convicted and sentenced to jail. Most have lost their right to practice. My lawyer said I could obtain more than half if we had evidence of adultery. He'd have to give up or face the consequences. I drew the line at blackmail. If he wanted to have affairs, I'd divorce him. That's it. What do you think?"

Peter was usually asked by divorced women about whether their deal was fair. He didn't want to get involved in other lawyers' cases, so he gave Edy his stock reply. "You did good enough, and good enough is enough. You acted honorably. You have nothing to regret."

Peter saw Edy as a combination of Alice Burns, the English professor, and Margaret Gould, the heiress, who were two of his former clients who testified at the trial. Edy always had a book in her hands, and if not an intellectual, clearly she was a highbrow. Like Margaret she exuded an aura of old family wealth. Alice and Margaret both rejected Peter's sexual advances. Edy, however, was turning friendly and seemed interested in him. She strolled with him through Adventura's gardens, arm in arm. They sat on a bench shaded by the sweeping branches of a Camperdown elm. Although they had just met, they discussed personal matters. Peter mentioned his own marriage blaming his infidelity for the divorce. His wife, he said, "was wonderful. If another, even half as good as Joan agreed to marry me, I would remain faithful."

Peter's remark about fidelity stunned him. Why did he vouchsafe a principle beyond his will to keep? And why did he say it to Edy? Because he had matured. He was getting old. He had a strange untested feeling. If he could win her over, he would remain constant. Devoted to only one woman. No longer a bee flitting faithlessly among roses.

Peter was right about Edy's change in attitude. She was warming up to him. Her mind raced. *He's big, active, and fun.* The field was circumscribed for a woman of sixty. *Of course, I'd never marry him. Why put marriage into my head? We've just met.*

On the walk back from the gardens, Peter, holding Edy's hand, invited her to dinner. "We'll dine at the Delano in South Beach. I'm told by one of my banker-clients it's a place not to be missed. If you say yes, I'll book a table."

"I accept dinner, but do you really want the Delano? It's expensive, jazzy, uptown. The crowd is young, hip, and beautiful." She squeezed his hand as she said with a smile, "Do you think two geezers will fit in?"

"I'm sure you will. I'll do my best. It will be a nice change from our fellow golden oldies."

The Bianca is the name of the dining room at the Delano. When Edy and Peter arrived to claim their table, the maître d' looked askance. They were above the average age by at least twenty years. Their dress also set them apart. The young women congregating at the bar wore outfits almost as revealing as bikinis. The men were dressed in open-collared silk shirts festooned with wild flowers. Peter recognized the shirts as the latest Tommy Bahama designs. He was a fish out of water, in a dark blazer, white shirt, blue bow tie, and while linen pants. Edy's dark red dress reached to her knees. It shouted: "I'm expensive," but also "I belong to a different generation." Although their age and appearance set them apart, Edy thought well of Peter for bringing them into this world. "We may look odd, but I feel secure. I like a man who's confident regardless of the surroundings. Thanks for choosing the Delano."

The waiter was attentive and smiled approvingly at Peter's choice of wine. Edy ordered zucchini flowers with heirloom tomatoes, mozzarella, and basil; Peter ordered grilled octopus. They both chose snapper as their main dish. He told the waiter to take his time bringing the food but not the wine. He asked for it right away.

The wine and food were above average, but the presentation was extraordinary. The linen, plates, utensils, flowers, and service justified the high price.

During dinner Peter told the story of his big break at Cahill and a summary of his career. He discussed his work helping battered women and his feelings of pathos for the victims. He thought for a moment about disclosing the disbarment trial. He decided against it for fear he would ruin an otherwise perfect evening.

Edy told of her privileged life and her determination to have a successful career. She briefly mentioned her marriage. Her children, she said, "all turned out well. They're in happy marriages and engaged in life. Nothing quite so boring as tales about grandchildren, so I'll avoid speaking about them. They spend a couple of weeks, over Christmas, with me. If I'm still talking to you, I'll introduce you."

Dinner lasted for almost three hours, during which they drank two bottles of wine. "I don't like to drive at night," Peter said, "especially after drinking. Too much traffic and too many wild drivers. That's why I took a cab here. I'll ask the waiter to alert the desk to have a cab at the door waiting for us."

On the cab ride back, Peter put his arm around Edy, and she snuggled close. They kissed again and again. As they got out of the cab, Peter popped one of his four Iron Mike pills. When they arrived at the door of Edy's apartment, she invited Peter in. *I'll just relax*, she thought. *What's the worst that can happen? And if it does, so what?*

The worst happened. The two geezers made love more ardently than any of the young folks they left behind at the Delano.

Before drifting off to sleep, Peter thought he would reveal his past. Then he remembered Philip Gross and the reaction of June Goldstein to his confession of being a sex addict, and he decided it was premature. *Why stir the pot?* The truth could wait.

Over breakfast on Edy's terrace, overlooking the Atlantic, Peter told her of his plan to alternate every two weeks between New York and Florida. "I've got an active law practice. Will you miss me when I'm gone?"

"Not immediately. In two weeks, I'm off for a month's trip to Myanmar, Vietnam, and Cambodia. I'm touring with a group of thirty. We've been traveling together for three years. Last year we went to Africa, the year before Japan. We all get along. I look forward to the trips. Now I'm ambivalent. I wish you could come along."

"I'd like to go, but I have responsibilities to my firm and clients. Five years ago I employed five lawyers, and now I've got ten. Rent and salaries for staff and lawyers add up to a big nut. It's all mine. I'm thinking of shifting the burden. There are three lawyers who were loyal to me during the Sturm und Drang. Never mind what the 'Sturm' was, maybe someday, if you're nice to me, I'll tell you. Anyway, when I return to New York, I'm going to make those three my partners. We'll each share equally in the profits. A true partnership in that sense, but there it ends. They'll have to work full time, while I take a month's trip to an exotic corner of the world. I'm supposed to go back tomorrow, but if you promise to spend the next few weeks with me, I'll postpone my return until you depart. I'll need to work part of every day, but you'll delight in a break from me."

"I won't, but I'll manage. I get immersed in a book, listen to music, write long emails, and play Scrabble on the Internet with others, some of whom I have never met. One lives in Australia! You know, last night I intuited that you have a deep, dark secret. It must be the 'Sturm' you mentioned. That's what got me thinking. I'll find out, even if I have to resort to devious ways."

Peter glanced at his watch, pulled out his cell, and called his office. He asked to speak with Joel Bernstein, Henry Greene, and John Harvest. "Listen fellows, a big change is in store."

"Let me guess," Joel said. "We're going back to representing women."

"Nah, I know," John said. "Our future is in M&A. You're giving a lecture on pitfalls in mergers. We'll invite all our investment banking clients. They'll start referring deals to us. We'll make millions. In a few years, we'll eclipse Skadden Arps and Wachtel Lipton. Right, Peter?"

"No, nothing so grandiose. I'm making you three guys my partners. The firm will be called: Morrissey, Bernstein, Harvest, & Greene. We'll share equally in bucks but not work. From now on I get to take six months off. You guys get your usual month. Agreed?"

When they all agreed, Peter named Greene managing partner and asked him to draw up an agreement, get the name changed on all court filings, and send a notice to their clients, and to all members of the City Bar Association. "There are other details, but I leave them to you. Let's get the change in place as soon as possible. Joel, you inform our associates about the change. You can assure them as business grows, they can expect to become partners. Fax me the partnership agreement. There's more good news to come. I'm staying in Adventura another two weeks. Someday soon you'll meet the reason. Have Gina relay my phone calls and send me work. You've got to work extra hard, make bigger fees to make up for my diminished share of profits. I've given up seventy-five percent. How am I to maintain my standard of living?" Joel, sotto voce, answered the question, "By trading the pool for your desk and making a real contribution." In an audible voice, Joel added, "Yes, sir, boss, I mean partner."

When Peter closed the phone, the smile on Edy's face didn't wane for a full minute. "Peter, I'm so proud of you. I'm so happy. I want the next few weeks to be joyous ones. Let's spend every night together, not making love but next to each other." Seeing the frown on Peter's face, she added, "Well, some nights we'll make love, but not more than once a week. I'm exhausted from last night's joust. You may move some clothes into my apartment. May I into yours?"

"You may as long as you come with your clothes." Peter picked Edy up, whirled her around, and kissed her twice. When he put her down, he laughed. It was infectious. She laughed. Joy reigned supreme.

The new partnership agreement was faxed to Peter promptly. He thought he'd get a draft and a chance to make changes. Instead, it was signed by Joel, Henry, and John. The instruction sheet asked him to return a signed copy by fax. *Strange,* he thought, *I gave them a big gift, not the other way around. You'd think they'd be thankful and deferential. Instead, they say "sign here and return." Well, I'll read it over and if I have changes, I'll make them.*

Peter had reservations about several provisions involving the rights of a majority in interest. It could accept or reject new clients, assign cases, enter into a new lease, provide for a mandatory retirement age, hire and fire lawyers and staff, and make all ordinary and necessary business decisions. The majority, not Peter, was in charge. The agreement could have vested powers in one partner. Many partnership agreements do. He knew the importance of preparing the first draft. He could then have said: "This is it. All that I'm giving up and nothing more." They would have signed. Having said they were equal partners and asking them to draft an agreement, he was stuck. His only hope: they would not oust him. Well, what if they did? He'd show them. He'd start a new firm, and they'd starve to death.

Peter did as instructed. He signed and returned the agreement.

Peter and Edy spent the next two weeks in a manner typical of long-married couples. They slept together, had breakfast together. Then they went their separate ways until the cocktail hour. Their time together was generally happy, but there were adjustments, accommodations followed by a touch of resentment. Peter had lived alone for almost all his adult life, Edy for the past five years. Now there was another person's interests to be weighed in deciding where to eat, whether to attend a concert, movie, or lecture. They were little things, but things that had to be resolved. Edy was the stronger of the two, and her will often decided. Peter found it easier to agree. Every so often she let him decide.

Peter had one concern. He was instructed to take one Iron Mike every two weeks. Its effect would last for about two weeks, but its power declined daily. Peter wanted to shine at every encounter. To insure success he took a pill each week. He rationalized that ignoring the clinic's instructions would not be harmful. During the month Edy was gone, he'd make up for it by not taking any pills. His average intake would be less than one pill every two weeks. When Edy returned he'd put sexual relations and Iron Mike on a biweekly basis. He thought about alerting the clinic he was planning to take a pill a week for a limited period of three weeks but decided against it. The issue did not seem important. Peter was more concerned about the changes in his office and their impact on him.

The first few days he heard frequently from the office. He received an important brief, which he revised. He negotiated, using his cell phone, while sitting in a lounge chair on his terrace, a settlement of a major case, and he talked to several prospective clients, making appointments soon after his return to New York. By the end of the week, the contacts had slowed. He called his secretary and asked about several cases. One she said was reassigned to "Mr. Greene." The other to "Mr. Harvest." Strange. Gina always referred to the other lawyers by their first name. Peter was the only "Mr."

Peter asked to speak with Henry first and then John. Gina put him on hold while she attempted to reach them. When she returned she said, "Mr. Greene is in court, and Mr. Harvest is on another line." Peter wanted to say, "tell John to kill his call," but instead said, with a touch of irony, "see if Mr. Bernstein will speak with me." Joel told Peter that the two cases had been reassigned, because personal attention was required. "We've upped our billing rate to yours. It would be bad business, we felt, to refer to us as substitutes."

Peter couldn't hold back. "What's this with Gina calling you 'Mister'? She always referred to you by your first name."

"We instructed her to change. It doesn't look good in front of clients for a secretary to be too familiar. Peter, I'm really busy. Anything else?"

Peter ended the call without saying goodbye. He was steaming. He thought a sauna and a massage would help. They did not. He complained to Edy. "Things are not going right in my office."

"That's because you're thousands of miles away," she said. "Once you're in New York, you'll be back in the saddle running the show. When I return we'll observe the routine of rotating every two weeks unless you feel it more important to spend more time in New York. I like New York."

The second week Peter received only several insignificant matters. He called Gina and asked about his mail and calls. She said, "Mr. Greene reviewed your mail, not the personal stuff, those I've saved for you. He answered the business matters. One of the two prospective clients called saying there was a new development. Mr. Bernstein returned the call. He met with the client, a Mr. Geneen who signed a retainer. Yesterday, Mr. Harvest spoke with the other prospect. They're meeting next week." Peter knew it would be futile to complain. His new partners were freezing him out. He wondered how long it would be before a mandatory retirement age was adopted. Would they chose sixty-seven, giving him four more years, or get rid of him immediately? What a damn fool he was. He violated his creed. *Never trust anybody if you don't have to.* Well, he'd be back in the office in a few days. Tomorrow Edy would depart for her Asian vacation. She'd have an exciting new adventure; Peter would be fighting once more to keep his head above water. Only this time *the struggle will be with the lawyers I raised, nurtured, and trusted.*

Peter drove Edy to the Miami Airport, with mixed feelings. He was sad to lose her for a month but welcomed the time alone.

He needed to plan his attack…to defeat what he was sure was a coup to dethrone him.

Peter arrived at his office Monday morning, an hour before it officially opened and went directly to the file room. All the cabinets were open. Only the drawer containing the firm's financial records was locked. His key worked. *Amateurs,* he thought, *they haven't bothered to change the lock.* He was about to take the ledger when he noticed a file stamped "confidential." It contained two documents: the fully executed partnership agreement and a memo referenced "The Plan." It bore the initials H.G. below the title indicating that Henry Greene was the author. On the last page under the heading "agreed to," appeared the initials of the three new partners.

> Our plan to leave Peter and start our own firm has been aborted by Peter's astonishing announcement. The risk of investing in a startup is great. We need capital (that means digging into our own savings—will my wife scream!) and hope that our cases and new business will follow. Staff, rent, and furnishings are just some of the many problems flowing from a departure. Now that we are partners we can eat our cake and have it too with one exception: we will have to carry Peter.
>
> We owe a lot to Peter. The firm's good will belongs to him as does all the furniture and equipment. Most lawyers on becoming partners have to chip in and pay their share of capital. Peter required no payment from us.
>
> I know he has not been productive and will be even less so over the next few years. Peter is now sixty-three. Has an IRA worth about $5 million and real estate worth at least that much. He won't starve regardless of what we do. I checked around. Between sixty-two and seventy is the norm for mandatory retirement. I'm amenable for a longer period but not more than seventy, but I recommend sixty-six. Here is my recommendation: We keep him on for three more years as a full partner. When he reaches sixty-six, he retires.

Peter returned the file and locked the drawer. He left the office and took a long walk north on Lexington Avenue. He weighed his alternatives. None made sense. *It's better for them to take over my firm. It's also better for me. If one lawyer leaves, it's not serious. If three senior lawyers defect, it's bad for all of us. How could I replace them and keep to my proposed schedule of working part time? Their takeover eliminates risk for them and for me as well. My timing was exquisite. I'll make a virtue out of necessity.*

Peter returned to the office at ten. He patted his three new partners on the back and greeted the other lawyers and staff warmly. He asked Henry Greene to meet in his office when he had free time. "Now is good for me," Henry said. When they were alone, Peter asked if his direction that Henry be the managing partner was agreed to by Joel and John. "There has been no formal agreement, but I've been filling that job, such as it is, by implied consent."

"Good," Peter said. "There's a few matters left to be settled. We need more space. The twenty-second floor is vacant. The commercial real estate market is soft. I know the landlord well. Our lease has only a few months left. With your permission I'll try to cut a deal for the whole floor at about what we're paying for two-thirds. It will give you room to expand. You, Joel, and John will be meeting with clients and need bigger offices. Mine is too large. In the new space, I'll take a smaller office. I'll still hustle business and pitch in, but at some point, my role must end. I think I'll be ready for pasture at seventy. Don't decide now. Talk it over, and we'll make it firm. I want you to know I'm very proud of all of you. I'm a lucky man to be able to turn over my practice to such competent lawyers. Now get out of here, and go back to business while I catch up."

Henry left but ten minutes later was back in Peter's office. "You're a generous man. We agree to seventy. I'll put it in the contract. We also would like new space. Joel and John told me to tell you how much we all owe you. I told them to deliver the message themselves. As for me, Peter, you have made me very happy. What else can I say?"

Peter closed the deal on the new space. He also obtained two new clients. Before a retainer was signed, he called in Joel in one case and John in the other and told the clients: "I'm always available to you, but the daily matters will be handled by my partners. Is that agreeable?" When the client said it was, a retainer was produced and signed.

Peter argued several motions in court. He won both. He negotiated a favorable settlement in one case and a fairly good one in another. He worked on briefs and helped in the preparation of cases for trial. When the month was up, his new partners were genuinely sorry to see him go. "Remember to come back to us in two weeks," Joel said. "We'll miss our senior partner."

Peter wrote frequently to Edy. He related the positive news about the office but omitted reading the confidential memo. He also said the truth over and over again. He missed her. Hated to be alone. Longed to see her face in the morning and again at night on the pillow next to him. She wrote beautiful letters describing the serenity of places and people formerly disrupted by war. She said: "I take solace in the knowledge that next year you'll be with me on our group's trip to India."

He called her as soon as he got back to Adventura and left a message on her answering machine. His message: "I miss you. Eager to see you. Please call." When a day went by without a return call, he checked with the desk and was informed she was "in residence." He sent a dozen roses with a note. "Breakfast, lunch, or dinner. I'll settle for a walk in the garden." Edy called. Her voice was as cold as an Arctic glacier. "I'll meet you in the garden in about an hour." She arrived later than that.

Peter asked about the trip. "It was wonderful until the last day. Peter, you're unmasked. One of my tour mates is a psychiatrist. We've been on several trips together and are friends. Last year she spent a week in Adventura as my guest. On the plane going, we sat next to each other. Same on the return trip. Her name is Helen Baker. Do you know her?"

For ten seconds he couldn't place the name. Then a shot in the gut. "Yes, she was Molly Dixon's shrink. She testified against me in the disbarment trial. Her testimony was skewed. She was biased. I'll bet her account to you was even more prejudiced, but you're not going to believe that. How did you get on the subject of me?"

"Disbarment? Molly Dixon? This is the first time I've heard about them from you. You bragged about helping poor women, victims of sexual attacks but concealed your many assaults on sparrows with clipped wings. How could you have sworn love and concealed a dark secret? You ask how did your name come up? On the plane over to Myanmar, Helen asked what was new. I told her I had met a dashing Irishman named Peter Morrissey. She said not a word. Then on the plane back home she held forth. 'I didn't want to ruin your trip, so I said nothing about Peter Morrissey. Now that we are on our way home, I'll tell you what I know about him.' She talked and talked. She asked if we had had sexual relations. I told her about our first date and what followed. She nodded and said, 'That's our Peter.' I was embarrassed, hurt. How could I have fallen for you? I broke down and cried right there on the plane in front of everyone. I never want to see you again." Edy walked away putting her hands over her ears. She didn't need to block her hearing, Peter had nothing to say.

He spent the next two weeks at Adventura hoping Edy would change. Duffy sent him the transcript of Baker's testimony on cross. He forwarded it to Edy with a note. "Dr. Baker never heard my side. Are you going to make the same mistake?" Peter did not know whether Edy read the transcript. He did not hear from her again.

He saw no reason to stay at Adventura. He cancelled his lease, packed his bags, and returned to New York. He wondered what dreadful event would fall upon him next. He did not have long to wait.

At Morrissey's next visit to the clinic, the doctor informed him: "Your latest test shows a decline in the functioning of your heart. The condition can be reversed with medicine and proper care. You cannot, however, continue in the program. For our own statistical study, how many pills have you taken?"

Peter answered truthfully. The doctor called him a "fool, idiot, moron." "No wonder you're in second stage heart failure. The disease is progressive once you enter second stage. You will have to be monitored every week."

The disease progressed rapidly. Within two months Peter was in the final stage of heart failure. His kidney function had failed. He was on dialysis. He was too weak to walk and spent most of his time in bed. A few months later, his heart stopped.

The funeral service was attended by his sister, his niece and nephew, and their families. They sat in the front row. The lawyers in his firm and their spouses and families occupied the second row. William Duffy and about a hundred other lawyers were present. Sitting alone in a back row was an attractive older woman—tall, slim with closely cropped white hair and blue eyes. She signed Edy Farnsworth in the Book of Remembrance.

18663073R00131

Made in the USA
Charleston, SC
15 April 2013